About the author

Orna O'Reilly grew up in Ireland and practised interior design for many years, both at home and abroad. She moved to Italy in 2013 to begin writing full time. Her award-winning blog, *Orna O'Reilly: Travelling Italy*, was begun while she was living close to Venice, from where she drew inspiration for her first work of fiction, *The Blonde in the Gondola*. Orna has been a contributing writer for magazines for several years and is now enjoying life among the olive groves of Puglia, in South-Eastern Italy, with her husband, Tom.

You can follow Orna's blog on www.ornaoreilly.com

Facebook: https://www.facebook.com/orna.oreilly

IN THE SHADOW OF THE OLIVE TREE

Orna O'Reilly

IN THE SHADOW OF THE OLIVE TREE

Vanguard Press

VANGUARD PAPERBACK

© Copyright 2021
Orna O'Reilly

A CIP catalogue record for this title is
available from the British Library.

ISBN 978-1-80016-130-6

*Vanguard Press is an imprint of
Pegasus Elliot MacKenzie Publishers Ltd.*
www.pegasuspublishers.com

First Published in 2021

**Vanguard Press
Sheraton House Castle Park
Cambridge England**

Printed & Bound in Great Britain

Dedication

For Tom

Acknowledgements

A big thank you to my husband, Tom, who gave me space to write while he stressed about our new olive farm here in Puglia and brought our very first harvest to fruition. Also, thanks to my two beta readers, Sue Hill and Tara Daly, who carefully read my manuscript in its early form, voiced helpful criticisms and were endlessly encouraging.

She was home at last. Back to her sweet trullo in Puglia with the olive trees poking their bushy heads over the high stone wall. She noticed how well the Virginia creeper had grown while she had been away, and her heart lifted as she heard her dogs scuffling behind the closed gate. As she swung it wide, slightly creaking on its hinges, they rushed to greet her, and she began to bend to hug them. But, to her horror, they both suddenly backed off and began to growl. She took a step back in fright and surprise as she realised, they weren't her beloved pets at all and, as she looked up at the man standing framed by the front door, she knew that this was a stranger. In her home.

CHAPTER ONE
JANET

Dublin
Eighteen Months Previously

'You're leaving *me*?' Janet was surprised at how calm her voice sounded. It was as though she were testing to see what the words tasted like in her mouth, now that she was finally saying aloud something she had been expecting to say for the past few months, ever since she had discovered that James was having an affair with the American woman.

'It's not working out any more. I'm not happy. Things are different somehow.' He managed to inject a note of self-righteous indignation and accusation into this statement.

His round, florid face, crowned with a black, shiny comb-over, was now flushed even more than usual. An air of nervous excitement emanated from his every pore. He didn't mention *her*; Cassie, her name was, but Janet always thought of her as "The American Woman" ever since she had moved into number thirty-four, three doors down, last year.

At first, Janet had quite liked her, having bumped into her in the supermarket on occasion when they had vaguely chatted. A single woman who seemed so independent until her teenage son got into a spot of bother at school, and James, who was his maths and geography teacher, had helped to sort things out with the headmaster. It hadn't been much really, just an incident behind the bicycle shed when Billy had got into a fist fight with another lad over ownership of a Mars Bar. The real problem was that Billy was a hulking lad with a fairly threatening manner, already almost touching six feet, while his opponent had been a lot smaller. And it appeared that Billy had been in trouble for bullying before. James had put in a good word for the boy and promised to talk to his mother.

'They live on our street,' he informed Mr Cassidy, the headmaster. 'She's a single mother, and they're new to the country. He'll settle down. I'll keep an eye on him.'

Mr Cassidy grunted that the boy had bullying tendencies, and the school was trying to implement a zero-tolerance regime for such behaviour. 'Okay. See what you can do.' His expression told James that he didn't hold out much hope of success.

James was actually thinking that Billy, being American and unusually large for his fourteen years, may have suffered from overexposure to growth hormones that everyone knew were in American beef. As far as he was concerned, Americans ate too much. Those super-sized portions he'd been served when he went to the US on holiday a few years ago had left him with the distinct impression that it was no wonder they were so large. And those sodas and milkshakes — about a million calories per glass. The kid had probably been raised on cheeseburgers and fries. He thought about his rash promise to talk to Billy's mother, imagining an ample woman with arms like hams. Perhaps he might even suggest that Mrs Hernandez might consider putting her son on a calorie-controlled diet.

Nevertheless, despite his misgivings and regretting already that he had volunteered for this unpleasant task, on his way home he parked his bicycle outside the wrought-iron gate to number thirty-four, undid the clip on his trouser leg, removed his helmet and walked up the path to the front door with, what he hoped, was an air of authority.

Having rung the doorbell briskly, he waited somewhat impatiently for the sound of heavy feet lumbering to respond and sniffed the air for the scent of fried chicken.

The door opened gently, and she appeared. The American Woman, Cassie. His heart literally skipped a beat, the way he had read they could do in the women's magazines that Janet left lying around in the bathroom. There she stood, small and olive-skinned, her huge brown eyes looking at him anxiously. Her long dark hair hung over one shoulder, and she was barefoot, with cerise-pink toenails. She wore a short cotton halter neck dress, and he could make out the shapeliness of her body underneath.

'Yes? What can I do for you?'

Her voice was soft, her full, moist lips were parted, and James's head filled, unannounced, with visions of all the things she could perhaps do for him if he played his cards right.

Putting on his most charming manner, he introduced himself and allowed her to sweep him into her home and into her life.

**

As Janet stepped off the bus the morning after James's announcement and contemplated another dreary day sitting in the back office of Jones & Sons Engineering, in a dreary building beside the main bus station in downtown Dublin, where she had been working for almost twelve years, she made up her mind. Just like that.

Sitting in the gloomy office, her chipped desk piled high with accounts and her inbox overflowing, with just a gas fire for company, she composed her letter of resignation.

'But why? Whatever will we do without you?' Mr Jones was aghast. His ageing hippie hairdo, long at the back and missing on the top, quivered with horror. Janet's resignation was the last thing he was expecting after all those years. And so suddenly too.

'I'm moving to Italy,' she announced, almost defiantly, in a voice that sounded a lot more confident than she felt. In fact, she was quaking inside. The idea of living in sunny Puglia had come to her while reading a magazine article on the bus. It was full of photographs of blue skies, white houses, olive trees and smiling people sipping glasses of pink wine in the sun. Looking out the fogged up, wet window at everyone swishing along the Dublin streets, leaning into the driving rain and wind, grey skies, resigned faces of her fellow passengers, then looking back at the magazine in her hands, she decided, quite simply, that she had had enough. She would move to the stiletto heel of Italy and live in one of those little cone-shaped houses called trulli. Apparently, trulli was the plural of trullo, and so, she would live in a trullo among the olive groves and begin life anew. She would heal herself. How this was going to be achieved would come to her when she got there, she was sure.

James had been as good as his word and had moved out straight away. It had been an easy move for him as he just had to carry his belongings three doors down the street, but it had been hard and humiliating for Janet. On her first night alone in their large bed, now her personal space, she stared into the darkness, wondering what the future would bring. Tossing and turning into the small hours, she remembered what her mother used to say to her when she was a child and sleep evaded her.

'Think about the presents you'll be getting from Santa for Christmas.' Her soft voice comforting.

Then she would relax, thinking of the Christmas tree, fairy lights and presents piled up at its base, and she would sleep. Now she calmed herself by imagining the olive groves basking in the Italian sunshine and finally drifted off, dreaming of her trullo in the Itrian Valley.

When the strangeness of the first few weeks after James's departure began to wear off, Janet felt surprisingly free. At first, it was the joy of a peaceful night's sleep without having to listen to his snoring and her freedom to sit up and read during the night if she felt like it. Having been a bookworm all her life, she was relishing the fact that she was able to read without being nagged to turn off the light when he wanted to go to sleep. Then she became aware of the fact that she had the bathroom to herself too and was free to leave the lid off the body lotion or toothpaste without being snarled at.

Her friend Marianne tried to be sympathetic. A successful economist, who had met Janet when they were at school together in Phibsboro, on Dublin's north side, who thought her own unmarried state a complete disgrace and was frantically trying to find a suitable husband before her rapidly winding down body clock ground to a halt.

Having met up at their local pub and found a corner table, they ordered two enormous glasses of white wine and a portion each of scampi and chips with a side of tartar sauce. Janet felt as though she had not eaten in days.

'Mmm... this is delicious,' she murmured as she dipped a chip into the glob of sauce on the side of her plate. 'Honestly, Marianne, I wish James had moved on years ago. I'm loving being on my own again.'

Marianne could not believe her ears. She looked at Janet, her lips a thin line of disapproval. 'How can you say that? A lovely man like James? A teacher and a good provider. Look at the beautiful home you have together. I don't understand you. Good husbands don't grow on trees, you know.'

Janet laughed wryly. Her sense of humour always came to the fore when she saw, as she thought, the crazy side of people she was fond of. 'I'm only forty!' she exclaimed. 'I've more than half my life ahead of me, with a bit of luck. I've been married to James for eighteen years, and now he's left me for a younger woman. Are you mad? He hardly qualifies for the "Husband of the Year Award", you know.'

'Couldn't you have persuaded him to stay?' Marianne was dogged. She had always been envious of Janet's marriage, which seemed so effortless, living in her comfortable house in Glasthule, on Dublin's south side, close to the sea. She was certain that she must have done something to drive James into the arms of one of their neighbours.

'Why would I do that?' Janet dipped a forkful of scampi into the tartar sauce, looking perfectly relaxed. 'For sure, I got a big shock when he announced he was leaving, but within a couple of weeks, I realised that I felt free for the first time in years. I looked at my boring job, solid marriage — as I thought — and saw nothing exciting on the horizon for, like, forever. No, I'm happy he's gone. Now I can start a new life.'

She raised her glass for a toast to her forthcoming adventure and realised her glass was empty. Already!

'I'll get this round.' Janet got to her feet and headed to the bar.

Marianne watched her friend. So tall and self-confident. Her long legs in skinny jeans that she herself could only ever dream of fitting into, her curly dark hair cut into a short bob, a butterfly tattoo on one shoulder, her low-cut blouse. Marianne watched a man at the bar begin to strike up a hopeful conversation with Janet's breasts and thought her friend did, perhaps, look a bit tarty, though she immediately quelled the disloyal thought. She saw Janet smile at the top of the man's head as she removed her breasts from his gaze and returned to the table with their fresh glasses of wine.

'What's this new life you're thinking about?' Marianne's curiosity was piqued.

'I've decided to move to Italy,' Janet announced without preamble.

'What?' Marianne took a large gulp of wine and almost choked on her last mouthful of chips. 'Italy? You don't even speak Italian. You're joking, right?'

'I've made up my mind. I need an adventure. Something completely new. I'm moving to Puglia as soon as the house is sold. I'm going to buy a trullo in the Itrian Valley and start again.'

'You're really serious, aren't you?'

'Completely.' Janet sensed her friend's discomfort and added, 'But think of all the lovely trips you'll make to Puglia to visit me when I'm settled. We'll have a great time.'

Somewhat mollified, Marianne said, 'I might even meet a gorgeous Italian hunk when I'm there. Keep an eye out for one for me.'

They both laughed like the old friends they were.

CHAPTER TWO
CLAUDIA

Anya was sixteen years old when Claudia first met Michel. They had been exploring the Rubens House in downtown Antwerp and, on exiting, decided to take a break at an outdoor cafe close by. They sat at a little table and did a bit of people watching while they sipped their coffee and savoured the tiny pastries that came with it. This was the sort of downtime mother and daughter had enjoyed over the nine years they had been alone together since Anya's father, Claudia's much-loved husband Philip, had died.

As mother and daughter sat together at that cafe table in Antwerp, they were unaware of the beautiful tableau they made. Both blonde and slender, the older woman, small and petite; the younger, willowy and long-legged, with hair tumbling down her back, blue eyes full of curiosity at her surroundings. They were suddenly aware that they had company. A tall, handsome, fair-haired man was standing over them.

'I am so sorry to interrupt you, but I wanted to tell you that this area has many pickpockets, and I couldn't help but notice that your bag' — he pointed to Anya's pink tote — 'is open and attracting some attention.'

Anya immediately checked her tote, which was hanging on the back of her chair. It was indeed open.

'Oh, goodness!' she exclaimed. 'I was sure I fastened it. I hope nothing has been stolen.'

The man smiled at them, noting the huge diamond on Claudia's wedding ring finger and her air of wealthy sophistication. 'I don't think so,' he said reassuringly. 'I've been sitting right here, and I would have seen if anyone had touched it.' He lingered. His accent was French, his voice smooth.

Claudia looked at him and gave him one of her famously dazzling smiles in return.

'Thank you so much,' she said. 'You're very kind to have pointed it out. Most people wouldn't have bothered.'

19

'You are very welcome.' He was charming and polished, his manner suave. His long, jean-clad legs were slim, and he was tanned and appeared to have what Claudia thought of as an athlete's body. 'May I sit down for a moment? I can see you are visitors. Are you waiting for your husband? Can I help you at all?'

He was so relaxed and natural, and the setting was so public that Claudia could not see the harm. There was a moment's hesitation, and she said, 'Of course. We've just been studying our maps and deciding where to go next. We've only got one more day, and then it's back home. And no, it's just us,' she added.

'Ireland?' His guess was not a difficult one, as he had spotted Anya's passport upon quietly opening her bag when neither of them was looking. He needed an excuse to talk to these incredibly beautiful, well-heeled women. *Girls, really*, he thought and licked his lips excitedly.

Before long they were — all three — chatting like old friends. Lunch together seemed inevitable, and before the day was over, they had swapped names and telephone numbers. Anya was thrilled.

'Oh, Mum!' she exclaimed when they were alone in their hotel room later that night. 'He's just fabulous. You will see him again, won't you? Please!'

Claudia relented easily. Michel, that was his name, Michel Reynard, quickly became a fixture in their lives. Two weeks and many telephone conversations later, Claudia flew from Dublin to Brussels, where she was met by Michel with open arms. He drove her straight back to his home, situated about half an hour from the centre of Antwerp, a pretty house with a roof terrace overlooking the peaceful Wijnegem Canal. He took her by the hand up the stairs to his bedroom, from where they emerged hours later to sit on the terrace, watch the sun go down, drink wine and eat delicious food, cooked by him, on a wooden refectory table under the stars.

That weekend, they strolled hand in hand along the tree-lined canal. It was all very romantic, and Claudia felt that, out of the blue, a new dimension had entered her life.

***

Michel was anxious to get married immediately.

'Why wait? We can get to know each other over the years.' He pressed her to marry him after they had only known each other for a few weeks. At first, she was reluctant — after all, she hardly knew him — but he besieged her with declarations of love and devotion, promising that he would make a good father to her daughter, who seemed to be spellbound by him. In the end, she was swayed by Anya's happiness.

Having been widowed for all those years, rearing Anya alone, she decided Michel would make a wonderful husband and a loving father to her daughter. She was sure that she would grow to love him, maybe even the way she had loved Philip. Perhaps it was more sensible, even more sane, to let their love grow over time. She was fond of him and felt good in his company. The fact that he was more than ten years older than she seemed to give him an air of superiority, and he appeared to be in control of the situation. She trusted him.

Anya hung on his every word and followed him around like a puppy, while he lavished attention on her, praising her every achievement and involving her in everything they did. They felt like a family, and Claudia rapidly felt herself weaken. Anything for her darling daughter.

Michel told Claudia that he had a son and daughter from his first marriage. Jan and Freda. According to him, their mother, his first wife, Magda, had influenced their daughter greatly and had destroyed the father/daughter relationship that they had once enjoyed. He appeared to be bitter about this and lost no opportunity to criticise his first wife. In fact, he seemed to hate her and painted an ugly picture of how she had behaved towards him.

When they were alone together, Michel persuaded Claudia to wear her hair in childish bunches or braids. She felt she looked foolish, having been accustomed to a more sophisticated style, but he insisted, just as he wanted her to always keep her body completely hairless, and she felt it was a small price to pay to keep her lover happy. He bought her frilly underwear and lingerie, even little frilly bed socks and white stockings with lacy tops, and it pleased him greatly when she wore them. His eyes would glaze slightly as he came towards her, his desire obvious.

And she desperately wanted to please him. He would make a perfect husband, after all.

He owned a flower import-export business and assured her that his finances were secure, though he admitted he had taken a hit when his previous wife, Magda, had left him and, as he said, 'Taken him to the cleaners.'

Relenting to his constant demands that they get married, Claudia decided to put her Galway home on the market and move to Antwerp as soon as possible. It sold immediately, much to her gratification, as it had been snapped up before it was even advertised, furniture and all. The moment she called the estate agent, he told her he had a buyer who wanted a house exactly like hers and in that very location. Within weeks, everything had been finalised.

Claudia walked around her beautiful home for the last time, touching the furniture that she had sold along with the house that had been her home for the past sixteen years, taking a last look at the bedroom she had shared so happily with Philip and, as she stroked his beloved leather recliner for the last time, she felt strongly that her life was about to change dramatically. She was entering unchartered waters, removing herself from her comfort zone, and she hoped that she had not made the greatest mistake of her life.

CHAPTER THREE
JANET

Janet loved to walk, long walks in the countryside or along the seashore south of Dublin. Now she was free to spend an entire day exploring the countryside when the weather was reasonably decent, her long, rangy stride covering the miles, feet encased in sturdy boots, her backpack containing water, fruit, sandwiches and her current paperback, slung over her shoulders, without having to watch the clock to be home in time to cook James's supper.

She had fully expected to feel lonely and was surprised to find that she felt somewhat relieved to be rid of James and his constant state of irritability. She realised how much of her life she had spent looking after him and catering to his whims and demands.

Her feelings of resentment and anger had been more difficult to deal with after eighteen years of childless marriage. After all, it had been James who had refused her pleas to have the baby she so badly wanted. When she accidentally fell pregnant early on in their marriage, she had wanted to keep her child and had begged James to let her have it, but he had been adamant. So, she had given in to James's accusations that she had broken her promise, and, under pressure and the threat of divorce, she had had an abortion. To this day, she felt the loss, knowing that this child, boy or girl, would be sixteen years old by now, when it was, almost certainly, too late for her. He was sharing his life with a younger woman who already had a child, albeit an oversized fourteen-year-old. The irony wasn't lost on her and just made her feel spurts of fury, which helped to keep her focused.

At one time, she had even begged to include a dog in their lives. But no. James said that dogs were dirty, made a mess, would dig holes in his precious lawn, bark all the time, and who would look after it while they were at work? So, she had acquiesced, and the subject was dropped.

She decided that she had been the best wife she could have been. Always loyal, even when they had the occasional massive row, which made her think of packing her bags and getting on with her life on her own. Well, okay, she thought. There had been that one incident, she didn't really like to think about it, when she had gone to Torremolinos for a hen party weekend, gone out clubbing with her pals, and had woken up the next morning with a strange Spaniard in her bed. It was just a one-night stand, after all, not to be repeated. James had never found out.

Now, she ran her hands through her dark, unruly curls and began to fling whatever James had left behind during his hurried, eager move, into black plastic bags, which she intended to dump. *Time to start again*, she said to herself and to the empty house.

Looking at herself in the bathroom mirror after dumping all James's unclaimed clothes and shoes, plus some photographs which she had torn up, and a framed wedding portrait which she had ripped down off the wall and smashed with the heel of her boot, she saw a cheerful, round, apple-cheeked face and dark lash-fringed brown eyes returning her gaze. She stood back to see a bit more of herself and decided she looked far too boyish. She resolved to buy herself some really feminine summer dresses in preparation for her move to the sun.

I'm going to knock those Italian men for six, she thought to herself, drawing herself up to her full five foot ten inches, marching off on her long legs to search for an estate agent. *I must sell this house soon.*

Finding a suitable local estate agent was straightforward enough, as the Victorian terraced house was in a sought-after area, close to schools, shops, buses and the Dart, that green train that travels the coast of Dublin, north to south from Howth to Greystones and back again. She and James had renovated the house completely when they had married, and it was in perfect condition. Half the proceeds would be hers, which she would invest in a trullo in Puglia.

She knew this was a wild dream, but she had taken to watching some of those TV programmes, where skimpily clad girls with unbelievable tans interviewed people who had moved to warmer climes where everything was less expensive, and the weather was mild and sunny for most of the year. If they could do it, so could she. She had some money invested from her parents' estate, untouched rainy-day funds, so she could afford to live without an income for a short while and pondered doing an online course in digital marketing, something she thought she would enjoy very much, and when she had her diploma, she could then, hopefully, work from home. Now she would have time to explore some interesting possibilities for her future.

Having just enrolled in an online course in the Italian language, she figured that when she actually got to Italy and immersed herself in the culture, she would be fluent in no time at all.

Every evening she would sit at the kitchen table, her long legs curled around the chair legs, with both her laptop and a bottle of wine open beside her, reading everything about life in Puglia, poring over every blog and article she could find online. She also tried hard to get a handle on how much her dream trullo would cost, looking up properties all over the Itrian Valley, or Valle d'Itria as it was called in Italian, where one could find many trulli for sale. Prices appeared to vary widely, so she decided she would find a place to rent first and then look around. There was a great deal she needed to learn before she invested her hard-won funds.

Dreamily, she examined photographs of The White City of Ostuni. It had a look that greatly appealed to her, with its clustered, narrow, alleyways paved in *chianca*. She felt she would be happy to live near such a charming town with its whitewashed buildings looking more Greek than Italian to her mind.

Finally, she found a small house for rent in the little village of Casalini, halfway between Ostuni and the beautiful hill town of Cisternino. The website advertised it as "a pretty townhouse in a picturesque village in the Valle d'Itria". She agreed to move in at the beginning of May for six months. As this was just four months away, she felt a real buzz of excitement as she began to plan her exit.

Janet was surprised at how quickly the house was sold. It took just three months of studiously avoiding walking past number thirty-four by turning right instead of left, as she normally did when she went out, to get to the bus stop or post office. This meant that she had to take a longer route around the block and her trips to the local supermarket ceased, in case she ran into The American Woman, Mrs Hernandez. In fact, planning for and thinking about her proposed move to Italy took up so many of her waking hours that she had no time for regrets or panic. She was on her way.

CLAUDIA

Claudia's late husband, Philip, had been ill for more than two years when he finally gave up the fight. It had been a gruelling time for the entire family.

Six months before Philip died, they decided to head to sunnier climes to see if it would help his illness. His doctor had suggested that some rest and sunshine might be a good idea, as it was a particularly wet summer in the West of Ireland, and he had entered a phase of remission. Philip, Claudia and Anya spent three peaceful months together in Puglia, down south on the stiletto heel of Italy. Claudia remembered their time there together with fond nostalgia; Philip pale and thin, sitting in the sun wearing a straw hat which seemed far too big for him, Anya full of the energy of a seven-year-old, and how resigned she herself felt to the fact that she would, most likely, lose her much-loved husband before too much longer. It was a precious and memorable three months.

After Philip's death, Claudia felt sad and lonely, confused by the fact that Philip's family seemed to think that she was in some way to blame for his death, and utterances like "under pressure" and "high maintenance" were regularly bandied about by his mother. It felt wounding and hurtful. To add to her sadness, her friends, for the most part, had deserted her too. Unable to understand why the dinner invitations had ceased so abruptly, she was unaware that it was her graceful beauty and air of vulnerability that stopped most married women from inviting her into their homes, should their husbands be distracted enough to be lured in the wrong direction.

Claudia found solace in writing romantic novels, pouring her heart and grief onto the pages. Her days were solitary, Anya was at school, and she spent her time at her desk, looking out on to her rose garden.

She was surprised when a publisher snapped up her first book, and the stories had flowed from her pen ever since. By now, she was a household name: Claudia Farrell, Ireland's top romantic novelist. She had kept her maiden name for writing and Claudia Barry, her married name, was an unknown, except to the inhabitants along the rugged shores of Galway Bay.

Now she was getting married again.

***

The wedding had been a quiet affair with Anya and her father, Sean, in attendance. Michel's twenty-five-year-old son, Jan, was also there, and Claudia found herself secretly relieved that this arrogant, swaggering young man — as she perceived him — lived far enough away in Liege not to be a frequent visitor. He arrived for the wedding in a navy suit, blond hair smoothed back, tall and well built, looking very like his father. His daughter, Freda, told them that she could not attend due to work commitments, which Claudia found odd, seeing as it was held on a Saturday. His mother, Hedda, was eighty years old and wheelchair-bound, so she was staying at home in Turnhout. His sister, Britt, made her excuses too.

Anya appeared to be entranced by Jan, who seemed happy to have a young admirer. Claudia had to admit that, despite her opinion of Jan, he and Anya looked wonderful together, both tall, blond, and strikingly good-looking, their lives ahead of them.

Claudia missed her own mother, who had died just a couple of years previously and could have done with her opinion on her change of circumstances. Michel, her new Belgian husband, was courteous to all and raised a toast to his beautiful bride. And Claudia did indeed look radiant in a creamy silk dress, with tiny flowers in her hair. Beside her, Anya, in pink, looked radiant too. The day was quite perfect.

Or so it seemed at the time.

After a couple of days, everyone returned home, including Anya, who was at boarding school in Dublin, and her father, who worked for a large wine importer. Sean hugged her when his flight was called, and she saw tears in his eyes.

'I hope your new marriage works out well and that you're happy with Michel. You must admit, you caught me off guard. It's all been so speedy!'

'You know how long I've been waiting for someone who can give me some stability and be a father to Anya.' She paused. 'You haven't warmed to him, have you.' This was more a statement than a question. Claudia knew that her father had always worried that someone would want to marry her for her money, as she had been left extremely wealthy after the death of her husband, Philip, and made a solid income from her writing.

'As long as he makes you happy, darling girl.' He hesitated, then added, 'Why did his daughter not come to your wedding? I think she lives in Lille, doesn't she? That's only a couple of hours away. None of his family was here, except for his son. Surely…' He trailed off, feeling guilty for bringing up the subject.

Claudia frowned. 'Michel and Freda don't seem to be very close since Magda left him.' Michel had taken great pains to paint his first wife as a scheming witch who had moved out as soon as Freda left home for university. Hence his straitened finances, as he told her constantly. His flower importing business was going extremely well, according to him, assuring her that his finances would resume their previous healthy state before long.

Anya came to stand beside her, waiting for her turn for a farewell hug.

'Love you, Mum,' she whispered. 'I hope you'll be happy with Michel. I'll see you soon.' They hugged, and Claudia looked admiringly at her beautiful sixteen-year-old daughter. She was doing so well at school. She hoped to study veterinary medicine at Trinity College in a couple of years. Claudia's heart swelled with love. It was hard to say goodbye, but she knew that Anya's grandfather would look out for her and that she would see her at every holiday and on visits to Ireland too.

Their first night completely alone since their wedding, he slowly removed the garter from her thigh that she had worn for luck, made passionate love, and they curled up together. Claudia was content. Until the next morning, that was.

She awoke to the sound of crashing and swearing and, as she opened her eyes, was stunned to see several clothes hangers flying through the air from the dressing room, accompanied by a loud stream of angry cursing. She heard words that she had never heard Michel utter before, a foul mouth that took her by surprise.

'I do not use plastic clothes hangers!' he screamed as they bounced and clattered against the end of the bed and around the room.

Claudia was stunned as he stormed through the bedroom, kicking the offending clothes hangers as he strode out, slamming the door behind him. She lay back down on her pillow and felt an ominous sense of foreboding. Tears edged from beneath her closed eyelids. Where was her cultured, wine-sipping husband who spoke like a Frenchman with pursed lips and unfailing charm?

This was a side of Michel she had not been aware of. She had never heard him shout and rage before. Crawling out of bed, as she picked up the offending hangers, she made a mental note to buy some wooden ones that very day. Anything for a quiet life, she thought, unwittingly setting a pattern that would quickly turn to poison.

CHAPTER FOUR
JANET

Finally, Janet packed up her house. She organised for most of it to go to the local auctioneer, some books, paintings and clothes to charity shops, and the balance of her most personal possessions went into storage, ready for the day when she would find her own perfect trullo in Puglia and get everything transported from Ireland.

Then, before she knew it, Easter had arrived, and she was boarding the aeroplane to fly to Brindisi.

Landing in Brindisi was the most exciting thing that Janet had ever experienced. Alighting onto the steps that had been pushed up against the plane, she looked around and saw the blue Adriatic Sea glistening beside the runway. Stepping onto Italian soil, albeit warm tarmac, gave her a jolt of pure pleasure, and she followed the stream of passengers pulling their wheelie-bags into the modern terminal building.

Hauling her enormous suitcase off the carousel in the baggage hall was hefty work, and she realised that she had taken James's muscle, what there was of it, for granted when such activity was required in the past. She would just have to get used to it, she thought to herself as she rolled it through the exit doors and followed the signs for the taxi rank. A taxi would cost a lot, as Casalini was about a forty-five-minute drive, but the bus would take ages, as it stopped at every opportunity along the way, and she wanted to arrive in style and as quickly as possible.

Exiting the airport terminal at Brindisi, she enjoyed the feeling of warmth. It was late spring, and she was looking around at the bustle of the arrivals area when a white taxicab drew up in front of her. The driver hopped out and, before she knew it, her suitcase was safely stored in the boot, and Janet was strapping on her seatbelt. Before she had managed to fasten it securely, the taxi drove speedily away from the terminal at — what she considered — breath-taking speed, screeching to a stop at the barrier, whereby the driver pushed in his ticket, pulled it out again and threw it into the front pocket of the car with several others, then he once more put his foot firmly on the accelerator and headed for the Strada Statale — the dual carriageway that runs up the coast from there to the city of Bari.

She was sitting in the back of the taxi, which drove at breakneck speed and, while several cars came up close to the back bumper, then swerved past, missing them by inches, or so Janet was convinced, she decided that she had never experienced such terrifying driving before. She wondered if she would ever become accustomed to it.

On her right-hand side, she could see the blue Adriatic Sea, while hills were beginning to appear on her left. This was the Murgia, the limestone plateau on which she expected to see hundreds of her beloved trulli nestled amongst the olive groves when they climbed uphill.

Taking the off-ramp for Ostuni, she was not disappointed, as she gasped at the sight of The White City of Ostuni perched high on three hills, with the huge sandstone-coloured cathedral sitting on the skyline. As they drove through the outskirts, passing a multitude of apartment blocks, she felt herself tensing as the taxi zipped straight through the roundabouts without yielding to oncoming traffic. She gripped the armrest. Perhaps giving way on roundabouts was not the Italian custom, she thought, trying to relax. The taxi driver rolled his window down, his arm dangling, as he called greetings to several people he knew. She realised that the only word she could understand was *ciao*!

She tried out her basic Italian on him, but he turned and looked at her blankly. Obviously, the "get by" Italian she had been learning online did not cover anything relevant, and the phrases she knew were, in particular: "Can you bring me the bill? Is it possible to pay by credit card? May I have a table beside the window?" She searched her brain for some suitable phrases and came up empty-handed. Well, she would soon learn, immersed in her new life in the Valle d'Itria.

As they exited Ostuni, Janet spotted her first trullo in an olive grove. Its pointy whitewashed roof with a round white ball on top peered over the fence, and she clapped her hands with glee, stopping in mid-clap when she noticed the taxi driver's eyes peering at her curiously in the rear-view mirror.

The sign said Casalini and, as they entered the village, the taxi turned left. This turn was executed at speed, without warning or indication,

31

throwing Janet to one side. As she righted herself, she could see that they were heading uphill into a street with a row of pretty terraced houses. The taxi ground to a halt outside a small house with three high steps up to the front door, which promptly flew open, and Janet had barely climbed from the car before she found herself enveloped in a fragrant hug by a large lady with improbably red hair.

'Janet!' the red-haired lady cried, bracelets rattling, as she released her from her soft, ample embrace. 'I am Donatella,' she announced. 'Welcome to my house.'

Luckily, Donatella spoke passable English, enough to make Janet feel welcome as she was handed the keys and given a list of instructions, including the days for the various bin collections and a dire warning about not turning on the dishwasher and the washing machine at the same time.

The next twenty minutes were spent explaining the lie of the land to Janet, pointing out the location of the nearest supermarket on the main street and telling her that the post office was just up the hill in a small piazza, beside which she lived herself.

Then she was gone in a flurry of purple chiffon and a flapping of silver sandals.

Janet had a look around. Her suitcase was sitting in the middle of the living room floor, where the taxi driver had put it. She would have to unpack it right there, as there was no possibility of managing to lug it up the steep steps to her bedroom.

The ground floor was open plan, with a small kitchenette in one corner and a wood-burning stove in the other. She noticed radiators and wondered how cold it got in winter. It was April now, and many warm months were ahead. A small square table, covered with a lace cloth, and just two chairs, sat underneath one of the street-facing windows, and there was a sofa staring at a television on the opposite side, overlooking a small garden, where Janet could see a paved area with a small barbecue and a wrought-iron table and chairs. Some terracotta pots containing herbs were lined up against one wall.

She spotted a door at the back of the kitchen and, upon opening it, was greeted by a set of steps leading downwards into the gloom. Pressing the light switch, a solitary bulb came to life, and she discovered that the steps led down to a small cellar, obviously for storing wine and other items that needed to be kept cool. There were hooks attached to the heavy overhead beams, which had probably been used to hang hams and a larder with a wire door for cheeses and eggs, she presumed.

But now to check out the bedrooms. She climbed the steep steps and peered into two small, cosy rooms with chintz furnishings and lace bed linen. One overlooked the garden, and the other had a bird's-eye view of the street. She chose the back bedroom, as she was sure it would be quieter than overlooking the street. She had been told that she was close to an extremely popular restaurant that was open six days per week and always packed. There would undoubtedly be quite a bit of traffic going up and down the narrow street in the evenings.

Opening her suitcase, she took out her sponge bag and a fresh T-shirt and headed upstairs to the tiny shower-room. As the water fizzed against her scalp and ran down her body, she had the feeling that she was washing away Ireland, James, everything she had taken for granted in her old life. It was a briefly unsettling sensation.

'Goodbye past, hello future,' she said aloud as her previous existence swirled down the plughole. Now she was going out to explore. She took her first step into the unknown.

The village of Casalini was intersected by the busy main road from Ostuni to Cisternino. On first viewing, it appeared to consist of just one street, a couple of shops, a pharmacy, a bakery and a bar. Always busy in the mornings with cars, trucks and tractors all jostling for parking space, by 1 p.m., it was like a ghost town when everyone headed for lunch, and everything closed down. After 5 p.m., it was busy again. Such was rural Italian life in Puglia.

Janet discovered that the little town was situated on a steep hill with the main street going across it, which meant that the streets on the right-hand side headed steeply downhill and climbed upwards on the left. All of the houses were painted white, and some trulli cones were to be seen here and there peeping out from among the flat roofs of most of the other houses.

From the outside, the main supermarket in Casalini appeared to be very small indeed. The glass door was protected by a mosquito curtain, comprising a set of dangling thin metal chains that one had to push

33

through in order to gain access. Fighting her way through these, she emerged into the cool interior, which was tunnel-like and much larger than she had expected. A white-haired old lady sat in a corner, nodding greetings at the customers, and the shop was full to the ceiling with every imaginable product. Washing powders and boxes of cereal were piled high on the shelves, which towered over narrow aisles. Vegetables were off to one side, apparently all local produce and fantastically inexpensive — just a few cents for a head of cauliflower! There was a small deli counter at the very back, containing fresh mozzarella, burrata — that creamy delight, so typical of Southern Italy — and cold meats waiting to be sliced, while behind it were huge baskets of freshly baked bread of all shapes and sizes.

Janet was surprised when a pleasant young man with spiked hair and an earring greeted her in English. He was obviously accustomed to dealing with the *Inglese* tourists during the summer months and seemed to know exactly what she would need. He lopped off a few slices of delicious ham, spooned some mozzarella into a small plastic container and picked out some of his best tomatoes for her. Then, as to the question of bread, he suggested a small loaf of Altamura, which, he said, was the best bread for making bruschetta. Janet picked out a bottle of primitivo — the best local wine, according to Gianni, the shopkeeper — and brought everything to the till, where his mother was now manning the checkout. His grandmother, as that was who the old lady in the corner turned out to be, was watching the proceedings with interest, nodding her head in approval.

Loading up two reusable shopping bags, she headed back to her little house and, having unpacked and put away almost everything, she cut a slice of crusty Altamura, piled it high with cooked ham, mozzarella and tiny tomatoes, poured a glass of full-bodied red wine and made herself at home at the kitchen table. She had left the door to the garden open, and sunshine flooded her new home. All Janet could hear was a bird chirping from the leafless fig tree outside. Peace. She had arrived.

One of the first things Janet did, within a few days of her arrival, was to get the bus to Cisternino to purchase a bicycle. A car would have meant leaving it parked on the narrow street, so it wasn't a priority at this point. It could wait. In the meantime, she needed some form of transport, so a bicycle seemed to be a good idea as it would have a double function: keeping her fit and enabling her to move about.

Cisternino is a white, beautiful hill town. When Janet left the bicycle shop, she pointed her new mode of transport towards Casalini, just a few kilometres downhill. It was an exhilarating ride, and she loved the feeling of the warm wind rushing by as she whizzed along. She had bought a purple crash helmet, and her curly dark hair peeked out below it as she negotiated the steep turns. She met a surprising amount of traffic on the road, not all of it cyclist-friendly, and she wondered if there were some safer back roads she should try to discover before she met a sticky end.

CHAPTER FIVE
CLAUDIA

Claudia was usually a strong and emotionally stable woman, but within a couple of months of marrying Michel, she felt weak and inadequate. Her writing was suffering too, as he always seemed to find something that she had apparently neglected to do as soon as she settled down, and her frame of mind was causing her an acute case of writer's block. She asked herself what she was doing wrong. Why could she never please him? It was obviously her fault.

She decided to take up flower arranging. Going to the storehouse where Michel's flowers were arrayed in buckets waiting to be sorted and delivered to the local florists, she was always aware of the different scents and colours and revelled in them. Picking out a few bunches of flowers and ferns, she returned to the kitchen and created three lavish arrangements. They looked beautiful to her tasteful eye, and she proudly displayed them in places of honour.

Michel arrived back for dinner.

'What do you think, darling?' Claudia stood proudly, waiting for his words of praise.

He laughed. 'What? You call these flower arrangements? You know nothing about flower arranging.'

Claudia felt humiliated and close to tears. 'Don't you like them?'

'They look ridiculous. Don't waste your time trying to emulate my colleagues in the flower business. You know nothing about the art.' And with that, he sat down at the dining table as though nothing had happened.

Claudia felt crushed. Her face was hot, and tears were not far away as she brought their meal to the table, serving him first, only joining him when he had uttered a grunt of approval. More often than not, he would shout at her that it was not hot enough, needing a minute in the microwave or back on the pan, or lacking in seasoning suitable for his discerning palate. In fact, at breakfast, just a couple of mornings previously, he had suddenly thumped the table with his fist, making everything rattle. 'Where is the marmalade?' he had roared while she cowered, anxious, terrified.

This evening, he had insisted that she make aioli, that garlic mayonnaise that he loved so much, to go with his fish, at the last minute. He then told her that, in the meantime, it had gone cold, and she was obliged to give it a minute in the microwave.

Finally, she sat in her designated place at the table. Her food had also gone cold while she had been making the aioli, and, anyway, her appetite was gone.

'What's the matter?' he asked. 'Are you not feeling well?'

'I'm fine. Sorry.'

'Maybe you need to take something for your nerves. I'll have a chat with my doctor. You're always so stressed. It's not good for you.' He reached for her hand. 'You'll be okay. Just let me look after you.' And he withdrew his hand, reaching for his knife and fork once more.

Michel was always cultured and charming to their friends, his friends, in fact. Hers were in Ireland, and she was stranded in Belgium, apparently friendless. She could feel that they thought she was a pretty useless human being, and as her self-confidence plummeted, she began to feel deeply depressed.

Take their honeymoon, for example.

Three months after they got married, in early summer, they went on honeymoon to the South of France, where Michel's best friend, Karl, had a house in the old town of Menton. One would think it a very romantic spot, but no. Not for Claudia, as it turned out.

Flying south to Nice, they picked up a rental car and drove to the picturesque town sitting on the shores of the Mediterranean Sea. Leaving their car in a nearby car park, they dragged their suitcases up into the old town, along the narrow, cobbled streets. Claudia was entranced by the tall, colourful houses jammed together as she took in the warmth of the air and the friendly atmosphere. *This is going to be wonderful*, she thought.

After about ten minutes, they arrived at Karl's house.

As Michel looked up at its façade, he turned to her suddenly and said, 'Last time I was here, I took a woman I met in a bar up to the top floor, and we had great sex. I found her very exciting. Beautiful, in fact.'

He licked his lips in a deliberately lascivious gesture and smiled to himself at the memory. And at Claudia's reaction.

Claudia felt as though her face had been slapped. Hard. She could feel her cheeks burning as she fought back recriminations and tears that were threatening to burst to the surface. This was their honeymoon, after all. As soon as Karl opened the front door, introductions were made during which she had found it difficult to speak at all. Their host had shown them upstairs to a charming room, where she collapsed, hot and speechless, on the bed. She lay there, staring at the ceiling.

'Yes. Do take a lie-down, baby girl,' he said in a calm, disinterested voice. 'You know how little things upset you. Have you got something to take for your nerves?'

Michel seemed utterly unperturbed by her shocked reaction to the sudden announcement of his previous sexual encounter and disappeared downstairs with a spring in his step, lured by the promise of a cold beer with his friend. She could hear them laughing and chatting, probably reminiscing about past conquests, she thought, as she lay there with her heart pounding, her face hot.

After four disastrous days in Menton, where Claudia felt deeply uncomfortable by Michel's casual attitude and closeness to Karl, who seemed unaware that she was even there, they headed to Dublin to spend a few days with her father and daughter.

Sean's house was in the upmarket area of Blackrock, south of Dublin. He had lived in the same house, virtually unchanged, since just after Claudia was born. It was her idea of the perfect home, this warm, comfortable house where she had grown up. Just arriving at the gate made her feel safe and secure. She hugged her father close when he opened the door, and Anya rushed from the kitchen to gather them into a group embrace while Michel stood by, smiling, his lips pursed in his charming French mode.

Michel was on his best behaviour during the visit. He hugged and praised Anya when she proudly showed him her latest exam results and was at his most agreeable to his father-in-law. Claudia felt uncomfortable when she noticed her daughter showing those results to her stepfather before she got to see them herself. Anya and Michel were becoming closer and closer. Claudia tried to see this as a positive thing, and she tried to overcome a slight disquiet at their mutual admiration. *Admit it*, she said to herself, *you're jealous.* She had been the sole parent to Anya for so many years that it was difficult to see her with another, albeit a stepfather.

On the last day, her father came to her as she puffed and panted over her suitcase as she tried to close it.

'Why is Michel not helping you with that?' he demanded, indicating with a gesture, her husband reclining on the sofa reading a book, with a beer at his elbow and Anya curled up beside him, her head on his shoulder, tapping on her mobile phone.

'Don't let him turn you into some sort of slave. You're not yourself since you married him, you know.'

'Really, Dad?' she pulled back her blonde hair, which had fallen over one eye, and looked at him. 'Honestly, I hate to ask him to help with anything. He always makes such a big deal of things. It's easier just to do it myself.'

Sean's face flushed angrily. 'That's all wrong!' He spat the words in a voice just above a whisper.

He crouched down beside her and helped her with the suitcase.

'I don't like this at all,' he said, putting his full weight on the bag and managing to fasten the zip. 'You need to stand up for yourself. Your mother would never have put up with this sort of treatment, I can tell you. I didn't rear you to be subservient to anyone.'

'Okay, Dad.' Claudia reached forward and put her arms around him. 'Don't worry. It's early days yet.'

Sean looked at her with a serious expression; his eyes, as blue as hers, challenged her. 'He's getting very close to Anya. Doesn't it bother you at all?'

Claudia was taken aback. Her eyes widened in alarm. 'What do you mean? He's her stepfather. They care about one another a lot.'

'Just keep an eye on her.' Sean stood up and tucked in his shirt, which had come loose at the back. Then he made his way back into the sitting room. 'Come, Anya,' he called. 'Let's get some tea on the go before we take your mum and Michel to the airport.'

Claudia got slowly to her feet, her father's words echoing in her ears.

A week after their return to Belgium, Michel and Claudia went to the town of Turnhout for the wedding of Michel's cousin Erik. It was the first time she had met Michel's daughter, Freda, who was there, as was her new mother-in-law, Hedda, wheelchair-bound and frail, and spoke not a single word of English. Claudia found it a boring, stuffy affair and was puzzled by the fact that Freda refused to sit near her father, preferring to huddle with various aunts and cousins, in particular with Michel's sister, Britt, with whom she appeared to be having an intense conversation.

She felt strongly that she and Michel were looked on with some suspicion and not a great deal of friendship. In fact, she felt that none of his relations wanted to have anything to do with them and treated them as outsiders. Although everyone was perfectly polite and formally welcomed her to the family, there was a certain warmth missing.

As they were getting up to leave, Freda appeared by her side. She had inherited her father's tall genes, but there the similarity ended, as not only was she large, with broad shoulders, but she had an unhealthy complexion, straight, mousey, shoulder-length hair and a look of self-consciousness. Claudia thought she looked shy and felt instant sympathy for the girl.

'I'm sorry,' Freda said. 'You must be wondering what's going on.'

Claudia was stuck for words, but she nodded in agreement.

'I'll write to you,' the girl said and turned away, her face pale. She did not speak to her father at all.

***

It was a very painful year.

'See this photograph?' Michel sat down beside her companionably. They were on their rooftop terrace, overlooking the Wijnegem Canal, having an aperitif. Claudia looked at the photograph. It was of the group of friends who comprised the wine club, which he attended regularly. She had met most of these people over the previous few months. It was difficult to keep up with all his old pals, what with his French group and his regular Freemason evenings, about which he was deeply secretive. Claudia did not mind the fact that she was excluded from all these clubs, as Michel did not seem to want her to be involved, though she did attend the wine group occasionally.

The one and only time she joined the French group for an evening speaking French, eating French food and drinking French wine, Michel laughed and sneered at her attempts at the language. She could understand it well from her schooldays and holidays in France over the years, but her grammar was rusty through lack of practise. However, she had thought that this group would help her to perfect her skills. But no. She felt humiliated and tense throughout the evening. Every time she tried to contribute, Michel would stifle a laugh and smile conspiratorially at his friends, a pained expression on his face as though she had just said something embarrassing. As her face began to feel hotter and hotter, she felt that tears were close and said nothing at all.

'Claudia gets easily upset. She's not well,' he told his friends. 'Come, chérie; I'll take you home.' He put his arm around her protectively as they left, everyone by now eyeing one another in bewilderment.

All the way home in the car, Michel told her how pathetic she was and how she had embarrassed him. As she wept, she decided she would never attend again. Nevertheless, once a month, he headed off alone and perfectly happy for his evening of French language and food.

Looking at his photo of the wine group now, she recognised most of the faces.

'Well,' he began, 'I slept with her' — he pointed at a woman she vaguely recognised — 'and with her and her and her, but not with Wilma. Look at her; she's too fat and ugly.' He threw back his head and laughed, obviously enjoying himself. And on and on he went. Claudia's face felt hot, and she knew tears were not far away. Her humiliations were coming thick and fast.

She felt anguished; tears rolled down her cheeks.

'I'll get you one of your pills.' He sounded solicitous. She had been taking Prozac for a while now. Michel insisted that her hormones were playing tricks with her mental health and had persuaded his own doctor to let him have some. 'I told him how easily upset you get. You'll feel better soon. You need to learn to calm down. You're really not well.'

'Maybe I should visit the doctor myself,' she ventured.

'Do you not trust me to look after you?' His voice was rising, and she felt herself cower inside, as she always did when he shouted at her.

Claudia felt as though she was going mad. Perhaps she was. She swallowed the pill that was given to her and tossed it back with a mouthful of wine, waiting for the numbness that inevitably followed. He was so patient with her emotional outbursts, after all. She would try to do better. He was only telling her a bit about his past, after all.

'Where's my ring?' Claudia asked Michel as they were getting ready to go out to dinner one evening. Anya was with them in Antwerp, and they were going to try a new restaurant that Michel had said was one of the best in town. 'My emerald and diamond one?' She rummaged around in her jewellery box.

Michel looked over at her with indifference. He was tying his tie in a large, flamboyant knot. 'You've probably just mislaid it. You're always putting things down and forgetting where they are.'

'Really? Do I do that?' She looked at him incredulously. She had to admit that since she had begun taking Prozac, plus whatever pills he gave her when she became upset, she had felt herself becoming slightly numb to life around her.

He laughed. 'You know you do.' He ran his hand over his already smooth jaw and checked himself in the mirror again. Obviously liking what he saw, he turned to her. 'It will turn up.'

Claudia was upset. 'It's my most precious piece of jewellery. My mother left it to me. It was her engagement ring. I would never just put it down and forget about it.'

'No?'

'No!' She looked once more in her jewellery box. 'It must have been stolen. Who would do such a thing? I mean, it's kept in the wall safe.'

'We need to go.' Michel put his arm around her. 'Put the jewellery box back in the safe, and I'll help you to look for it later.'

'We need to call the police!' Claudia was now becoming upset. She had had to take an extra tranquilliser earlier, as Michel told her she was becoming too hyper when Anya arrived home. She had not felt that she was upset, probably just excited at seeing her daughter. But Michel knew her moods, and she trusted him.

'Let's decide later when we've had time for a proper look.'

'But it's gone! It must have been stolen! It's worth a fortune.'

'Let's talk about it later.' He took her by the elbow as though she were unable to descend the stairs without assistance. At the bottom, she saw Anya, a frown on her face. 'Your mum's not herself,' he said to her, his voice low, confidential. 'I need to pop back upstairs for my jacket, just take her out to the car, and I'll be right out.'

He mounted the stairs, two at a time, and entered the bedroom. Crossing to the wall safe, which he quickly opened, he took the missing ring from his pocket, placed it in a prominent place on the metal shelf beside the jewellery box and locked it again. Then, picking up his jacket from the bed, he slipped it on, smiling to himself as he hurried downstairs and joined Claudia and Anya in the car. Anya was pensive on the drive to the restaurant, while Claudia stared ahead as though in a trance, but Anya soon cheered up as she sat beside Michel, and he chatted to her about school, praising her lavishly when she told him about her latest triumph in getting an A-plus in maths.

Claudia was on edge all through dinner.

'What's wrong, Mum?' Anya was concerned at Claudia's distracted state. She opened her mouth to speak.

'Your mum is fine,' interrupted Michel. He spoke soothingly. 'She's not herself these days, and she's very thrilled to have you home.' He turned to Claudia. 'Isn't that right, darling? You're not well at the moment.' He turned back to Anya. 'It's women's things,' he said, and Anya nodded, though she really did not understand what was going on.

Returning home that evening, Claudia went straight to the wall safe to have another look. There on the shelf, right beside her jewellery box, was the emerald and diamond ring. She snatched it up just as Michel entered the room.

'It's here. My ring.' She held it up for him to see.

'I told you it would turn up, darling.'

She fell into his arms, sobbing. He stroked her hair. 'Let's go to bed. You need to rest. I'll talk to the doctor again tomorrow. Perhaps you need a stronger medication.' He led her to the bed, a glint in his eyes.

***

Meanwhile, Michel's son, Jan, was driving Claudia insane. Like a shark who can scent blood in the water, he seemed to have realised that she had become weak and vulnerable, arriving regularly with a huge bag of filthy sheets and general clothing items for her to wash. She was furious about this, but Michel loved to see Jan arrive, and they would go walking together while she was left with a few machine-loads of washing. If it had just been the washing, she could probably have coped, but it was his indolent and disrespectful manner that got under her skin.

On several occasions, she noticed him look at Anya with a closed expression on his face that Claudia found difficult to read. On one occasion, she found him loitering outside Anya's bedroom door while she was inside getting ready for bed. She asked him what he was doing there and watched him saunter towards his own room without answering her question. She was convinced that he could be a bad influence, apart from the fact that he was almost ten years Anya's senior, but she seemed to idolise him, almost as much as she did Michel.

Claudia was deeply annoyed by Jan and his constant intrusive visits. She was supposed to be writing, not washing this lazy young man's clothes and bed linen every couple of weeks. Unfortunately, there was a regular train service between Liege and Antwerp, and he arrived regularly and often unannounced.

If ever she mentioned her reservations to Michel, he would dismiss the subject, shouting, 'It's his home!'

CHAPTER SIX
DAISY

She was childlike. A waif, whose auburn hair parted in the middle and fell in waves on either side of a small, pale face from which peered two anxious brown eyes. She spotted Janet the moment she walked into Caffe Negroni, beside the park in downtown Ostuni.

She saw a tall, slim, dark-haired woman in white leggings and a flowing, red chiffon blouse, sitting on the fringes of the usual expat group, sipping a glass of white wine and looking lost.

'Hi! I'm Daisy.' She introduced herself to Janet and pulled out a chair, inviting herself to sit down beside her. 'I've seen you in here a few times. Are you English?' Her accent was cut glass and, as Janet thought to herself, *la-di-dah.*

Janet immediately recognised her new acquaintance as an original hippie, dressed in boho-chic, with a thick beaten silver bangle above her elbow and a draped Balinese shawl.

'Hi, Daisy. No. I'm Irish, from Dublin. My name is Janet Casey. Pleased to meet you.' Janet stuck out a friendly hand, and Daisy took it gratefully, holding onto it for a few moments longer than necessary while her eyes scanned Janet's face, seemingly searching for clues. Finding that her close scrutiny provided her with the information that the object of her interest appeared to be friendly and was not about to bite her, she released Janet's hand and sat down opposite her, gesturing to the waiter, with one tiny beringed hand, to bring her a spritz.

Daisy was a regular at Caffe Negroni and, with her posh accent and eccentric style of dress, accompanied by a slightly absentminded air, was looked on as not really "one of us" and excluded from becoming close to any of the other expats on a personal basis. But she seemed to neither notice nor care and carried on happily chatting to anyone who would listen.

She discovered that Janet had stumbled on Caffe Negroni by chance. Apparently, on Janet's second visit to her new bank, she had needed an urgent bathroom break. As was her custom, rather than barge into a bar looking for the loo, she ordered a coffee and then enquired, politely, if she could use the bathroom. On one of her subsequent visits there, she noticed a large gathering of English-speaking people sitting at a group of tables, all leaning in having a good gossip. She had wandered over to them and introduced herself, and they had promptly invited her to join them, and Janet had the distinct impression that they were thrilled to have a new person to listen to their tales of woe.

The expats, over an Aperol Spritz, a glass or three of wine or a few beers, used these occasions to complain bitterly about Italian bureaucracy and imagined slights and grievances held against the inhabitants of the town and its environs. Though this annoyed Janet quite a bit, and she could find no good reason to join in, she nevertheless found herself drawn there, just to speak English and fraternise with other expats on a regular basis.

Their constant griping, after a few weeks, began to make Janet feel uncomfortable, but they were living here, and she felt she could learn a lot by spending some time in their company. She was there, sitting on the periphery of this intense group of, mostly, English women, when she was aware of this small, thin waif, wrapped in an exotic shawl, looking down at her. It was Daisy.

'Do you live here full time?' Daisy began their first conversation. She looked nervously at Janet as though expecting her to refuse to answer. Her little face looked uncertain.

Janet felt herself warm towards the other woman. 'Yes. I'm renting in Casalini and looking for a trullo to live in full time. You?'

'Oh! I'm looking for an apartment in the historic centre of Ostuni.' She leaned forward, and Janet could see that Daisy was a fair bit older than she looked at first glance. Not quite so childlike up close. 'I want to live here full time too. It's time I put down roots. I've been travelling the world for the past few years. Have you been to India?' She babbled on.

The two women chatted amiably for quite some time.

'What brings you to this part of the world?' she asked.

Janet was accustomed to being questioned as to why she was in Ostuni. 'I've been here for more than two months now, and I'm just beginning to settle down. Let's just say, at this point, I'm trying to get my bearings.'

'Wow!' exclaimed Daisy, crossing her thin legs. While flicking back her wispy hair, she picked up her spritz and prepared for conversation. 'That means we're in exactly the same position. My dear, so many people who live here have been giving me advice. I'm completely confused and don't know who to believe. Everyone sounds so negative. They all seem to think I'm going to be taken to the cleaners.'

Janet chose her words carefully. 'I wouldn't waste a moment of my time listening to negativity. I would just prefer to get out there myself and make up my own mind about both the property I want and decide whose qualified advice to take. But no negativity.' She took a large gulp of her spritz and crossed her long legs with a flourish, as if to emphasise her independence.

Daisy looked at her admiringly. She was not, it seemed, accustomed to hearing positivity in Caffe Negroni. Janet seemed to have found a new friend.

Over the next hour, Daisy regaled her with sad stories about trying to purchase the home of her dreams. Having found a shoulder to lean on, she proceeded to tell Janet about one nightmare scenario after another: the apartment with an illegal bathroom; the one so tiny, one would have to walk sideways past the loo and bidet to get to the shower; the apartment with no heating; the estate agent who sold an English lady a trullo with an illegal extension which turned out to be unsaleable as a result, apparently a fairly common occurrence, according to the chat from the expat group. And on and on.

'My dear, you have no idea the trouble I've had! Nobody wants to sell anything in a straightforward manner here.' Her lips quivered with emotion, and she took an enormous, fortifying swig of her spritz. Janet was horrified to see Daisy's eyes fill with tears, and she looked away, feeling embarrassed. She realised that she had little time for such a display of emotion and looked on it as self-indulgent.

Perhaps I'm becoming hard, she thought to herself for a moment. This practical woman who had weathered the storm and had started a new life alone in a strange country had little time for negativity in others.

However, she could not help but feel slightly protective of her new friend.

'It will happen, Daisy. The right property will come along. Wait and see. And stop worrying about it. Just enjoy being here for the moment.'

Daisy looked at her new friend admiringly. She could see that Janet appeared to be overwhelmed by all the negative talk. Caffe Negroni was possibly the most popular hangout in Ostuni for expats and a place chock-full of negativity. Daisy paid close attention when Janet told her that she really didn't think it was her scene.

This sort of negativity could be contagious, and they both knew that, in time, they needed some more positive people to hang out with. Surely it was possible to meet a different sort of expat. They resolved to find another bar, and Janet insisted that, as soon as she found her feet, she would begin to give Caffe Negroni a miss, but for now, it seemed to be the "in" place to meet if one wanted to know what was going on. However, this was absolutely not how either of them wanted to live their lives here in this friendly corner of Southern Italy.

Janet placed her glass decisively on the table and rose to her feet.

'I must go,' she said, and Daisy got up too, draining her glass as she rose and putting it back on the table with a clatter. They walked to the door together. Daisy — Janet noticed — was a bit wobbly on her little feet. Outside the bar, a magnificent Pugliese sunset was in progress, and the palm trees in the nearby park were darkly silhouetted against the deep-orange sky. They sighed happily in unison.

Donatella's daughter lived in Ostuni, and whenever she visited her, usually a couple of evenings a week, she offered Janet a lift. She always picked her up later on for the ten-minute drive back to Casalini. Now, she was parked a little way down the street, waiting for Janet and studying her phone. Her tiny, battered grey car was covered in dust. It was now summer and a dry, dusty time of year, with steel-blue skies and high temperatures during the long lazy days, when tourists from Northern Europe visited Puglia in their droves to hang out on the pretty beaches and throng the narrow streets and tempting restaurants of the little towns every evening.

Donatella looked up as they approached, and Daisy was introduced. Janet could not help noticing the contrast between tiny Daisy with her wispy red hair, childish figure, and reserved demeanour, with her dark, ample-bosomed landlady, who was loud in her pleasure to see that Janet had made a new friend.

Bidding each other goodnight, having swapped numbers and email addresses, with promises to meet again soon, promises that Janet was unsure of but needed to see how this new friendship evolved. Daisy was not really Janet's type of person as most of her close girlfriends were down-to-earth, practical women, not dizzy types at all. But they were all back in Ireland, and she was alone in Italy. A friend was to be valued, after all.

Daisy, for her part, walked along the street and down the little laneway to where her tiny bedsit was located. It had been described as an apartment when she had been told about it by an estate agent who had befriended her. When she saw how tiny it was, she was shocked and upset but too timid to tell her "friend" that she did not like it. Anyway, she figured, she would not be there for too long. Something would come along soon.

CHAPTER SEVEN
CLAUDIA

Two of Claudia's old friends from Galway came to visit. They were both well-known writers — one a poet with a real talent for putting rhythm and fun into the most mundane everyday matters.

They stayed for dinner, and Claudia pulled out all the stops. She, herself, was an excellent cook, and they ate and drank until after midnight. She felt alive and stimulated. Perhaps she was getting better.

All three women talked about their writing careers and, as the evening wore on, Claudia could see that Michel was feeling left out. She tried to involve him in their conversation, which was about people they knew, books they had read and various current Irish topics, mainly from the world of art and literature.

She noticed that he was drinking heavily and felt unaccountably nervous. This was not good.

And she was right. It was a disaster.

After her friends had left to return to their hotel, with kisses and promises to catch up again soon, Claudia turned to Michel with a smile.

'Wow! I really enjoyed the evening,' she exclaimed happily. 'It was lovely to be able to catch up with the girls.'

Now she saw that he was visibly drunk. With great difficulty, she managed to help him to climb the stairs. Being a foot taller, she realised that it was perilous, but she persisted, and, finally, they reached the upper landing and the safety of their bedroom.

While standing in front of her basin in her nightie, brushing her teeth, he entered the bathroom.

'How dare you!' he suddenly shouted.

Claudia was speechless. What had she dared to do? She had had the first normal evening in months, really enjoyed herself and did not feel stupid for a change.

'You tried to humiliate me,' he roared. 'You thought you could make me feel inferior by talking about books and exhibitions and all the things

I know nothing about. Well, I know how stupid you are. You may fool those bitchy friends of yours with your pseudo-intellectual chatter, but I know what you're really like.' His voice rose to full volume.

As Claudia stood still, frozen to the spot, toothbrush still in her hand, he reached for her hair and lifted her bodily from the floor. The pain was intense, and she screamed.

It was just for a few seconds, but enough to frighten her greatly. She fled to the guest bedroom and locked herself in. She could hear him stumbling around and muttering viciously about what he was going to do to her if he got his hands on her. She was terrified and spent the rest of the night huddled on the guest bed, dozing occasionally and sobbing bitter tears. Was this what her life had become?

Next morning, the matter was not discussed at all. Claudia drove to the supermarket and, as her head touched the headrest in the car, the ache she felt on the back of her scalp reminded her of how her life was spinning out of control.

She resolved to try to be stronger in future.

***

'I'd like you to become more involved in my company.'

Michel surprised Claudia greatly with this statement. Though her money was supporting them, and she had paid for major alterations to the house out of her own funds, he had steadfastly refused to let her see even a bank statement. 'That's not for you to worry about. I'll take care of things.' His voice rose. 'That's what I'm here for.'

Claudia had previously always looked after her own finances but had acquiesced to Michel's insistence that he must be in charge of all matters to do with money and, by now, she was so deeply depressed that she just wanted to be allowed to lie on the sofa every afternoon. Michel kept telling her she was menopausal, though she was barely forty years old.

She was lying there, trying, but failing, to read a novel. Her mind just did not seem to be able to absorb anything these days. Perhaps it was the Prozac, which was, ostensibly, supposed to help her to cope with the menopause, or whatever it was that was causing her such stress. Nonetheless, these words registered.

She sat up on the sofa and asked, 'Really? In what way?'

'I think it's time you invested in our future.' He had on his charming face, the one that she didn't often see unless they were in the company of his friends. The face where he pursed his lips and spoke with an exaggerated French accent. She had thought it was quite sexy at first, but not anymore. He had stopped using it within a couple of days of their marriage, so she was surprised to see it directed at her out of the blue. She felt a momentary surge of hope. He was actually speaking to her as if she were a competent adult, not a cowed, nervous wreck. 'I would like you to put some of your money, which is doing nothing but sitting in a bank, into our company.'

He said it as though he were bestowing a great favour on her. She tried to concentrate.

'How much do you want me to invest?' she asked anxiously, smoothing her tousled blonde hair and trying to concentrate.

Claudia had already eaten a big hole in her finances since they had married, just six months previously. His house had been run down, in disrepair and needed redecorating, plus a great deal of new furniture in order to make it acceptable to her. Her delicate touches were now everywhere, and it breathed understated elegance, which it had certainly not done before, with its dated seventies décor and a great deal of dark, heavy furniture. She had hated it, feeling that its darkness added to her gloomy thoughts. But the refurbishment had cost a great deal, and she needed to get a new book out soon, or she would begin to notice the large dent in her savings. Her lack of ability to concentrate was now causing a problem. For the first time in her life, she felt helpless. Trapped. Vulnerable. Unrecognisable as the strong, capable woman she had been less than a year previously.

The figure he mentioned made her take in a deep breath. He added, 'But it would only be for a few months. Then you can have it all back, with interest.'

Timorously, Claudia ventured, 'For that amount, perhaps I'd need some security. I have to think of Anya's future, and this money was left to us by her father, Philip.' She continued, breathing deeply. 'It's technically hers, and I put it aside for her college fees. I just can't afford to hand it over without some safeguard in place. I know you understand.

We'd need to have some kind of legal agreement drawn up; I think.' Even in her drugged and depressed state, her brain was obviously functioning on some level. The thought of Anya's money disappearing down the plughole, which appeared to be Michel's business, was intolerable.

For a moment, anger and indignation flashed across Michel's handsome face, and he looked as though he was going to make an angry retort. Then he thought better of it, aware that Claudia was, though depressed and under his thumb, far from stupid.

'Of course! We'll make an appointment to see my solicitor, Graham, this week.'

Claudia had met Michel's solicitor at their wedding and found him to be an overbearing, overweight man who spoke to her as though she were a child. He had obviously taken his cue from Michel.

A few days later, she found herself on the other side of the desk to morbidly obese Graham, with Michel by her side, leading the conversation.

'Of course, if Claudia signs over this money to the company, she thinks she will need some security.' Michel gave a dismissive chuckle, man to man, as though she were being unreasonable and a bit silly. The "little woman".

Graham looked concerned. 'What security do you have, Michel?' he asked dubiously.

'Just the house. Our home.' He turned his charming, pursed-lipped face to Claudia. 'I suppose, as it's our home, that would be no problem.' He genuinely thought that he had her firmly under his thumb.

'Okay,' she responded. It sounded like a good plan, as she had already invested what was possibly close to its market value in its extensive renovation. 'Let's do that then.'

Graham looked at them pompously over his reading glasses. 'Michel. You do understand, don't you, that if you lose this money, your house will belong to Claudia? You can't afford to get divorced, or you'll be out on your ear!' He laughed, a man-to-man sort of laugh that made Claudia cringe. Suddenly, as though light had penetrated her addled brain, she realised that she was, hopefully, about to regain some control over her life. Michel obviously thought that she was incapable of ever leaving him, so strong was his hold over her.

'Of course not!' She smiled, as lovingly as she could manage. Michel squeezed her hand confidently. The documents were drawn up, and she signed on the dotted line, as did Michel, as he signed their home over to her, so confident was he that she would never leave him. He had her under control, after all. He patted her paternally on the hand.

Claudia still had some money. She owned a cottage in the West of Ireland, which was home to some long-term tenants. The title deeds were in her safety-deposit box in the bank. It was her rainy-day money and gave her a feeling of security, even after agreeing to hand over such a huge sum to Michel.

As the days went by, Michel continued to attempt to import and export flowers for Antwerp's busy flower markets and shops, propped up by the large sum of money he had received from Claudia. She noticed that he was becoming louder and even more bad-tempered than usual and seemed deeply stressed as the days went by. She got the strong impression that the business was going badly once more. She thought to herself that perhaps he was not as bright as she had imagined in the beginning. Very few people were, in her opinion.

She decided to pay a visit to Ireland to see her father. Anya was on a school break, and Sean was keen for them to visit. Afterwards, she would bring her daughter back with her to Antwerp for a couple of weeks.

Two days before she was due to leave Antwerp, the postman put a letter in their box. It was addressed to Claudia.

Claudia studied the envelope, turning it over in her hands. A French postmark. The handwriting small, neat and slightly backhanded. Who did she know in France? Could it be the promised letter from Freda? She resumed her seat at the dining room table, where she had been having breakfast before the arrival of the postman and poured another cup of tea. She felt herself tense up as she opened it and slowly unfolded the single, tightly written sheet of paper.

As she reached the bottom of the page, she tried to digest what she had just read. Her stomach heaved, and she began to pore over it again as the full horror of what she was reading hit her like a hammer blow. Before she had time to read it again, or to fully digest the contents of this damning report, she felt, rather than saw, Michel behind her as the letter

54

was whisked from her hands, and he strode from the room carrying it in two fingers as though it were something highly contagious. She hadn't heard him come up behind her, so riveted was she at the content of this explosive revelation.

Gathering herself together, she rushed after him into the kitchen, where she was just in time to see the letter tossed into the stove and burst into flames.

'Why did you burn it?' she screamed at him furiously, trying to get to the stove as he held her back effortlessly with one hand. He was silent, his mouth set into that familiar grim line of disapproval. Moving away from the stove in tandem, Claudia was conscious of how helpless she felt beside this tall man, who stood a foot taller than she did at six foot four inches in his stockinged feet. He towered over her menacingly, a strange expression on his flushed face. Was it guilt? Embarrassment?

'It was my letter,' she insisted. 'I've been waiting for it for months. Freda said she would write to tell me why she wouldn't speak to you at Greta's wedding. It's disgusting. The poor girl.' She fought to sound calm, but her voice quavered dangerously.

Michel strode from the room, refusing to respond. She rushed after him once more.

'Is it true? Did you do what she said?'

He said nothing, just kept looking at her, his face a mask.

With that, he was gone, the door slamming in his wake as he strode from the room and out the back door where she saw him stride stiffly to the storeroom where he kept his stock of flowers: row upon row of buckets full of sweet-smelling, colourful blooms, mainly chrysanthemums, which he grew himself. She stood in the doorway, looking after him coldly. The horror of what she had just read finally hit her, and she rushed to the bathroom, where she threw up violently. She swore that once this was all over, she never wanted to see or smell a chrysanthemum again.

Looking in the mirror over the basin, after she had splashed her face with cold water, she saw a pale, ghostly vision with red-rimmed blue eyes. Her blonde hair was flat and damp, and she ran her fingers through it. Opening the cabinet over the basin, she withdrew the plastic bottle full of Prozac and, on an impulse, lifted the loo seat and emptied the entire container into its depths, flushing a few times to make sure they were completely gone. A moment of anxiety about what she had done was replaced immediately by a renewed sense of purpose. She was going to regain control of her life.

Still feeling shocked, Claudia thought about Anya and her stomach clenched with fear. Michel was her stepfather, whom she trusted to help give her daughter a safe and happy home after losing her father so young. She would have to have a mother—daughter chat the next time they were together. And she would need to look carefully at her present situation, only having been married to Michel for less than one year. But how could she stay under these circumstances?

So, finally, the letter had arrived, and it was damning evidence about her new husband. Claudia felt that the words in the letter were stamped on her brain forever. It chronicled some years of sexual abuse inflicted on Freda by Michel when she was a young teenager, which had been so traumatic she had twice attempted suicide; the second time had, apparently, been a very close call. While still a student, she had checked into a hotel and taken an overdose of sleeping pills. Miraculously, the hotel owner had discovered her in time. Freda had left her wallet at reception and, on trying to return it to her and hearing no response to his knocking, the owner had decided to open the door and leave it in her room. He then discovered Freda lying unconscious on the bed with an empty packet of pills and a bottle of whisky on the bedside locker. She was rushed to hospital, and her stomach was pumped. She hadn't attempted it since and had not told Claudia the details of that first attempt.

Claudia recalled two particular sentences in that terrible letter. Verbatim. The words were tattooed permanently on her brain.

Often, when I would get home from school and go to my room, Papa would come and lie down on the bed beside me, open my school blouse, feel my breasts and much more. He said how much he loved me in my school uniform. It was unbearable.
And
He knew how deeply this was affecting me, but he wouldn't stop. I was too terrified of him to tell anyone.

Freda was unmarried, now thirty years old, with no real friends, no children, living a solitary life in Lille. Her mother had moved to South Africa with her new husband, so she was alone. Her life was a deeply unhappy one. Claudia's heart ached with sympathy.

Her visit to Ireland was therapeutic. Freshly off anti-depressants without medical supervision, she felt energised, though perhaps a bit manic from time to time over the first few days. Each time she sat down for more than a few minutes, she found herself up again and pacing. Every morning she walked the leafy streets of Blackrock and Mount Merrion, down to Seapoint and to the old seawater swimming baths, which had been very popular in her father's teenage years. By degrees, she began to feel more in control of her life. She would pop into Starbucks, in what had once been Blackrock Post Office, overlooking the old baths, wondering if her father had dived from the metal platform, a now rusty monument to the fact that time moves on. She pondered her future. What on earth was she going to do? She really could not stay with Michel under these circumstances. Her life had become a living nightmare.

She spoke to Anya about Michel, trying to find a way to ask her tactfully if he had ever touched her inappropriately. It was a dreadfully embarrassing conversation and confusing for Anya, but at least Claudia felt reassured that such a thing had never happened and resolved that Anya would remain unscathed by her stepfather.

Sean came to Claudia the morning they were leaving. It was obvious he had something important to say, just the way his blue eyes looked anxious but determined.

'If you decide to divorce Michel, you have my full support,' he announced. Claudia was taken aback, as she knew her father had strict ideas about marriage and divorce. She had broken down in tears the previous evening and told him how unhappy she was, leaving out the sordid details. She was reluctant to burden her already anxious father any more than was necessary. However, what appeared to have clinched the deal was the fact that Sean's dog Rowland, a miniature Pinscher, hated Michel with a passion and constantly barked at him. Michel had taken a few kicks at poor Rowland on their previous visit, and Sean had witnessed a couple of these incidents. And Sean was firmly convinced that Rowland was an excellent judge of character.

'Thanks, Dad.'

CHAPTER EIGHT
CLAUDIA

She returned to Antwerp with Anya, only to find Michel uncommunicative and moody. He barely spoke to her but turned his charm up fully in Anya's presence. Claudia could see that her daughter was confused. She tried to make things as normal as possible during her daughter's visit, but it was complicated. She and Michel got into bed together at night with their backs to one another on either side of the bed. The horror of what she had learned had managed to destroy the last vestiges of what she had felt for him.

Once more, she insisted that they talk about the entire matter of Freda, but all he ever said was, 'I used to drink a lot back then.' No denials, then.

That weekend, Jan arrived. When he had phoned earlier, and Claudia heard Michel talking to him on the phone, she had mouthed, 'Not this weekend. We need to talk.' But he had almost completely ignored her pleas and said, 'Maybe next weekend would be better.'

Jan arrived anyway, emptying out his washing on the kitchen floor as usual and swaggering to his room, wearing a set of headphones.

Claudia had reached breaking point and, stepping over the mountain of washing, strode after him.

'I thought your father made it clear that this weekend didn't suit us?' She stood, finally, to confront this arrogant young man.

At that moment, Michel emerged from the study to find his wife and son standing in the hallway face to face. Jan appeared to be unruffled as he removed his headphones from his ears, letting them casually drop to the back of his neck, a slight sneer on his lips. Claudia was in an aggressive pose, hands on hips. Michel stopped in his tracks and listened to the conversation.

'I'll come here any time I want. This is my father's pad.' Jan's voice was smug as he looked down at her from his considerable height, similar to his father's.

That was the end of Claudia's restraint.

'Well, have I got news for you!' she said, stabbing her finger towards him. 'This is *my* pad now, and I want you to leave immediately.' She turned on her heel and stalked off. She never saw him again.

Anya had arrived for the tail end of the conversation and was distraught. 'Mum! How can you tell Jan to leave? I don't understand. Why is it not his home anymore?'

Claudia put her arm around her daughter's shoulders. 'Trust me,' was all she said as she looked into her daughter's face. 'I have no choice.'

Anya stormed off to her bedroom and slammed the door in the manner of any normal sixteen-year-old girl.

Later, after the front door banged and Jan had gone, never to return, Michel came to find her. She was upstairs in the bedroom, trying to regain her composure.

Before he could open his mouth to berate her, she pre-empted him, turned around and said coldly, 'I'm going to get a divorce.'

Michel stared at her disbelievingly. He walked towards her threateningly and put one of his large feet on top of her small ones.

'Nobody walks out on me,' he roared as he punched her hard under the chin and her head snapped back. She screamed in terror. He was about to do it again when Anya burst into the room and flew at Michel.

'Don't hurt Mum!' She tugged hard at his arm and began to cry.

Michel stepped back from Claudia and looked at Anya in horror and, with what Claudia felt, was embarrassment. He actually managed to look sheepish at his lack of self-control.

'Anya!' he exclaimed as the two women left the room, their arms around each other.

Claudia went downstairs with Anya and hugged her tightly when they reached her room on the ground floor.

'Mum! I've been so scared recently. The way he looks at you. As though he hates you.' She paused, then said, 'Why does he hate you? What have you done? Can you not make more of an effort?'

At that moment, hearing the accusation in her daughter's words, Claudia knew she had to get away from Michel and his influence over Anya as quickly as possible. Away from this house in Antwerp. She had married Michel, thinking he would protect her and be a father to her daughter, but it seemed that she had put both of them in jeopardy. Their security and prosperity were at risk. She needed to think.

He still thought she wasn't serious about leaving him. The previous night she had placed a row of pillows down the middle of the bed, as he had refused to move out to the guest bedroom. He threw the pillows angrily on the floor, so she had spent the night perched on the edge of the bed, eyes wide open, afraid they would touch, feeling revolted by his presence.

She would have happily moved into the guest bedroom but felt that it would be akin to admitting that he still had some power to manipulate her into backing down over her desire for a divorce. As though it were still his "pad". Also, it would have added too much drama to Anya's already over-dramatic weekend. She could not add to it further.

Next day, Claudia put Anya on her flight back to Dublin, having rung her father, who was pleased to have his precious granddaughter back so soon. Then she went to the bank to take her passport and all documents from her safety-deposit box. She had found a divorce lawyer, and she wanted to set things in motion immediately. She hadn't a moment to lose.

Claudia had met this officious female bank teller before and had felt that she disapproved of her in some undefinable way. Now, with a martyred sigh, she carried the safety-deposit box to the desk where Claudia inserted the key and withdrew her personal documents — passport, birth and marriage certificates — on automatic pilot, her mind preoccupied.

As the teller began to take it back to the vault, Claudia suddenly realised that all was not what it should be. She frowned, trying to think what could be wrong.

'Come back, please,' she called to the teller, who looked impatient, feathers ruffled, but brought it back to the desk where Claudia was standing. 'I need to open it again. Something doesn't look right.'

She reopened the box and looked in. The title deeds to the cottage in the West of Ireland were missing.

'Someone's been into my safety-deposit box!' she exclaimed. The teller looked defensive. 'Who has been given access to my box?' Now strident and confused.

'Well…' A moment of self-righteousness and the teller, chin raised, informed her that Michel had taken out her safety-deposit box a few days previously.

'What?' Claudia was incredulous. 'But I gave nobody permission to access it.'

'We've known Mr Reynard for years.' The teller looked offended, her colour rising. 'When he asked for your box and said he had your permission — and he had the key — of course, we gave it to him.' The teller was gabbling now.

'Get me the manager.' Claudia was now furious. The gaslighting was over. She was back in control. She realised that Michel had controlled her by making her feel stupid and unworthy for the past year. She had read an article about gaslighting and knew now that she had been a victim. He was a con man, a common thief, and a paedophile to boot. She shivered, suddenly feeling as cold as ice.

The bank manager, Mr Janssen, sweaty-palmed and nervous, was summoned from his inner sanctum to deal with this angry Irishwoman. He told her that Michel had brought him the title deeds while she was in Ireland and was in the process of raising money against them. Claudia was horrified at the subterfuge and crookedness of the arrangement. Of course, her keys had been hanging on a hook in the kitchen while she had been away. She had never imagined that such blatant crookery could possibly be at play.

Mr Janssen assured her that Michel had insisted that it was all with her knowledge and approval. He had taken a photocopy of her deeds and returned the originals to Michel. Then he went on the offensive, worried that she would try to sue the bank. In fact, that was his main preoccupation, and he instructed his secretary to type up a letter stating that Claudia absolved the bank of any responsibility and that the matter would be dropped. She probably should not have signed it so readily, but she just wanted this whole sorry mess to end as soon as possible.

She then immediately closed her account and moved to another bank right across the street. Mr Janssen appeared to be relieved to see her go, mopping his brow with a large handkerchief as he scurried back to the safety of his office.

On her arrival home, she confronted Michel.

'Where are the title deeds for my cottage in Connemara?' she demanded. 'I know you stole them from my safety-deposit box. I've just had a major run-in with Mr Janssen. Give them to me.'

Michel laughed. 'Oh no you don't, my girl. I'm hanging onto them. What other insurance do I have?'

His arrogance shocked Claudia to the core.

'You're not going to get away with this, Michel. If you don't give them back to me, I'm going to the police on Monday. You've stolen them from me, and I want them back immediately.' She was by no means sure she would call the Belgian police. He was the Belgian here, a man in charge of his home, or so it would appear on the surface. She would probably be looked on as hysterical, but she kept her shoulders square and a stern expression on her face.

He turned on his heel and left the room in feigned indignation. She looked in dislike at his back as he exited. 'You're my wife. What's yours is mine,' he flung over his shoulder. It looked as though he was going to try to brazen it out.

Claudia spent the entire weekend searching for the title deeds. They had to be hidden in the house, she thought as she hunted high and low, drawer by drawer and cupboard by cupboard. Michel moved into Jan's bedroom at her insistence, but she knew by his confident attitude that he thought she would come round soon. She needed him, after all. How would she manage on her own? He was quietly confident.

On Sunday afternoon, when she had pretty well given up her search, he came into the kitchen where she was sitting drinking a large mug of tea. He had the documents in his hand.

'Here.' He threw them on the table and stormed out. 'They were hidden in that stupid Cordon Bleu recipe book you brought with you. I knew you wouldn't think of checking there.' The smug expression on his face infuriated her, but she snatched the documents before he could change his mind. She had had enough. It was over.

Immediate divorce was inevitable, and Claudia pushed hard for it to be over quickly. Her lawyer asked her the reason for such speed and seemed to sense that there was something odd about the entire thing. She used "irreconcilable differences" as the reason for the divorce and refused to mention the child sexual abuse and the fact that he had tried to steal her money. She just wanted the entire charade to end. Immediately.

Claudia wanted nothing from Michel except her renewed sanity and persuaded him to leave and go to live with his ancient mother and unmarried sister, Britt, in Turnhout for the time being, while she put the house on the market and proceeded to get on with her life. He had nowhere else to go. It was now her house, and she wanted him to move out. His flower import-export business was finished due to his foolish decisions. She wondered how his first wife had coped with him for so long. He now had no income whatsoever. All he possessed was his ancient Renault, a few still life paintings and the clothes on his back.

He closed his business, sold his car and paintings in order to raise some cash and, despite his pleading and crocodile tears, Claudia refused to assist him further with his debts. It was over.

Arriving at the railway station, Claudia stepped out of the car to see him off. As she turned to go, he wheeled around to face her, eyes glittering.

'This is not the end.' His jaw was clenched, and he towered over her threateningly. 'Because of you, I've lost my home. I'd still be there only for you, no matter what you may think. Don't ever relax because I'll be back. Your worst nightmare has yet to begin.'

With that, he turned on his heel and, dragging his suitcase — given to him by Claudia the previous Christmas, a premonition that he would need it perhaps — hoisted it onto the train and disappeared. Claudia let out her breath. She felt as though she had been holding it for the past year.

Michel watched her from the carriage window. He saw her slim figure, clad in a cream trench coat, turn and stride away. He noticed a man give her an admiring look and was overwhelmed by a feeling of anger and bitterness. As she left the station with a spring in her step, he looked at her with undisguised venom.

'Next time we meet, Claudia,' he said out loud, 'I'll make you regret the way you destroyed my life. That I can promise you.'

***

After the house on the Wijnegem Canal in Antwerp had been sold, Claudia couldn't bear to go back to Ireland in, as she imagined it, disgrace. Only one year of marriage to Michel, and that had ended in disaster. Being a reserved and private person, she decided she could not bear the inevitable questioning from family and friends.

Having thought long and hard about it, discussing it at length with Anya and her father, her thoughts moved to a possible life in Puglia, in the South of Italy. She remembered her time there with Philip and Anya all those years ago: the wonderful light, the coral sunsets, the friendly people. A chance to start again where nobody knew about her shattered life. Somewhere to regain her soul, become strong and get to know herself again. A place where she could write in peace. The vision buoyed her up and gave her a feeling of optimism.

Maybe she would even stay there permanently, she thought. In the meantime, she wanted some time to herself to reflect on how her life had turned into such a disaster.

She had spoken at length to her cousin, Olivia, who had recommended she start her Pugliese adventure by staying a couple of weeks at the hotel where she herself had stayed on a previous visit. This traditional, family-owned hotel, high in the hill town of Ostuni, with wonderful views of the Adriatic Sea, would be the perfect place to begin. Using that as her base, she could look for a house or apartment to rent while she decided whether to settle there permanently and, if so, to begin her search for a new home.

Anya was about to return to boarding school for another year and promised she would fly to Southern Italy during the holidays and was adamant that Claudia should take time to heal and learn to live with herself. Claudia thought she must have done some good in life to have such a wonderfully loving and understanding daughter and held her close at the departure gate in Dublin Airport.

'See you soon, Mum.' Anya was relaxed and hugged Claudia back. 'Enjoy Puglia!' She remembered, though not very well, her stay in Ostuni all those years ago and knew from her aunt Olivia that it was a particularly beautiful and peaceful place. She hoped her mother would begin to relax after the past couple of stressful years, meeting and marrying Michel, selling her home in Galway, getting divorced, then having to sell the house in Antwerp, among strangers. It was a lot for Claudia to handle, and Anya hoped she could begin to be happy in her new life.

Anya fought down feelings of resentment towards her mother. She knew deep down she was being unfair, but she had loved Michel almost as much as the father she remembered only in flashbacks. He was always so kind. He would take her on his knee and stroke her back and her hair when she was upset and needy. She missed him. But she loved her mother and could see that he had made her unhappy. It was all so very confusing.

Being unaware of most of the facts regarding her mother's short-lived marriage to Michel, all that hurt and horror, a dark, disloyal side reared its head as Anya wondered why her mother could not have tried harder. She still felt that the blame must lie with her, so clever, cool and controlled, not with sweet Michel, so loving and caring. She wondered if there was any chance that they could get back together when her mother had calmed down and realised what she had given up. For what? A life alone? She could not understand the logic. Why had Michel begun to act as though he hated Claudia? What on earth had she done? She thought a lot of it had to do with the banishment of Jan, but she was unsure of the facts. Being a normal teenage girl, Anya sighed at how difficult and stubborn her mother could be.

All the same, as she watched her mother's neat figure in slim jeans and a black jacket, her blonde hair held back in a chignon, walk towards airport security and a brand-new life, she felt a wave of love and sympathy for this brave little woman who had been through so much.

And was about to go through so much more.

CHAPTER NINE
JANET

Determined to explore the area carefully while keeping an eye out for a suitable trullo for sale, Janet either cycled or walked on a daily basis. She was feeling physically fitter than she could ever remember.

'All that great food,' she said to herself, as she perused the local markets in Ostuni and Cisternino. The fruit and vegetable sections were always a riot of colour, with everything freshly picked by the local farmers. Open-sided vans, with shade cloth attached to the sides to protect their produce, immaculate displays of fish, meat and cheese of every description, and it was possible to purchase a pair of palazzo pants, a sturdy pair of shoes, a sweater or a cotton nightie for just a few euro each, all at the same time among the clamouring stalls. Janet loved the hustle and bustle, the wonderful smells of frying fish and roasting chicken while listening to the local women haggling over the price of potatoes.

Before long, Janet got to know the various stallholders and was always greeted with suggestions of what was best as soon as she arrived. She loved their open friendliness and began to settle into her new life like a duck to water.

Her favourite way to spend a morning was to take a stroll through the nearby olive groves. As it was summer, the tracks were dusted with a fine white powder. When a car or tractor passed, this powdery surface formed a sandy, white cloud which, when it settled back down, left her eyes and lips feeling gritty. Prickly pears — known as Fichi d'India — hung over many of the stone walls, and apricots were in abundance. Fig, cherry and almond trees were everywhere among the thousands of olive trees that populated the landscape.

The white cone of a tiny trullo peeked out from the olive grove as she walked past on her morning stroll. She admired this little house every day and was always struck by its quaintness. She wondered what it would be like to live in such a pretty house. Until now, she had never ventured inside a trullo that was actually inhabited. There were many derelict trulli dotting the countryside of the Valle d'Itria and, though she had nervously peered into many of their dark interiors from time to time on her long walks, she had never seen how it would be to actually live in one that had been renovated.

Early one morning, while strolling through the olive groves not far from Casalini, Janet noticed that the gate to her favourite trullo was open, and she peered inside. It was charming, with flower pots dotting the stone patio and placed on each step leading to the roof. An old lady, small and thin, with snow-white hair, was bending over, showering them with love and water, a small tan-coloured dog at her feet, oblivious to Janet's curiosity. The little dog suddenly looked up and spotted her lurking in the gateway and ran towards her, barking furiously, as she backed away, walking briskly out of range. How she had longed to look inside, but there was no *For Sale* sign to be seen anywhere, and she did not want to appear to be intrusive. On subsequent visits, the gate was firmly closed, but Janet was greatly attracted to this little house and felt it tugging at her heartstrings when she, almost unconsciously, found her feet taking her in its direction.

As she was passing by one morning, the gate opened, and a car emerged. It was an ancient Fiat 500, and the old lady was behind the wheel, peering anxiously at her as though she were in the way. When she got out to close the gate behind her, she noticed that Janet was still there and blinked at her in surprise. The little dog, who was sitting in the front of the car with his paws against the side window, barked warningly at her, then began to dash over and back across the front seats in order to bark from both windows in rapid succession.

'*Buongiorno*!' Janet found her voice. In her improving Italian, she managed to compliment the old lady on her pretty trullo. 'I pass this way a few times a week,' she informed the surprised woman. 'I just love your home.'

'Thank you!' The old lady beamed at her from behind her spectacles. 'I have noticed you walking by many times. Would you like to come in for a coffee the next time you're passing?'

Janet clasped her hands together in delight, and a friendship was born.

The old lady then tried to hush the little dog and introduced herself as Margherita. 'I don't get many callers,' she confided. 'I look forward to your visit.'

They agreed that Janet would call on the following Friday for coffee and a piece of apricot crostata. Janet helped her to close the gate and headed off with a spring in her step as her new friend crunched the gears of her little car and chugged down the lane in the opposite direction, the dog still barking furiously, now through the back window.

***

A warm breeze embraced Janet as she walked along the stony track. Olive trees, showing the tiniest clusters of bright-green baby olives, peered over the stone walls as they had for hundreds of years. Fig trees leaned temptingly towards her, dangling their heavy fruit. She felt a sense of peace descend on her for the first time in many months.

'*Buongiorno!*' She greeted Margherita as the little dog sniffed around her feet, checking her out. '*Permesso?*' She knew what to say when entering someone's house and was rewarded by the old lady's response.

'*Prego!*' said Margherita and introduced her to an excited Gigi, as that was the dog's name.

'I've never been in a trullo before,' Janet confessed, as she dipped her head slightly under the low doorway and stepped onto the flagstone floor trying not to trip over Gigi, who appeared to be acting as tour guide, running ahead and looking back enquiringly whenever she paused to admire yet another feature of Margherita's beautiful home. Having been built with limestone, the trullo was surprisingly cool inside.

From the outside, the pretty house appeared to comprise two trulli with a central room joining them together.

'Come and have a look around,' invited her hostess, waving her hand in a welcoming gesture. Janet noted the small windows in the trullo sections and the huge fireplace with the old pot-bellied stove in the corner of the kitchen. Through a stone arch, she could see a fairly large room with a dining table and sofa, while leading through yet another arch, she found herself under the dome of another trullo, which was a bedroom,

69

barely containing a large bed covered in floral throws and pillows, off which was a small shower-room.

There was a small, shady veranda with a small barbecue at the side of the house, accessed from the kitchen.

Janet had a good look around and fell in love with the tiny house on the spot. It was, she felt, like walking into a dream. *Her* dream. She remembered how she had felt that day in Dublin, when she'd sat on the bus, rain pelting down outside, while she read about Puglia and allowed herself to dream about another life for the first time. This was what she had visualised then, to the letter. She sighed, a mixture of delight and envy in equal parts.

Outside, the garden was perfection itself. Some olive and various fruit trees dotted the grassy expanse. She spotted some artichoke and tomato plants in a neat vegetable garden off to one side. An old green wooden bench was parked underneath the largest olive tree, on top of which sat a fabric-covered box of sewing and a paperback book waiting for their owner's return. Beside the bench, in the deepest shade, was a small dog bed which Gigi promptly dived into, as though Janet might claim it as her own.

Behind the old olive tree, she spotted another tiny trullo. She moved closer and saw that it was used for storage and had been fitted with a metal security gate.

'That's where I keep all my garden tools.' Margherita had come up behind her and noticed her curiosity. 'I like to keep it securely locked. You never know!' she added.

How perfect it all is, Janet thought, gazing wistfully at the peaceful surroundings and the pretty garden, silent except for the twittering of some birds calling to one another from the branches of the fruit trees. She couldn't remember ever feeling so envious before in her life.

Waving goodbye to Margherita and her new canine friend, crouching to give Gigi a final pat, Janet walked along the hot powdery road to Casalini, wishing the little trullo were hers.

***

Daisy was over the moon. Yes, she often became overexcited, but this was different. She looked like the cat that got the cream.

'I think I may have found the perfect place to live!' she exclaimed, her face alight, little hands waving as she and Janet met at Caffe Negroni a few days later.

'Tell me all!' Janet was delighted for her friend as they made their way to a corner table. Several expats, sitting huddled together at three tables which they had pushed together, looked up briefly and said hi and ciao as they passed, carrying their glasses of Aperol Spritz. Janet thought they looked as though they were enjoying a scurrilous piece of juicy gossip, which was probably a fairly accurate assessment.

'Now tell me!'

There were always problems when Daisy was involved. The girl seemed to positively invite trouble.

'Well,' she began. 'it's the sweetest little apartment I've ever seen!' She enthused, clasping and unclasping her little hands together on her lap. 'A little jewel. It belongs to a lady who is moving to Rome to be near to her son and grandchildren. She's selling up completely.' She took a long draught of her spritz and continued. 'It's got great views of the coast; it's up high in the historic centre here in Ostuni. Right at the top.' She gave an excited little squeal for emphasis.

'That's wonderful!' Janet was genuinely pleased for Daisy, and they began to plan for when she could go up to the old town to have a look; give a second opinion.

'Well...' Daisy sounded hesitant. 'I know you'll think I'm crazy. I mean, you're so much more sensible than I am.' She gave a little laugh and lifted her palms as if to fend Janet off. 'But I've already put in an offer and paid a ten per cent deposit.' She sat back in her chair wearing the expression of a naughty convent schoolgirl who's just been found by the nuns stealing apples.

Janet was stunned. Daisy was normally so indecisive about everything, and now she had found her future home, perhaps, and was planning to move in there as soon as possible. Just as soon as her offer was accepted, that is, and the legalities had been formalised. 'Wow!' was all she could find to say. 'Erm, I don't want to rain on your parade or anything.' She hesitated before continuing. 'But did you get an engineer

71

or anyone independent to have a look? You know — check it over before you agreed to purchase it?'

'Oh no!' Daisy told her. 'My estate agent is wonderful. He would never lead me astray. He told me that he would do all the translating and that he uses a notary when it comes to the final paperwork. When all that is organised, I'll bring in the balance of the funds from my bank in London.' She sounded so full of confidence and optimism that Janet didn't have the heart to make any negative sounds.

'Well. Let's raise a toast then.' She lifted her glass of spritz, only to find that she had already drained it in the heat of the moment.

CHAPTER TEN
CLAUDIA

Claudia was no stranger to fame, but in the Farrell family, her cousin Olivia had always been the exotic one, a legend. A famous interior designer, whose life of privilege and luxury had crash-landed just a few years previously but had come bouncing back again with her recent marriage to Count Niccolò di Falco in Venice, and she was now officially a contessa.

Olivia had always appeared to be aloof and otherworldly, but all that had changed since Niccolò had entered her life, and she was now throwing a lavish celebration at their palazzo on the Grand Canal.

Equally well known in her own right, Claudia, as one of Ireland's top novelists, regularly saw her books sail to Number One on the bestseller charts.

The invitation to Olivia's wedding celebration in Venice was a wake-up call for Claudia. Like an electric shock. What would she wear? How long would she go for? The list seemed endless. She was looking forward to this in a way she hadn't looked forward to anything for the past couple of years. Her new life in Puglia was deliberately quiet and uneventful, and she couldn't even remember the last time she had really dressed up.

Olivia had just got married in a small civil ceremony in Venice. She and her new husband, the handsome, aristocratic Conte Niccolò di Falco, were now ready to celebrate with family and friends.

Arriving at Marco Polo Airport on the outskirts of Venice, Claudia rolled her bag along the walkway leading to the water taxi rank a few minutes from the arrivals hall. It was a bright spring day with Easter just around the corner. The taxi skimmed across the Venetian Lagoon, with all its bobbing boats, water buses and taxis; wide blue sky and shimmering water giving her a feeling of exhilaration which continued long after she had found her hotel and checked in. The dark wooden floors creaked underfoot as she climbed a few short steps from the reception desk to her bedroom, which was old-fashioned in style, with a tall wrought-iron bedstead and velvet curtains. The bathroom was modern, chic, and immaculate.

The wedding celebration was scheduled for the following day, so Claudia decided to spend her free time exploring. Not having visited Venice for many years, she decided to wander over to St Mark's Square to see the Basilica and the Doge's Palace. Olivia had told her about her favourite walk along Riva degli Schiavoni to the church of San Pietro di Castello, where she planned to sit for a while on — what she considered to be — "Olivia's bench". Her cousin's story had attracted a lot of media attention. In fact, there had been so much publicity after the strange death had occurred that a book had been written about it, which had gained her a certain notoriety. After the dramatic events leading up to her relationship with Niccolò, things had settled down, but she had now managed to ignite further attention because of her recent marriage.

Claudia strolled past the smart cafes in St Mark's Square, where small orchestras played Vivaldi for the clientele as they sipped the most expensive coffees in "Europe's drawing room". Many of the tourists thought it was worth it, but Claudia — though enthralled by the atmosphere — kept on walking.

That night, she dined alone. She had been invited to join various uncles and cousins in town for the party, but she wanted to absorb Venice by herself. Tomorrow would be the time to resume family life in the bosom of the Farrell family when questions about her brief marriage to Michel would inevitably be brought up. Claudia's and Olivia's fathers were brothers, and there were several uncles, aunts and cousins to catch up with and who, she knew, wanted to see her, perhaps even to interrogate her. She shuddered at the thought. But not today. That was hers.

As she sat in the restaurant eating white polenta with creamy baccalà and sipping a glass of excellent pinot grigio, she reflected on her new-found solitary life, which had begun to heal the sadness and the lasting effects of the terrible abuse she had suffered. She thought she was beginning to regain her true self at last, but it was going to be a long process.

Next morning, as Claudia's water taxi ferried her to the palazzo on the Grand Canal, she allowed herself a moment of reflection. Her first couple of months in Puglia had been tranquil, and she had decided to make it her permanent home. Having rented a small apartment in a square close to the public park in Ostuni, she had begun her search for a new home, but, so far, she had not seen any property that had piqued her interest.

The Grand Canal was, as usual, busy with myriad floating modes of transport. From the traditional gondola flitting by with loved-up couples on board, to the packed vaporetto ferrying passengers from one floating bus stop to the next, to the red fire engine rushing past followed by a police boat, the activity was endless. Along the sides of the canal, lined with beautiful churches and palazzi, tourists flocked in their droves.

The atmosphere in Venice is difficult to describe in words. Old buildings loom overhead; ancient stones on the bridges over the narrow, winding canals are warm and worn under one's hand; smells waft from kitchen windows and the fish and vegetable markets tantalise; restaurants full of people eating, drinking, gazing, taking photographs and selfies; washing hanging from racks attached to window ledges flapping idly; colour is everywhere; cacophony and bustle of boats passing, accompanied by the ever-present sound of water splashing and the screams of the seagulls as they swoop over the canals, make it a feast for the senses.

Claudia was dressed to kill. At least, that's what she told herself, hoping it was true. A few weeks previously, she had driven to a town called Cassamassima near the city of Bari, where the largest shopping centre in Puglia was located. There she had found an elegant, backless, pale-blue silk floor-length dress, which she had dressed up with a long string of pearls and matching earrings. She had draped the pearls down her slender back, and they almost reached the curve of her waistline.

Her platinum-blonde hair was swept into a simple chignon, and the colour of the dress enhanced the blue of her eyes.

As Claudia's water taxi pulled up to the dock at the foot of the tall palazzo, other boats were arriving at the same time. Some were taxis like hers, and others were obviously expensive motor boats, privately owned, gleaming in the sunshine. The well-heeled passengers were alighting onto the wooden dock and entering the ground floor of the palazzo through a tall wrought-iron gate.

Claudia had heard all about it from Olivia, who had met Niccolò, her husband, a wealthy Venetian count, while renovating this magnificent palazzo: Palazzo di Falco, the five-hundred-year-old home of the ancient, aristocratic di Falco family. Now Olivia was a contessa and hoped to start a family as soon as possible. They were both blissfully happy. This would be a celebration to remember.

As she exited the lift onto the piano nobile — main floor — of the palazzo, to the welcoming sound of a string quartet and the muted conversation of elegant guests, she saw Olivia coming towards her with arms outstretched, ready to gather her favourite cousin into a hug.

'Claudia!' She greeted her cousin with a warm hug, then pulled away, looking enquiringly into her eyes. 'Are you all right, darling?' she said softly, her luminous green eyes concerned.

Olivia was looking wonderful, Claudia thought. Her ivory-coloured lace gown with a plunging neckline emphasised her tanned cleavage and natural voluptuousness. Her blonde hair was piled high in an elaborate twist, adding to her glamourous appearance. She was a lovely woman in every way.

'I've been better, to be honest, Olivia. Coming to terms with everything hasn't been easy. But I'm so thrilled to see you happy; that has cheered me up enormously.'

The two women, their blonde heads close together, brought many admiring glances from all around them. Two beautiful women, who were similar enough in appearance to make them look like sisters. Their fathers were brothers and, though Olivia's mother, Lucia, was Italian, hence her olive skin and softly voluptuous figure, Claudia's late mother, Pamela, had been a small, delicate woman with a pale complexion and almost white-blonde hair. The result was Claudia, a paler and less curvaceous version of her cousin, but just as striking to look at. Though neither of them was tall, they still managed to stand out in a crowd and certainly turned heads wherever they were.

'Come and have lunch with me tomorrow,' Olivia said. 'Then we can chat, just the two of us. Niccolò will be going to the villa in

Galzignano with his cousin, and I'll be here on my own. I'll get Maria to prepare something simple. I'm longing to catch up.'

Claudia squeezed Olivia's hand gently. 'I'd love to.'

It was the unanimous opinion of the Farrell family that Olivia and Claudia were its most beautiful and successful members and, as such, were treated as objects of undying interest, mixed with a modicum of inevitable jealousy. They were all concerned about Claudia's recent bad luck in her second marriage, while delighted about Olivia's charmed life. They eyed the two women and gossiped among themselves, leaning in and wondering what now for the golden girls, who were an endless source of diversion, as far as they were concerned.

'Mum's over here.' Olivia took Claudia's hand and walked over to Lucia, Olivia's mother, who was holding court with a group of Italian ladies, all obviously thrilled to be speaking to the mother of the bride. Lucia looked radiant, as only the mother of the bride can be when her daughter is marrying a handsome, super-rich aristocrat.

She turned to hug Claudia. 'How lovely it is to see you!' Lucia's Italian accent was stronger than usual, probably due to the Prosecco she was sipping and the bevy of Italians who surrounded her. Claudia's father, Sean, hovered in the background with his brother, Daniel, Olivia's father. Her parents were in an obviously happy mood now that Olivia had finally married her count after having lived with him "in sin" for the past two years. Daniel and Sean were close, and their daughters were important to them, though Daniel had been known to give Olivia a hard time when she and her first husband split up.

The palazzo was gorgeous, and, at the first opportunity, Claudia wandered off to have a look around and to marvel at her cousin's talent. She had seen before and after photos and was deeply impressed. It was a masterpiece of understated elegance. She brought her glass of Prosecco along and wandered down the long corridor where the bedrooms were situated. It was hard to imagine that this hallway previously had a wood-patterned vinyl floor covering before Olivia had got her hands on it.

The tall walnut doors to all the rooms stood open and welcoming. Only one door remained locked. Niccolò and Olivia had still not managed to break the taboo set when Niccolò's beloved daughter, Sofia, had died. This had been her room, and it remained untouched, even after all this time. It felt, to Claudia, as though a miasma of sadness lingered around the doorway. Preoccupied, she turned away and bumped straight into a tall, dark gentleman in an impeccable suit. At least, it was impeccable until Claudia's Prosecco spilt down the front and over his expensive-looking silk tie.

He stepped back quickly and looked at her with undisguised annoyance.

'What on earth are you doing here waving a glass of wine around?' His eyebrows rose. 'One of Olivia's Irish friends, I imagine.' He sounded highly unimpressed by such an idea, exuding disapproval from every pore.

Claudia bridled. 'I'm terribly sorry.' She looked up at him with studied hauteur and drew herself up to her lofty five foot four inches. He must have been about a foot taller than she was, but she had her pride. 'Would you like me to get a cloth from the bathroom?'

Her blue eyes met his brown ones and held a dignified challenge, though she was deeply embarrassed, watching the front of his shirt beginning to cling to his chest. His tie was a mess, probably a write-off, she thought.

'No, thank you.' He was obviously annoyed, but he was now looking at her differently. Something close to interest and curiosity. 'I think I can manage to dry myself.' He looked at her sternly, and she noticed that his longish black hair had two distinct silver wings brushed back over his ears, giving him a professorial appearance.

She walked away, or rather stalked, trying to look poised, though, in reality, she was mortified. His gaze seemed to burn a hole in her back. She would keep away from this man for the rest of the day. Keep a low profile.

Re-entering the enormous salon, she made a beeline for the group surrounding her cousin.

Olivia looked radiant. Beside her stood her new husband, Niccolò. He looked the happiest Claudia had ever seen him. They made a beautiful couple, standing among family and friends, hand in hand.

Claudia had met Niccolò in Dublin recently for the first time at a family party, and she was immediately charmed by his quiet intelligence, quite apart from the fact that he was probably the best-looking man she had ever laid eyes on. An image of the man she had drenched in Prosecco just a few minutes previously popped into her head. What a loser! It was just half a glass, for heaven's sake!

CHAPTER ELEVEN
CLAUDIA

Waking up late the next morning, Claudia luxuriated in the tall four-poster bed at her hotel. Nestled among the soft pillows, she looked around the room, which was decorated in classic Venetian style, with gilded mirrors and rich velvet drapery. She could hear the noise and bustle from the canal outside. Slipping out of bed, she crossed to the window and revelled in the sight below. The canal was sparkling blue, and action packed. It seemed that life was moving along at high speed while she had been having a lie-in.

It had been a late night. Olivia and Niccolò's celebration had been a lesson in how to do things in style. Claudia remembered the fabulous dinner, glittering crystal, fine wines, exotic foods… her thoughts came to a standstill as she remembered the silver-winged man she had drenched in Prosecco earlier, sitting at the next table, and she gave a quiet grimace. She saw that he was eyeing her with what appeared to be a look of disdain on his handsome features, and she looked away in embarrassment.

Glancing at her watch, she realised that she had a couple of hours to kill before the di Falco motor launch was due to collect her to bring her down the Grand Canal for lunch with Olivia. Not being in the mood for breakfast, she decided to take a vaporetto out to the island of San Michele to see the di Falco tomb for herself. This was where Niccolò's daughter, Sofia, had been laid to rest, along with several generations of his family. She had read about the unique island in the Venetian Lagoon and wanted to see it for herself.

Tying her hair back into a casual ponytail and donning a pair of cream chinos and a navy T-shirt, throwing a jumper over her shoulders, as the early spring weather could be deceptively cool, she strolled to the vaporetto stop at Fondamente Nove, the floating bus stop closest to the cemetery island.

Purchasing her ticket, she verified it by passing it over a little machine at the entrance to the floating metal structure, waiting for her vaporetto. It arrived with a roar of reverse-thrust and a puff of diesel fumes, causing the bus stop to sway from side to side. It was already packed with visitors on their way to the island of Murano to see the glass factories. The island of San Michele was about halfway between Venice and Murano. She stood to one side, trying not to be struck by a backpack being worn by an overexcited tourist in unfashionably baggy shorts and canvas sandals, despite the fact that he was standing directly under a sign which clearly advised passengers to remove their backpacks and store them at their feet while on board.

A quick trip out into the lagoon brought the vaporetto to a bouncing stop, banging hard against the jetty that led onto the island. Cypress trees stood tall over the red brick walls, and she walked down the short path to the entrance of the famous graveyard, where thousands of Venetians have been laid to rest. She was greeted by the sight of a metal rack from which hung several small watering cans which visitors could use to water the flowers on the well-tended graves.

Claudia knew that the di Falco mausoleum was among those of the old Venetian families, and she had no difficulty in locating them. They stood in a long, formidable row along one side of the graveyard, facing the myriad rows of crosses and headstones that made up most of the area.

As she approached, she noticed a man standing in front of one of the tombs. She did not pay a lot of attention to him as she scanned the row for the name di Falco. Suddenly, noticing the silver wings on his black hair, she realised that it was the man from yesterday's celebration and froze. She could see that he was in deep contemplation in front of the di Falco tomb. She stepped back hurriedly, hoping not to be noticed, and backed straight into a rack of watering cans. They toppled over with an enormous, rattling crash, and he looked around. There was no escaping his disbelieving stare. She cringed inwardly as she righted the stand and hung the watering cans back on their hooks, banging them together in her haste, before turning and walking hurriedly away, her face hot and red.

Luckily, there were plenty of tombs to hide behind, and she lurked in another part of the cemetery for a while before emerging cautiously.

He had gone. She approached the mausoleum, looking around before mounting the steps to its glass door. Fresh flowers had been placed in a vase, and she wondered if he had known Sofia or had been close to other di Falco relatives who were interred there. She considered that a probability, as he had been at the celebration the previous day.

Back at the hotel, all thoughts of the silver-winged man put to one side, Claudia donned a light linen dress and canvas wedge-heel shoes. Checking herself in the mirror, she noticed that her eyes were tired. *Too much Prosecco yesterday!* she thought.

She went downstairs to wait for Marco, the di Falco boatman. He arrived punctually and led her to a shiny mahogany motor launch with cream leather seating inside a long cabin. She decided to sit outside at the front and chat to Marco as they wove their way up the Grand Canal. She tried not to dwell on her embarrassment that morning at the cemetery. Hopefully, she would never bump into that man again. She cringed as she remembered the incredulous expression on his face as she tried to reorganise the watering cans that she had knocked over. Now, she put it out of her mind.

The boat nudged up against the wooden dock at the base of the di Falco palazzo. Marco gave Claudia his hand to help her to alight and pointed her in the direction of the steps to the lift, which would bring her to the main living area. She remembered the cramped lift from the previous day: wood-panelled with brass fittings and warning signs telling passengers not to transport large domestic appliances upstairs in its tiny interior. *As if!* she thought, as she eased herself inside.

As she stepped out into the grand, pillared interior on the main floor, a small, dark woman came to greet her, introducing herself as Maria, the housekeeper. Claudia had noticed this little bundle of energy bustling about the previous day and had already figured out that this was the famous and indispensable Maria, who had been with the di Falco family for several years.

Olivia came rushing forward to hug Claudia, and Maria stood back, watching the cousins embrace. *How beautiful they are*, she thought, as she returned to the kitchen to finish off the preparations for lunch.

'Come!' Olivia took Claudia by the arm and guided her out onto her long terrace overlooking the Grand Canal.

Claudia was spellbound by the view. On her right, was The Accademia Bridge, which was busy with tourists taking selfies at the top, with the enormous church of Santa Maria della Salute in the background. To her left, she had an unobstructed view of the gondolas, vaporetti and utility vehicles that wove their way up and down the canal. 'Stunning!' she said, resting her hands on the old stone balustrade as she peered down at all the activity beneath.

'I have some interesting news for you.' Olivia began as Maria served up traditional *Risi e Bisi*, a fresh pea risotto, and poured a glass of chilled pinot grigio for each of them. They lifted their glasses in a toast to each other. 'To your new life in Puglia.'

'To your new married life. I hope you'll be very happy, Olivia. Niccolò is a lovely man in every way.' She took a sip of her wine. 'He adores you. But you know that.' She smiled at her cousin, who smiled back in agreement. 'What's the interesting news?'

'I may, just possibly, have found your perfect home in Ostuni.' She paused, uncertain for a moment, worried that she might be overstepping the mark. She continued. 'I don't want to interfere in any way, you know that, but a friend of Niccolò has just finished renovating a palazzo there and has been offered a dream job in Rome. Out of the blue. He wants to sell it as it is. Almost finished and apparently, just needing decoration and general furnishing. He's not looking to make a huge profit, just to cover his costs. He's keen to move to Rome as quickly as possible. Perhaps you'd like to take a look when you return?'

'Of course!' Claudia was intrigued. 'Tell me more. As you know, I've been trying to find something suitable for the past couple of months, with no result. I'd love to see it.'

'If you like, I can phone him after lunch, and you can set up an appointment. But only if you want to.' She looked anxious. 'I hope you don't think I'm sticking my nose in here. I know how independent you are, but this just seemed, perhaps, to be exactly what you are looking for. The location is perfect with views of the Adriatic Sea and within walking distance of the old town. I must say, it sounds wonderful.'

Claudia felt a shiver of excitement. It sounded perfect.

After lunch was over and their plates of fresh fruit had been consumed, they moved to the big sofas in the sitting room to relax with an espresso. Maria looked crestfallen when they both declined her offer of homemade biscotti to go with their coffee.

'The palazzo looks wonderful, Olivia.' Claudia looked around the luxurious room, the tall walnut doors, the marble pillars and the newly restored terrazzo floors.

'Thank you.' Olivia paused, and her voice took on a serious tone. 'I'm sure you noticed that Sofia's room is still locked and untouched.'

Claudia nodded. 'Yes. I saw that yesterday. How is Niccolò now? Is he still grieving deeply?'

'Niccolò will always grieve the death of his daughter.' Olivia was pensive. 'But he has decided to take a positive step towards our future, and our next plan is to try for a baby of our own and to redo Sofia's bedroom.' She paused. 'These are big steps for him, so we're taking it slowly. He's incredibly emotional.'

'It's a pretty big step for you too.'

'Yes, I know. When I was married to Steve, it never even occurred to me to have children. They just didn't enter into the equation. We were both too busy with our high-flying careers and living the perfect life, or so I thought. I would have been a terrible mother back in the day.' She paused. 'I was actually far too self-centred to have welcomed such an intrusion into my perfect life.' She gave a bitter laugh. 'But it's different with Niccolò. We've discussed this at length. I was worried that he might be too scared to begin fatherhood again after what happened.'

Claudia reached over and took Olivia's clasped hands in hers. 'Whatever you and Niccolò do with your future will be good. I know it. You two were made for each other. He adores you, whether you have a baby or not. And you'll be fabulous parents.'

Olivia visibly relaxed. 'Thank you, Claudia. You've been so strong this past couple of years. I know what you've been through.' They both sat back and looked at each other. 'How are you doing, you know, emotionally, these days? Are you really happy to be in Ostuni?'

Claudia smiled. 'I'm fine. Life is peaceful. I love living there. It feels like home already. Everyone is so friendly, though I haven't begun to make any real friends yet. I know that will happen in time.'

'Would you like me to phone the owner of the palazzo for you? I can set up a meeting for when you get back.'

'Yes, please!'

Olivia reached for her mobile phone and dialled.

After the brief call, Olivia gave Claudia the telephone number and details of Niccolò's friend from Ostuni. Claudia promised to contact him the moment she returned.

***

Claudia took just one look around the palazzo on Via Mazzini in the heart of Ostuni and knew she had to have it.

The owner met her outside and brandished a set of keys. Claudia looked up at the palazzo towering above. It appeared to be three storeys high, with a long, narrow terrace along the front with a wrought-iron railing, backed by three tall dark-green shuttered French doors. Above these were a further three much smaller windows. The stone was mellow and cream coloured. At street level, a dark-grey metal roll-up entryway was situated to one side and a high wooden front door, with a glass fanlight overhead, was in the centre of the façade. He produced the longest key, which looked old and had a family crest in the shape of an eagle with its wings spread, stamped into the bow. He opened the door, and they entered.

'Palazzo dell'Aquila,' he announced. 'The Palace of the Eagle.'

Claudia gasped. In front of her was a vast area with room for at least two cars that could enter and exit through the motorised up-and-over metal gate. The floor was cobbled. Twin marble staircases with ornate iron balustrades curved upwards on either side of this vast vestibule and, at the top, she could see a tall walnut door in the centre, which was, apparently, the entrance to the living area of this grand old house.

Shivering with excitement and anticipation, Claudia mounted the sweeping stairs on the left-hand side and approached the entry to the main floor. The owner inserted another long key and swung open the door, revealing a square vestibule leading to the vast interior. He strode to the tall windows and opened them and the outer shutters, the huge room filled with light. To the front of the palazzo was a large salon that led out onto the terrace. This had been renovated and now included a kitchen to one side, its tall glass doors giving a view of the Adriatic Sea in the distance. Behind the salon were three large bedrooms, all with en suite bathrooms, and an impressive sitting room with a dining alcove, which led out onto a larger terrace at the back of the house. This second terrace looked out over a charming walled garden, full of flowers, climbing plants and huge terracotta urns. Hidden away from busy Corso Mazzini, it was quiet and full of chirping birds. *Heavenly!* she thought.

A further set of stairs led to — what had once been — the servants' quarters. These had been converted into a large study under the eaves and two other rooms, which were empty at this point, but which Claudia could imagine being another study for Anya and a walk-in wardrobe to accommodate her vast collection of shoes and bags.

The lofty ceilings and large airy rooms, plus the view over the Adriatic Sea, clinched the deal as she fell instantly in love with this beautiful house.

It was perfect. Claudia put in her offer on the spot, which was accepted.

Perhaps the quickest property transaction ever, took place within a couple of weeks, and she moved in straight away.

Her new life in Puglia was beginning. What could go wrong?

CHAPTER TWELVE
JANET

The weeks slid by, along with the hot, dry summer. Janet found the climate wonderful, as there almost always seemed to be a light fluttery breeze to keep things pleasant. She invested in a small electric fan for the house in Casalini and, spurred on by Daisy's hoped-for success, she looked at every house she could find for sale within her limited price range.

As she was not working, she had to be careful to budget until she found something to do to bring in some small income. Teaching private English classes was what she had in mind, but her Italian needed to improve a great deal first and, of course, she had just enrolled for her promised course in digital marketing online.

By now, she had queued at the *comune* — municipal offices — to receive her essential fiscal code, or tax number, required by everyone who lives in Italy; then she had opened her first Italian bank account. She decided to apply for residency. Being an EU citizen, this would be simple and, before she knew it, she had her *Carta d'identità* and her new driving licence, which, being an EU licence, had been simple to exchange.

Janet began to feel as though she had really arrived. Her next move would be to buy a car. She buzzed with excitement as Donatella drove her to Cisternino to pick up her second-hand, fire-engine red Fiat 500. Driving back to Casalini, parking her car outside her rented house, she felt exhilarated.

With more freedom to move about and properly explore the area, Janet began to visit the beaches near Ostuni. She joined fellow swimmers on the long beach at Pilone, which was watched over by one of several small towers that studded the coastline, and she loved walking the sandy beaches that led from Torre Guaceto to the turtle sanctuary. Along the way, she often popped into the cool, blue Adriatic for an impromptu swim when the going got hot or sat on the beach reading her latest paperback novel while munching on a bar of chocolate.

She still walked past the little trullo among the olive groves and often popped in to visit Margherita. They had become firm friends and spent lots of time chatting about their past lives.

She was fast becoming attached to little Gigi and began to wish she had a dog of her own. All that unconditional love was an appealing thought. She began to take doggie chews along with her on her regular visits to Margherita, and the little dog would rush about excitedly when she arrived. Janet would lie back on the sofa with the chew in her pocket and wait for Gigi to leap up and sniff it out, digging it out of her pocket with practised skill. It made her and Margherita laugh with delight.

Margherita had been a teacher before she retired about ten years previously. She had worked in a primary school in Ostuni, and her English was excellent, luckily for Janet. Her husband, Giorgio, had passed away about five years previously, and she appeared to be quite content to live alone. She had three sons, her favourite, the youngest Mimmo, on whom she doted. He came to lunch once a week and regularly brought his wife and children to visit, which always cheered her greatly.

Janet gathered that the other two sons lived up north somewhere and were rarely mentioned except when Margherita was talking about something from many years ago when they were children. Otherwise, she seemed to have dismissed them from her life. And they had dismissed her in turn, for whatever reason, from their lives, Janet thought but did not say.

When Janet told her about James and his liaison with The American Woman, Margherita tut-tutted sympathetically and told her she would find another husband soon.

Oh no! Janet was horrified at the thought. As far as she was concerned, she couldn't trust a man as far as she could throw one. 'No! I'm very happy to remain single for the rest of my life,' she declared firmly, wondering when she would be called back to Ireland to finalise her pending divorce. Apparently, James was planning to marry The American Woman and become a stepfather. She tried not to feel bitter and almost succeeded.

Margherita said nothing but nodded wisely, if disbelievingly.

***

One morning, as Janet sat in the corner of a local bar having a cappuccino while availing of the bar's free Wi-Fi, she was joined by Daisy. Her new car was parked outside in the sunshine. She thought she had never felt happier.

'I'd love to have a dog.' Daisy's eyes lit up at the thought as she spotted a little cream-coloured puppy of indecipherable breed sitting under the next table, head up, ears standing to attention, quivering with concentration as he watched his owner lift her fork from her plate and put it back down again, as he waited for the smallest cake crumb to fall from the table, checking the floor in vain every time this happened — which was often as it was a huge piece of cake. 'You see that little guy over there?' She pointed. 'Most of the local dogs look like that; only the size and hairiness, varies quite a bit. But they've all got the same sweet face.'

Janet looked. She would love a dog too — all that uncritical love. But she couldn't have one in her rental, or could she?

'Daisy. Where do you go to get a dog here? Is there a dog rescue place? I can't afford to buy a pedigree pooch, and these little guys are so sweet.'

'I know of a kennel,' she responded enthusiastically. 'We'll make a plan and go together.'

'I'll chat to Donatella and let you know what she says. I mean, if I can have a dog here at my rental, I won't hesitate for a moment.'

The idea took hold, and the following week, Donatella, Daisy, and Janet all climbed into the red Fiat 500 and headed off to the local kennels. Daisy sat in the back, being by far the smallest, while pink chiffon-clad, perfumed Donatella sat up front shouting directions. Driving towards Ostuni, they turned left up a narrow hill and arrived at a large gate. As they emerged from the car, several dogs of varying shapes and sizes rushed to bark at the trio through the bars.

Unfazed, Donatella rang the bell with a long purple nail and the gate was opened by a tall, well-built man with curly black hair and eyes that Janet immediately identified as dark and brooding. He certainly did not appear to be particularly welcoming.

'*Si?*'

Donatella took over completely, and she chatted away in the local dialect, which, to the ears of Janet and Daisy, was incomprehensible. The dark man began to look more relaxed.

'This is Angelo,' she announced, and they all shook hands. 'He's a vet, and these are his kennels.'

Janet was immediately attracted to this tall, languid man with the brooding black eyes. She could feel the immediate attraction she felt for him hit her low in her stomach. She looked at him directly and realised that the impact was mutual. He looked away in apparent confusion and ushered them in. The dogs swirled around the women's ankles, sniffing their greetings as they wove their way through the canine throng. Janet had never seen so many wagging tails in her life. There must have been about twenty dogs there to welcome them.

'He has some sweet puppies for you to see.' Donatella was bubbling with enthusiasm as she strode into the compound containing several dogs, all barking enthusiastically at the new arrivals, vying for their attention.

Angelo led the way, his long legs clad in jeans, effortlessly strolling through the throng of excited dogs, to a caged area in which several puppies were yapping plaintively, looking for attention. One small tan-coloured dog ran towards Janet and began to whine, trying to lick her hand through the bars. Janet fell in love immediately.

Bella! Beautiful, she thought. *This little one is so utterly sweet!*

And so, half an hour later, Janet, Daisy, Donatella, and newly named Bella, resting contentedly in Donatella's lap, headed back to Casalini. Janet, quite apart from having a new puppy, had Angelo's telephone number in her pocket. He had given it to her 'in case she needed to discuss the care of the puppy and her further vaccination requirements'. She planned to call him in a few days. Not too quickly. One doesn't want to appear too eager, after all.

***

Of course, Janet phoned Angelo a few days after their initial meeting. They arranged to meet for a coffee at Bar 900 in Ostuni. She arrived on time to find him seated at a table in a shady corner in the outdoor area, staring at the screen of his phone. She walked to the table, running her hand nervously through her tousled curls. He looked up, immediately getting to his feet and shaking her hand formally.

There really are no words to describe an instant physical attraction. Janet and Angelo sat for some time discussing the care of puppies, but it was merely a formality, and they both knew it instinctively. When they parted, having arranged to meet the following evening for an aperitivo, Janet knew that this new relationship was going only one way.

They got just halfway through their Aperol Spritzes at a bar in Casalini, before they rose and walked hand in hand to Janet's little house, shedding their clothes with abandon as they headed up the steep steps to her bedroom, much to Bella's fascination as she watched from her little basket beside the stove.

Janet had never known such raw pleasure. She and Angelo stayed there until morning, and neither of them slept for more than half an hour that night. They were like drowning souls that had been thrown a life-raft and could not get enough of one another.

Where could they go from here, Janet asked herself the following day. She barely knew him. What did she think she was doing? Had she gone crazy? But then she thought about his tanned, smooth skin, muscular physique and gentle hands that performed magical tricks on her hungry body, and she figured that it did not really matter. They would just take it one day at a time. For the moment, this could only be classified as lust, and it would do her fine. She was not about to fall in love with the first sexy Italian male that crossed her path. This would be easy. She was in control.

CHAPTER THIRTEEN
JANET

Early one morning, as she walked along the dusty lane which took her past the trullo, Bella trotting beside her, she noticed the blinds were drawn, and the car was missing. Normally, Margherita was out watering her flowers at this hour, and Janet had mentioned that she might pop in and share a coffee that morning.

That's odd, she mused. The car was always there in the driveway, and Margherita never stayed away overnight. She tried the handle of the gate, and it opened easily. *And the gate is unlocked. Even odder.*

She knocked tentatively on the front door, but there was no reply, and she turned for the gate, just as Gigi came bounding around from the back garden.

'Hey, little man!' She greeted the little dog, who was quivering nervously. 'Where's your mistress? Are you here on your own?' He replied in tiny whimpers as he greeted Bella with his usual sniffing routine, which seemed to cheer him up, and they went dashing off together. Janet was mystified and a little bit uneasy. Margherita never went anywhere without Gigi. She went around to the back garden and saw that he had a bowl of water and some kibble beside his bed. Both little dogs lapped up a quick mouthful of water, as dogs always do when they have been rushing around and turned their attention to her once more when they saw that she had turned to leave. Gigi's face was anxious, and his ears were up, listening for words of reassurance.

Saying goodbye to Gigi, Janet returned to the gate, wondering why the house was locked up and why Margherita was away so early in the morning. She knew it was none of her business and that she shouldn't interfere, but she decided to phone anyway to check that all was well. On the other hand, if she were away, she would not want a phone call at seven thirty. She decided to phone her later on.

Arriving home a couple of hours later, Janet decided that this was a respectable time to contact Margherita. She pulled her phone from the pocket of her cotton cargo shorts and dialled.

'*Pronto!*' A male voice answered her call. Janet was flustered. Her telephone Italian was not too good, but she decided to soldier on.

'I'm looking for Margherita,' she said in halting Italian. 'She's not at home, and I was wondering if she was away. We were meant to have a coffee together this morning.'

'This is her son, Mimmo,' informed the voice on the other end of the call. 'I am sorry, but my mother is in hospital since last night. She had a bad fall and is unconscious.'

Janet was deeply shocked. 'Oh, my goodness!' she exclaimed. 'Can I go to see her?'

'I am sorry. No. Not at the moment. What is your name? I can telephone you later today when we have some news.' He was polite and unemotional. But what could Janet expect? He didn't know her; they had never met. He was hardly going to break down and sob to a complete stranger on the other end of the phone. But still, Janet thought he didn't sound anything like upset enough for her liking. They agreed to talk later on.

Janet flopped down in her kitchen chair and, elbows on the table, put her head in her hands and fought the tears back. Margherita was — other than Daisy — her only friend here in Italy. Angelo did not count. Not yet anyway. Their sporadic get-togethers appeared to be purely physical, and she didn't feel that she knew anything about him at all, let alone on an emotional level. He was very distant and uncommunicative, but she was not looking for a serious relationship, so it suited her just fine.

However, she suddenly realised how fond she had become of the old lady. On hearing this news, she felt as though she'd been punched in the stomach. Bella lay across her foot to give her comfort. She patted her gratefully.

When the phone rang late that evening, Janet looked at the caller display and saw that it must be Mimmo, as the call was from Margherita's phone. Her teeth were clenched as she answered the call, and she was so tense she could hardly utter '*Pronto*' as a feeling of dread overwhelmed her.

'It's Mimmo,' the voice informed her calmly. 'My mother has regained consciousness but is very unwell. She will be staying in hospital for the time being.'

'May I go and visit her?' Janet's anxiety for her friend made her voice high and quavery.

'I am sorry, but nobody is allowed to visit,' Mimmo announced. 'She is gravely ill, and the doctors have told us that she will not be going home again. When she is discharged, *if* she is discharged, I should say, she will go into a nursing home. She will be unable to look after herself anymore.'

Janet was deeply shocked. 'I don't understand.' She ploughed on, though she felt as though she had lost Mimmo's attention. 'When can I see her?'

'I don't know.' It sounded as though the conversation was winding down.

'What about the dog? Gigi?' she enquired. 'Is there somebody looking after him?'

'The dog will be sent to the local kennels. There is nobody to look after him. I have been topping up his bowls with biscuits and water since yesterday.'

'Could I take him home and look after him?' The words were out of her mouth before she had time to think. What would she do with two dogs in her rental home? What would Donatella think? But she knew that Donatella would not mind being the compassionate soul that she was.

'Are you serious?' Mimmo sounded interested in the idea; she could tell by the way he asked the question. 'Where do you live?'

'I'm renting in Casalini while I look for a new home,' she ventured. 'I only hope that my landlady doesn't mind, but I can't bear the thought of little Gigi being sent to kennels. He's such a sweet little guy.'

'A new home?' Janet could almost hear the wheels turning in Mimmo's head and held her breath as she knew, she just knew what was coming next. 'Are you looking for a trullo?'

'Well… yes, actually.'

'Do you like my mother's home?' There. He had said it.

'Of course!' Janet said, her heart in her mouth. 'It's the most beautiful home I know.'

'We will be selling it, of course.' Mimmo sounded pragmatic, at the least. 'Perhaps we should meet to have a chat.'

'Yes. We should meet. I'll go over early tomorrow morning to collect Gigi, and perhaps we could meet then.'

They agreed that she would collect Gigi early and meet him there at seven a.m. to have a chat. It was all completely surreal as far as Janet was concerned.

Janet barely slept that night. First and foremost, she was deeply upset at the news about Margherita. Secondly, she didn't know if she could afford her beautiful trullo as she was still waiting for the sale of her house in Ireland to be completed. Her brain whirled with all these new stresses, she who had announced to herself — and anybody who would listen — that, on leaving Ireland, her days of stressing were over. Now she knew neither what to think nor how to deal with this brand-new situation.

Morning dawned with a steely-blue sky and a day that promised to be hot and dry, not a breeze today to ruffle the branches of the olive trees. She drove from Casalini to the district — called a *contrada* — where the trullo was located.

Mimmo's silver four-by-four was parked outside the gate when she arrived. As she entered the property, he emerged from the trullo and approached her, while Gigi rushed past him to greet her with whimpers and licks.

Mimmo was quite short and considerably overweight; his stomach spread like an apron over the belt of his battered, blue jeans, though she could see that he had once, perhaps, been a good-looking man. Now, apparently in his mid-forties, he looked as though he spent most of his time eating pasta and eschewing any form of serious exercise.

He had made a pot of coffee and produced two cups and a sugar bowl from the cupboard over the sink in the tiny kitchen. Her coffee was poured, and the cup was slid towards her on the wooden table top.

'How is Margherita?' Janet asked anxiously. 'Is she any better today?'

Mimmo was carefully examining the contents of his coffee cup as though he did not want to meet her eyes. 'A little better,' he said as he threw back his coffee in one swallow. 'But she is very confused, and the doctor is not permitting visitors who are not family.'

'Will you tell her, if you get the chance, that I send lots of love and wish her a speedy recovery?' She added, 'Tell her I will visit her as soon as it's permitted.'

Mimmo nodded his assent and got straight to the point.

'You would like to purchase this trullo?' he enquired, with no beating around the bush.

'I would love to,' Janet replied, then added, 'But I am still waiting for the money from the sale of my house, and I don't know how much money you want for it anyway. Perhaps it's too much.'

'We can do a deal,' he announced. 'You can rent the trullo for the moment and, as soon as the money arrives from your house, we can finalise everything.' He mentioned a large sum of money which made Janet wince.

'I'll have to look at my finances. I hope I can manage it.' She was apprehensive but excited at the same time as she began to make mental calculations. *Yes, I can just about afford it,* she thought to herself.

They stood up and shook hands with an agreement to speak to one another the following day. He told her that if she was not interested that he would be putting it on the market immediately and expected to get even more than the eye-watering sum he had mentioned.

'It's possible to move straight in here without having to do anything to the house,' he told her, which she already knew, as she considered it picture-perfect.

'Do we need to have an agreement drawn up?' Janet asked anxiously.

Mimmo waved a hand casually in the air. 'No,' he said. 'I trust you. The trullo will be yours when you get your finances organised. Until then, you can rent it for a nominal sum.'

Janet had a fleeting thought, *but do I trust you?* Then she looked around her new home and put it out of her mind. Whatever happened, she would manage.

Mimmo looked content.

CHAPTER FOURTEEN
JANET

The day Janet moved into her trullo in the Valle d'Itria, near the old white city of Ostuni, was a moment of heart-stopping joy.

She had spent the early part of the morning putting down the back seats in her little car and piling all the clothing and books, which were her only possessions, into the back. Gigi and Bella's basket went onto the floor on the passenger side, followed by the two little occupants, who sat there together, ears up, looking expectant.

Waving goodbye to Donatella and promising to see her soon, she put her car in gear and pulled out onto the main street, turning right towards her new home. Before she had gone very far, both dogs were up on the passenger seat, sticking their noses out through the window, enjoying the breeze.

Her first thought, driving through the gate of her trullo, was that her dream home in the Valle d'Itria had become a reality. Feeling a moment of guilt that this wonderful event had occurred in her life at the expense of her friend Margherita, she wondered when she would be able to visit her. She had struggled with these confusing feelings of guilt, mixed with delight, at the thought of moving into her little trullo.

She spoke to Mimmo regularly to ask about his mother, but all he ever said was, 'No. She can't receive visitors. No, she is too ill and wouldn't recognise you anyway.'

Opening the car door, she stepped out into the winter sunshine. The sky was cloudless, that particular colour of blue that Janet now thought of as "Pugliese Blue", as she pulled the door key from her bag and entered her new home.

'We're home!' she informed the dogs as they bounded ahead of her into the trullo. They seemed to understand and dashed around, sniffing everything from the floral chintz sofa to the brass bedstead and back again, panting with excitement. Janet placed their bed in its old position beside the stove, and they immediately leapt in. She had originally thought of getting a second basket for Bella, but the two little dogs refused to be parted and liked to be curled up together into one furry ball.

Dragging her belongings out of the car, she made short work of putting her clothes away and placing her books on the bookshelves alongside Margherita's. Mimmo had told her she could keep them along with most of the furniture, and Janet had a feeling he was not exactly a bookish person anyway. He had removed Margherita's clothing and anything he felt might be of value, leaving the rest.

Janet's honeymoon with her new home was, she felt, far more exciting than her first few weeks of marriage to James. Not having lived with him before they got married, she had been shocked to find how irritable he was, always becoming revved up by the most insignificant things like, for example, the fact that she did not always put her clothes away at night and sometimes lost a sock in the wash. She did not believe in getting overexcited by what she considered trivialities, but he was pernickety and insisted on perfection at all times. Without his constant nagging presence, that she had once thought she could not live without, she felt nothing but relief. She could not wait to know that their divorce had been finalised, and she could move on with her life and never have to think about him again.

The trullo, with its pretty garden, gave her constant joy. She had found a local man, Leonardo, to help her with the heavy stuff, such as pruning her eight huge old olive trees and doing the tilling and fertilising that were such an important part of maintaining her lovely property. Next October or November, she longed to see her first olive harvest, as this year had not been productive. Mother Nature was, apparently, giving the trees a year off.

Once every week or so, Angelo would arrive with a bottle of wine, have supper with her and, usually, stay the night. Their relationship seemed to suit both of them very well. Janet was not yet ready to commit to a serious relationship and, it seemed, Angelo felt the same way. They got on well, and their friendship was something that felt right to Janet. He filled a need, for the moment. Everything in good time, she thought, but she always looked forward to his visits. It prompted her to keep herself looking good and not to lapse into becoming a solitary dog-lady, as she was afraid it would be only too easy to let things go.

After she had queried him about vaccinations for the dogs, he told her that, as he was a vet, he would organise everything for her. He had a surgery in the centre of Ostuni, and his practice was mainly focused on small animals: dogs and cats. He told her he far preferred the animals to most of their owners, 'Present company excepted, of course.' He laughed.

She found a good hairdresser, finally, after a couple of false starts.

Her first hairdresser was a man, a showman. After she had had her hair washed by a friendly girl at the basin and had been shown to the maestro's chair for a cut, he told her to stand up and proceeded to jab at her head with a pair of scissors. Apparently, this darting and diving man, who used the scissors as though he were taking part in a fencing tournament, had decided that he was a celebrity because he had once been interviewed for television. After all the drama, the cut was not great; in fact, Janet thought that it looked exactly the same as before she had subjected herself to this ridiculous performance. She hurried home.

Her second attempt was with a young man, dressed from head to toe in black, who sported a tall quiff on top of his dark head, a pointed beard, and spectacles with red frames. *Oh no!* she thought. *Not another wannabe celebrity!* He cut her hair quite nicely, but then he persuaded her to allow him to "enhance the colour", and it turned out a strange shade of red that looked completely unnatural, though he insisted it looked wonderful. Furious, she left, vowing never to return, especially after he argued with her, insisting that that was exactly what she had asked for.

However, it was a matter of third time lucky. She finally found an unpretentious woman with a nice, airy salon just off the big roundabout in Ostuni, where the road begins its straight eight-kilometre dash for the town of Ceglie Messapica, a town famous for its excellent restaurants. Janet then settled down, she hoped, to a lifetime of well-cut and coloured hair. Now she could relax and put her previous hairdressing traumas behind her.

Janet paid a monthly rental to Mimmo, and he still paid the electricity bills as the property was in Margherita's name and would remain so until she had paid for it in full and the title deeds had been signed over.

Soon after she moved in, her first water delivery arrived. As the Valle d'Itria is located on a limestone plateau with no rivers, all water, if it does not fall from the skies and get collected in a tank, comes from deep boreholes more than three hundred metres deep. As Janet's trullo did not have its own *pozzo* — borehole — she was obliged to order her water and have it delivered.

She could hear the ancient truck groaning and rattling its way up the lane long before she saw it arrive at her gate. On its back was a big oval-shaped metal tank filled with precious water. It clanked through her gate and the delivery man, Tommaso, climbed out. He was a warm, friendly old man who chatted to her in almost incomprehensible dialect as he unrolled a long rubber pipe with a nozzle, dragged it over to the small manhole covering her cistern and filled it in just a few minutes. Having paid him and waved him goodbye, she realised that she had known nothing about the finer details of living here before she had jumped in and committed herself to achieve her ambition of living in a trullo. No amount of online research made up for actually living in one. She realised that she was on a sharp learning curve.

As the end of the year approached and the leaves fell, resulting in bare trees and grapevines like gnarled, blackened stumps, Janet soon realised that a trullo could be a damp place to live in during the colder months. She had not realised that Puglia is humid in winter, where mists from the Adriatic and Ionian Seas envelop the olive groves and low hills after dark. For example, she had noticed, after visiting Donatella in Casalini late one evening, that her car was drenched in dew, and she had to use the windscreen wipers before she could drive away. Every morning the ground outside her trullo was wet, and the walls dripped with streaks of water as though it had rained in the night. The grass was sparkling with drops of moisture, the olive trees were in their element, and the sky was blue overhead.

As a result of this winter humidity, she battled with what the locals referred to as *muffa* — mould. Over her head, in the topmost part of the cone in the trullo which comprised her bedroom, the ceiling had turned black, and her black suede boots had, in turn, become blue. She was horrified. She rang Donatella, who arrived within the hour, laughed merrily at Janet's inexperience, got out the ladder, mixed some bleach with water and wiped it all off with a big cloth on the end of a brush.

Janet invested in a dehumidifier, which she left switched on in the bedroom trullo section of her home, more or less permanently, over the winter months. Luckily, she managed to brush the *muffa* off her boots, and all was well — yet another notch on the learning curve of her new life in a trullo in Puglia. She relaxed and learnt to accept it, regularly airing out her clothes and keeping the windows cracked open during the daytime.

Leonardo taught her a lot, too. She now knew the laws about when it was necessary to ensure that grass and weeds were cut and during which months it was forbidden to light a bonfire. She knew to keep her pots of lemons in a sheltered south-facing position, as the cold wind from the north, the tramontana, could kill them in winter when the weather, on occasion, became surprisingly cold. Having imagined Puglia as being warm all year round, the cold snaps which occasionally hit the region came as a surprise. One day Janet would be out walking in short sleeves, the next in a warm fleece and woolly hat. Winters could be unpredictable, but mostly the weather was sublime, with a high blue sky and an occasional stray cloud that had, apparently, become separated from the pack.

She rediscovered her love for cooking. James had been a big fan of fish fingers and oven chips with baked beans or mushy peas, which was hardly a challenge, but which Janet accepted, as it was so easy to throw together after a long day at the office. He also enjoyed regular takeaway pizzas and Chinese food, which Janet found to be too greasy for her taste. She preferred Thai food, with chicken satay being her favourite. So, she had got out of the habit of cooking many years ago, except when friends came for dinner when she would pull out all the stops.

Now she was on her own, and the markets, with their fresh fruits, vegetables, meats and fish selections galore, made her feel close to euphoric. She was in her element and began to follow recipes from various Italian websites online. She found new vegetables such as broccoflower, a delicious yellow-green combination of cauliflower and broccoli, which she loved and, of course, the glossy aubergines, courgettes and peppers were — to her mind — out of this world. She learnt to make a perfect ragu — a pork and beef mincemeat sauce with carrots, onions and celery, that required no less than three hours to cook on her stove top, puffing its mouth-watering smell into every corner of her cosy trullo. She would freeze most of the ragu when it had cooked and regularly cracked open a portion to have with pasta.

An organic supermarket supplied just about everything else she could possibly want. In fact, she had not realised how many organic and biological items one could find until she visited this friendly shop. Pasta, eggs, snacks, washing liquid, bath oil, the selection seemed endless. There they would wrap her purchases and carry them to the car and, even though she protested that she could manage fine, they always insisted.

There were many good wine shops — *enotecas* — around. She loved to try out new wines and soon established which shops she enjoyed visiting most. She began to learn about the various primitivo, fiano and verdeca wines, with malvasia rosato a personal favourite of hers. The staff loved to see her arrive, discuss their latest finds and would regularly gift her a bottle to take home to try.

A large *pasticceria* — pastry shop — on a narrow side street in downtown Ostuni regularly lured her inside. Pastries, large and small, colourful, creamy and delicious, caused her almost orgasmic delight as the assistant would fill a little golden cardboard tray with however many she chose. She usually opted for the smallest tray, but when Donatella was visiting, she pointed to the larger one, as the sweet tooth of this generously proportioned lady was legendary. There was also a corner with a few tables, where one could sit to have a coffee to accompany whatever delicacy one had purchased, and Janet often found herself there, checking the news on her phone, sipping cappuccino, and biting into a pastry.

Janet's favourites were the famous Pugliese cream-filled pastries called "nuns' breasts" — *tette della monache.* These came with different fillings: cream, chocolate, and pistachio. She would sit there at her favourite corner table and bite into one of these super-sweet cakes, revelling in the sensation of creaminess in her mouth, always closing her eyes for the first bite. The owner of the *pasticceria* often came to sit with her. Angela and her husband had owned this wonderful pastry shop for more years than they could count, and it was famous for its *pandoro* and *panettone*, those huge, soft cakes so popular in Italy at Christmas, and at Easter, when they are dove-shaped and called *colomba*.

Just up the street from the *pasticceria*, Janet found an immaculate cheese shop, all white and gleaming chrome, where they had a selection of delicious Pugliese cheeses to choose from: burrata, oozing buttery cream, mozzarella balls and twists, fresh ricotta, pecorino fresco and hard cheeses of every description. She loved the little cheese balls wrapped in *prosciutto crudo* and considered them one of her particular weaknesses. The assistant would wrap her portions in silky greaseproof paper and pop them in a biodegradable bag for her to take home.

She especially enjoyed cooking for Angelo at the weekends when he was most likely to visit. She began to look forward to the winter evenings spent with him in front of the log fire, drinking her favourite primitivo wine and chatting comfortably, always ending up in bed together.

Thus, Janet began to find a level of contentment in her life that she had never experienced before. She realised that she was perfectly happy with her own company, most of the time, never bored as long as she had a good book to read and, apart from Angelo, Daisy and Donatella, she did not spend much time nurturing new friendships. *All in good time*, she thought. The dogs were her greatest comfort, with their unjudgmental love. They walked together every day, along the lanes that cut through the olive groves, rarely meeting a soul.

CHAPTER FIFTEEN
JANET

Janet had been living happily in her new home for just over three months when she received a double dose of news. First of all, her divorce was about to go through. She was anxious to get this over and done with, though she had been both looking forward to and dreading it at the same time. The thought of meeting James again was not a pleasant one.

She thought about her personal effects in storage in Dublin and made a mental note to arrange to get them sent to Puglia, though the non-essentials would have to go as her trullo was tiny. It was strange that items she had once thought she could not live without had become irrelevant in her new life.

Just as she was planning her trip to Dublin, she had a call from the nursing home where her grandmother was staying. Her beloved gran was dying, the matron told her. She had contracted pneumonia, and her doctor said that it looked as though she would not survive much longer. If she wanted to say goodbye, she should come soon.

***

'I've got to go back to Ireland for a while,' Janet confided to Daisy over an aperitivo in Caffe Negroni that evening. It was late winter, and Ostuni was bathed in a grey mist, suiting her mood, and it was cold and humid.

'Why? What's up?' Daisy asked, taking an overly large swig of hot, aromatic China Martini, which was her special winter tipple. 'You're going away?'

Janet sighed. 'My grandmother is dying. I have to see her, try to be with her and comfort her as best I can. She has nobody except me.' She felt sad when she thought about her long-lost family. 'As you know, my parents passed away several years ago, and Gran has outlived almost everybody. I'm the only one left who's close to her, so I feel I need to visit her soon. Say goodbye, I suppose. Not that she'll register my presence, but she has always been a sweet, gentle soul, and I want to be there for her, if possible.'

Daisy clasped Janet's hand, eyes filling with tears, her sympathy obvious.

Janet continued. 'My divorce is about to go through, and I need to meet with my solicitor and attend to all the legalities. I have to get my finances sorted out too. I can't buy my little trullo from Mimmo until I get my share of the money from the sale of the house in Dublin.'

'Oh goodness! What an ordeal for you!' Daisy squeezed her hand harder. For such a tiny person, she had a strong grip. Janet winced slightly.

'Poor Grannie. She's been living in a residential home on the outskirts of Dublin for the past eight years. She's completely lost to dementia.' She looked down, and Daisy thought she looked a bit guilty. 'Honestly, if she had her full senses, I would never have been able to leave her there and come over to live in Italy. Actually, I considered bringing her to live with me here, but that was just a thought. I couldn't manage to look after her now the way she is. She doesn't know whether I'm here or there. I ring her every week, though. We have the same conversation every time.' She withdrew her hand from Daisy's firm clasp in order to pick up her glass of red wine and check her phone. 'I'll be heading off in a couple of days on an open-ended ticket.'

'What about your trullo?' Daisy asked. 'And the dogs?'

'Daisy. That's why I wanted to see you this evening.' She paused. 'How would you feel about house sitting for me while I'm away? I know there's not much hope of your being able to iron out the contract on your apartment any time soon, and your rented room in town is not exactly paradise.'

Daisy had had nothing but problems regarding the title deeds on her longed-for little apartment in Ostuni's historic centre. The seller appeared to be taking her time and to be getting some sort of sadistic kick from leaving Daisy dangling in mid-air. Apparently, there was not even a certificate of habitation for the property, a legal requirement, or not, depending on who you spoke to. Also, even if the legal glitches could be ironed out, there was still a great deal to do in order to render it fully habitable. Daisy wanted to redo the bathroom, install a new kitchenette and some form of heating for starters, and she was becoming increasingly frustrated and anxious.

She was stunned to be asked. 'You mean, stay at your trullo with your dogs for a while? I'd love to. Oh goodness, I'd absolutely love to! Fabulous!' She waved her hands about, as she always did when she was excited. Janet took this as a promising sign. 'Have you any idea for how long? Two weeks? Three?'

'Daisy, I honestly don't have a clue. It might be a month, probably more. I must attend to my divorce, and I don't know yet how that's going to play out. I need to make sure that I get my finances in order. As I said, I need to pay for my trullo.' She smiled happily at the thought. 'Right now, I'm paying a small rent to Mimmo with a view to paying him when my money is available. It's vitally important that I attend to this now; otherwise, who knows what will happen in the long-term.' She ran her hand through her hair as if trying to organise her thoughts.

'I can come any time, darling!' Daisy was envious of Janet's beautiful new home and was thrilled at the thought of staying there for a while. And she adored the little dogs. What fun she would have!

'Fantastic!' It was now Janet's turn to feel pleased. 'This means I can leave Gigi and Bella at home while I'm away. If you had said no, I was going to leave them at the kennels with Angelo, but this is a much better plan.'

Daisy responded with a wide smile.

'How about you come on Monday? I have to leave early on Wednesday morning to catch the flight from Bari to Dublin. Donatella will mind my car for me while I'm away and will drive me to the airport. When I return, I'll get the train to Ostuni and a taxi home.' Lovely Donatella had become her best friend in the world since she had stayed at her little house. She mothered her Irish friend, feeling she needed looking after. And she was probably right, Janet always told herself.

She continued. 'If you come on Monday, I can spend some time showing you where everything is, including the dogs' routine, feeding times and so on. There's the rubbish collection too, which days for plastic and all that. Plus, stuff like where the fuse box is located, in case you have a power-out.'

Daisy was thrilled. She leaned over and hugged Janet. 'Oh! How wonderful! Oh, darling! I would love to become a house sitter. And a dog minder. And a plant waterer...' Her little hands waved in the air, and her big brown eyes were alight with excitement.

Bidding one another goodnight, with a parting hug, the two promised to meet on Monday.

Janet was actually dreading this trip and knew that every part of it would be difficult, and she would need to be strong. First of all, she needed to say goodbye to her grandmother, her last surviving family member. Tears sprang to her eyes as she made up the bed in the second room, which was to be Daisy's for the next month or so. She decided that the best way to get through the ordeal was to focus on her long-term goal, which was her new life in Puglia. This would be her incentive for putting her old life behind her, once and for all. When she returned, she would begin to make an effort to meet more people, go out more. Spring would be here soon, and with it, a renewed vigour. She felt both optimistic and anxious at the same time.

James wanted to marry The American Woman, Cassie, as soon as possible. He would adopt her son Billy, and they planned to live happily ever after. He had even implied that they hoped to add to their family. That he seemed happy to consider such an event gave Janet a deep feeling of bitterness at the injustice of it all. But then she would think of her trullo among the olive groves of Puglia, and her mind would become calm, her spirits would lift. She would run her fingers through her wild curls and think only of the future.

CHAPTER SIXTEEN
DAISY

House sitting for Janet! How fabulous! Daisy thought as she packed up her few bags and prepared to move out of town and into Janet's trullo. She did not have a car of her own; in fact, she had not driven for several years, so she would use Janet's bicycle to get about, and Donatella would pop up to see her occasionally to check that she was all right and did not need anything.

The tiny one-roomed apartment which she had been renting for the past few months had become claustrophobic. It was at the bottom of a narrow alleyway in Ostuni, about fifty metres from a busy street; really more of a bed-sitter consisting of one dark room with no space for anything except a bed, a tiny stove and sink and an enormous brown wardrobe, which dominated the cramped space. There was minimal daylight via the lace-covered glass panels in the front door, which, when the weather was warm, she had to leave open for ventilation. The bathroom was the tiniest that Daisy had ever seen and, when the shower was used, not only did Daisy get wet but so did everything else.

'Anyone could just stroll in when I'm washing,' she confided to Janet over a spritz at Caffe Negroni one evening. 'I only agreed to stay there while I was looking for a place of my own. I had no idea it was going to take so long.'

Five days later, Daisy was dragging her bags along the cobblestoned lane towards Corso Vittorio Emanuele II, where she piled them higgledy-piggledy on the footpath and waited for Janet to arrive to pick her up. Little did she know how much this short journey was to change her life. Getting into that red Fiat 500 was only the beginning.

But for now, she was happy.

***

Daisy was excited. Very excited.

It had all begun one evening, about a month after she had begun house sitting for Janet, as she relaxed in the setting sun outside a bar in the main piazza in Ostuni, Piazza della Libertà. The sun was beginning to slip behind the tall houses surrounding the piazza as she adjusted her woollen Kashmiri shawl — the early spring evenings were still cool — sipped a glass of white wine and flipped through an Italian gossip magazine that someone had discarded on the chair beside her. She could barely speak any Italian, apart from important words such as *vino* and *ciao*, but she recognised all the "celebrities" and "stars" with their blank, wrinkle-free features staring vacantly at her from the pages. *My goodness! Is that really Madonna?* she thought to herself, as the almost unrecognisable face smiled up at a darkly handsome man, apparently her new lover, who had to be a least thirty years her junior. She took another sip of wine and settled down to study the photograph. What on earth was Madonna wearing, for heaven's sake.

Janet had been away for more than a month at this point, having buried her grandmother just a week after she had returned. Now she was bogged down in the hassle of getting her money signed over and all the last-minute haggling with James. She had told Daisy that every time she saw him now, The American Woman was glued to his side, constantly looking up at him with adoring eyes. It seemed that Janet wished she could afford just to walk away; then she would think about her pretty trullo and remember why she needed this money so badly. The thought had kept her going, and Daisy was utterly happy in her continuing role as house sitter.

As she browsed, she was suddenly aware that there was someone blocking her light, and she looked up. Above her stood a tall man in an open-collared shirt, a pullover tied around his broad shoulders, and a pair of chinos. The first impression Daisy got was, *He must be a runner, with a body like that.* She smiled up at him and raised her glass.

'May I join you?' His accent was French, and he was looking at her intently. Before waiting for her reply — she was speechless for a moment — he sank into the chair next to her and raised his hand to summon the waiter, who was hovering nearby.

The waiter stood over them, holding his tin tray with an enquiring look on his face.

'Another?' The man looked briefly at Daisy and said, 'Another of those for the lady and a Peroni for me.' The waiter sped off across the cobbled street, dodging a speeding Vespa. These piazza seating arrangements had just opened up in anticipation of the Easter holidays. In winter, the bars and cafes served drinks inside only, but during the tourist season, tables and chairs were hauled onto the piazza to accommodate the increased volume of visitors. The different cafes had their individual colours so you could know which bar or gelateria your drinks were coming from. Theirs were marked out by red cushions on white metal chairs, and there were little piles of paperback novels placed strategically on the tables. Red rugs had been provided, and Daisy had one of these partially draped across her lap. The ice cream parlour next door had blue-and-white checked cushions, so there could be no confusion between these establishments, an essential requirement.

The man was looking at Daisy intently. 'Do you live here, or are you just visiting?' His silky French accent was giving her goosebumps.

'Oh, I live here,' she replied, looking at his arm resting beside hers. His golden skin was tanned, and she felt a shiver of desire shoot through her body. She found herself wanting to touch that arm with its blond hairs. 'But I'm house sitting at the moment. My friend — girlfriend,' she added quickly, 'is away at the moment. It's a lovely trullo outside town. I'm waiting for my new apartment to be finalised.' She realised she was giving far too much information to a total stranger, but there was something authoritative about him, she thought, the way he was listening so intently to what she had to say.

'You are very pretty and, I think, quite dangerous.' His voice was smooth and sexy. He had obviously noticed her reaction to him and how her face had suddenly flushed.

Daisy was aware that his interest in her had been piqued and wondered why. And had he really called her "dangerous"? That had to be a first, as Daisy had never considered herself anything other than ordinary. To add to that, she felt that she was not exactly looking her most glamorous. She also admitted, though reluctantly to herself, that she was no spring chicken either. She thought of Madonna and how she managed to snag all these handsome men, but then that was Madonna, with her wiry body, her fame and vast wealth. Not little Daisy, with her wispy red hair and brown eyes, a legacy from her Spanish grandmother.

He asked her all about the trullo. Did she have neighbours? She told him no, not another house for at least five hundred metres, and anyway, it was behind a high stone wall.

'Come!' he commanded. 'Let's get something to eat. How about that bar over there?' He indicated a small osteria across the square, and they made their way there, finding a cosy corner to sit at a small table and eat fish.

Dinner together was merely a formality. His hotel room was close by and, before too many hours had passed, they ended up there together.

Daisy had never experienced anything like this before. No clumsy lover, this man was obviously experienced and gave her pleasure that night as she had never experienced before. He kept calling her "my baby girl", which made her feel small and vulnerable. Which she was.

Waking from her tumbled sleep, she looked at her watch and leapt out of bed.

The man put out a hand to restrain her. 'Don't rush off, ma chérie. Stay a while.'

'Oh! I must go! My friend's two dogs will need to be fed and watered.' She was sitting on the side of the bed, trying to pull on her jeans at high speed. 'I have a responsibility.'

'How will you get back? Do you have a car?'

'Oh lord!' she exclaimed. 'Look at the time. I can't call for a lift at four a.m. What was I thinking?' Daisy was feeling very hot and bothered. She had hoped to cadge a lift back to Janet's trullo with Donatella at about ten p.m., but she had completely forgotten in the heat of this overwhelming passion. Donatella was probably wondering what had happened to her, though surely realised that she had had a change of plan. She should have phoned her. *Oh dear!* she thought. *Now what am I going to do?*

'I can drive you.' He looked at her unconcernedly. He was stretching his long, golden limbs languidly. 'I have a rental car parked right outside. Come back and lie down beside me for ten minutes, and then I'll drive you home.'

As he undressed her once more, Daisy was overwhelmed with desire for this gorgeous man. It was like a dream.

But not for long. The nightmare was about to begin.

***

As soon as the man arrived at Janet's trullo, where Daisy was greeted by two frantic little dogs, things began to become slightly strange.

As she crouched down to cuddle Gigi and Bella, the man stood back, admiring the trullo and its surroundings.

'It is so quiet here. So private.' He observed. 'In what direction is the nearest house?'

'Down that way.' Daisy, who was now being licked half to death by the two little dogs, who were whining and yapping their joy at her return, pointed to a clump of tall cypress trees. 'At the bottom of the hill we just drove up. I've never met them, but I think they're English. I met an English lady out walking her dogs the other day, and I'm fairly sure that's where she lives.' The sun was making a speedy ascent, and the trullo was bathed in the early morning light. 'I think a Belgian couple live over there.' She pointed vaguely in the opposite direction. 'I haven't actually met any of them yet.'

'So, they're not likely to drop in to see you then?' More a question than a statement.

At his voice, both dogs stopped mid-lick, and their hackles rose. Gigi growled deep in his throat. Never one to be left out, Bella joined in, and they both voiced their displeasure at this stranger in their home with a couple of sharp barks and backed away from him.

'Hey, guys!' Daisy quietened them. 'It's okay. This is my new friend.'

Standing up and going to fetch their bowls to rinse them, she said, 'Sorry, I've never heard them growl at anyone before. I don't know what's got into them.' Gigi was now barking furiously at the man and gave a couple of experimental lunges at his ankles. He frowned and gave a small kick in Gigi's direction, which made him bark even more furiously.

As Daisy began to put some kibble and water in their bowls, she was aware that the man was following her every move. She had greatly enjoyed her night of passion; it had been quite a while since she had taken such pleasure from, what she assumed, was a one-night stand as usual. But now he could go. Real-life could resume, and she could consign this episode to history.

He did not go, however. He stayed for breakfast. Daisy was now tired and longing for a shower and a nap, but he had seemingly taken over.

Just as she was thinking of asking him to leave, as though he could read her mind, he beckoned to her. 'Come and sit on my lap, baby girl. You're tired. Let me hold you.'

He looked so handsome sitting on Janet's chintz sofa that she was drawn irresistibly into his arms. Ten minutes later, they were in bed, and he was doing things to her that nobody had ever done to her before, at least, not in a long time, and the wrought-iron bedstead was being put to the test as it creaked and groaned beneath them.

After that, it was only a matter of a couple of days before he had moved into the trullo with his few possessions, and Daisy was his willing slave. He made her feel beautiful, young, desirable, and she yielded to his demands happily, in a haze of desire. The only blot on an otherwise perfect situation was the fact that Gigi and Bella loathed him and spent their time growling and barking at him. She noticed that he occasionally aimed a kick at Gigi and decided to ignore it. All would be well. Janet would return soon, and she would get on with her life. She was sure that this relationship was temporary and that he would soon leave. In the meantime, she would relax and enjoy the episode before he wandered back to wherever he came from.

The man was very vague about where he was from. 'I'm French,' he told her when she asked. 'Maybe I will stay here.' He told her that he was independently wealthy. A trust fund, she gathered. Every few days, he would leave her for a few hours and disappear, where she did not know, but he always brought home delicacies, wine, and flowers. Then he began to buy her underwear. Frilly. She thought it made her look ridiculous, but he seemed to find it exciting, so she went along with the idea. For now. It was just temporary after all, and it was nice to be fussed over for a change.

Occasionally, she thought about Janet. When would she return? What would happen to her relationship with this gorgeous man then? But, as he whispered intimacies into her ear, she soon put these matters out of her head. She felt as though she were under some sort of spell. Perhaps he would come to live with her in her new apartment in the old town of Ostuni, but she doubted it. Her certainty that this was a fleeting romance, kept her sane. Anyway, her apartment would be far too small for the two of them.

One morning, as Daisy climbed out of bed and pulled back the curtains to greet a sunny day in the olive groves of the Valle d'Itria, she felt warm and complete. She pulled a Japanese silk kimono over her nakedness and looked at the pale blond head on the pillow beside hers. One tanned arm was flung over where she had been lying, and she felt a warm glow at the fact that she was still a desirable woman. She had long ago given up hope of such a relationship.

By day, they walked through the olive groves with the little dogs rushing around their feet, sniffing at every single twig and tuft of grass, leaving their territorial mark wherever they went. He cooked for her every evening, and she felt special and cherished. He asked her to tie up her hair in little bunches and liked her to wear white ankle socks and as many frills as possible. He bought her two pairs of baby doll pyjamas which seemed to affect him greatly, as when he looked at her dressed in them, his face would flush, and his breathing would change gear. If Daisy found this at all odd, she never said it, either out loud or to herself. It was enough to have him there, admiring and desiring her.

He had taken over all the shopping and had asked her for her credit card. 'I'm sure you want to pay your own way,' he said as she gave it to him, along with the code. She trusted him.

He soon began to show his disapproval for her misdeeds in many subtle ways. A look. A gesture of impatience. A reminder that she was just a little woman after all. Inferior to him, a man. He wielded an insidious power over her that made her feel as though she never needed to have another original thought, that he would do her thinking and deciding for her.

That morning, as Daisy spooned ground coffee into the cafetière, exactly the number of spoons that he insisted on or he would become angry with her, she realised that the dogs were not in their baskets. *That's odd*, she thought as she opened the door and stepped outside. Perhaps he had let them out earlier. Calling them yielded no result. She began to panic, rushing into the bedroom and waking him.

'The dogs! Gigi and Bella! They're gone.' She began to dress, picking up the clothes she had discarded the night before, overwhelmed with panic and guilt. 'Where could they be? I need to go and search.'

He sat up in bed and lazily stretched. 'They'll be around somewhere.' He sounded relaxed. 'There's no cause for alarm. You'll see, they're okay, wherever they are.'

Finally, pulling on a pair of trainers, Daisy dashed out the front door and began calling the dogs in earnest. 'Gigi! Bella!' She ran around the garden, looking for them. 'Where are you?'

She opened the gate and ran out onto the laneway. 'Gigi! Bella!' There was no sign of the dogs whatsoever. She returned to the house, shoulders slumped, leaving the gate ajar in case they returned. She had no clue how to handle this problem.

She would phone Angelo at the kennels. Perhaps they had wandered off, and someone had handed them in. Or she could call over to the English lady down the hill. Perhaps she had seen them. Yes. That was the best idea. In the meantime, her lover was sipping coffee and looking at his iPad, seemingly unconcerned. She told him what she planned. 'I'll chat to the English lady. Perhaps she's seen them. Otherwise, I'm sure Angelo will do something to help to find them.'

He looked at her, his face stern. 'Fussing about them isn't going to help,' he said in his smooth French accent, pursing his lips the way she loved him to. 'If they have wandered off, they'll come back. I'll handle it. It's too soon to call anybody yet, and I'll do it later if they don't come back by themselves. You're not to stress yourself. You know how you get, baby.'

Daisy almost screamed in frustration but restrained herself when she heard his words and saw the expression on his face. 'But how did they get out in the first place?' she asked him. 'There's a high wall around the property. I'm definitely going to have to talk to Angelo. I'll give him a buzz immediately.' She looked up at him, towering above her and, all of a sudden, felt a deep disquiet. She could see a strange glint in his eyes and immediately stopped talking. She would have to deal with this in her own way. Something was wrong. The first stirrings of unease began to assail her, and she wondered, not for the first time, what it was he wanted from her.

He said, 'I'll make a fresh coffee for you.' He began to press the buttons on the coffee machine. 'Here,' he said, placing it in front of her as she picked up her phone. 'Have this first. Take a few minutes to calm down before phoning him.' He sounded reassuring, and she had a glimmer of doubt.

As she sat and sipped, she thought about her situation. Here she was, house sitting for her friend Janet, with a strange man living amongst her possessions. She had not spoken to Janet since the man had moved in; she had felt guilty about that, not having mentioned it to Janet in their weekly emails. Perhaps she had presumed on their friendship, she was unsure. Now Janet's beloved dogs had gone missing, and she agonised about what she should do. Perhaps she should contact her about it. She knew she should, but Janet was in the middle of a turbulent time in Ireland, and she did not want to bother her. First of all, she would do everything she could to locate them herself. She looked up at the man and noticed that he was looking at her with a quizzical expression on his face. Suddenly, she was overcome by drowsiness. His face blurred.

He caught her as she began to slide to the floor.

CHAPTER SEVENTEEN
CLAUDIA

Claudia threw back the door onto the terrace overlooking Corso Mazzini and revelled in the mild spring air. The sun was just setting, and she could see the Adriatic Sea over the flat rooftops that stretched downhill below her. The town now glowed pink as it absorbed the last rays of sunshine.

Technically, she was camping these days indoors. Her magnificent palazzo, already beautifully restored, was in need of a great deal of furniture and decorative touches. Currently, she was using just a few of the huge rooms, two for sleeping, one for her and one for Anya, and one for cooking and relaxing. Her first essential purchase had been a gigantic four-poster bed in painted white wood, which she had draped in simple white muslin. She had also bought an equally gorgeous bed for Anya's room. Next, she had bought a hardwood chestnut table and six chairs for the kitchen, which she had placed strategically in front of the glass doors leading to the terrace. The vast terrace was high above the street, with three sets of tall French doors all leading from the main floor of the palazzo. Two led from the huge salon and the third, behind which she now sat, was from the kitchen.

On the terrace, she had placed a small wrought-iron table with just two chairs, as the space, though long, was narrow. She had been advised that the wind here in Ostuni could be quite strong at times and, as she did not want her furniture to end up on the cobblestones of Corso Mazzini, she purchased the heaviest set she could find. On the large rear terrace, she placed a long table, also made of heavy wrought iron, and eight chairs. For now, she just wanted to purchase the essentials and see what came to mind after she had been living here for a few months.

She had begun to furnish the enormous salon, and a sweet lady from Ceglie Messapica, about twenty minutes away, was currently making curtains. Antonia was the soul of efficiency, and Claudia felt confident leaving this mammoth task in such capable hands.

The ceilings were high and vaulted, built from limestone in the traditional style of Puglia. This new home, dating from the late eighteenth century, had been a lucky buy, thanks to Olivia and Niccolò's connections, and she had been in a position to purchase it outright. She loved it and was convinced that furnishing it slowly would be a true project. She was feeling a renewed energy and love of life.

While Claudia had waited for the house in Antwerp to sell, she had resumed writing and had launched a blog about life with a husband who happened to be a gaslighter. She was amazed by the level of sympathetic response she received from fellow "gaslightees" as she thought of them. She hadn't known it was so prevalent. Most of the letters were heart-breaking to read, full of stories of subtle, and not so subtle, bullying and aggression to which these women had been subjected and had convinced themselves they were becoming mentally unsound. She decided to incorporate these experiences into her new book, which she had just submitted to her publisher. It was called *Gaslighter*.

She looked at some of the emails she had received from women who had been broken by their husbands and partners but had — somehow — survived.

This letter struck a chord.

My husband told me he was going to visit the mobile blood bank to give blood. He was gone a long time, and it was bedtime, so I got into bed and fell asleep. But something woke me up. We lived in the country in a remote location. It was a very quiet night, and I could clearly hear his car approaching the lane to our house. There was a cattle grid at the end of the lane, and normally, I would hear the clang-clang of the car crossing it, but this time I could hear that it kept on going.

I looked at my clock, and it was just two a.m. I got out of bed and looked out the window. We were on top of a hill, and I could see the lights of the car heading up a dead-end road towards a local hotel. I decided to go and have a look, as I had been suspicious of his late nights for some time while I was at home looking after two babies.

I checked on the children, and they were both sound asleep, so I thought I could leave them for ten minutes while I checked on why my husband's car had gone past our driveway. I pulled a jacket on over my pyjamas and rushed out to my car, heading down the drive and up the

118

road where he had gone. I drove to the front of the hotel and couldn't see his car. Then as I turned to go home, thinking I had been mistaken, my headlights picked out his white car at the far end of the car park.

As I approached carefully, my lights lit up his car, and I saw him sit up in the driver's seat. He was not alone. Beside him was a girl with long dark hair. They sprang apart as I approached. I had never previously had such an emotional reaction to anything in my life before, but in that moment, I could have killed him. Both of them, in fact. I know I could have, and I now understand what a "crime of passion" means. I put my foot down and accelerated into the side of his car.

There was pandemonium. The girl jumped out of the passenger door and began to run. I wanted to kill her. Really. I reversed and tried to drive forward, possibly to mow her down. Who knows? But my husband pulled his car in front of mine, whereby I drove into it once more. I noted that she had run into the hotel, and my husband began to drive away. I followed him at speed, keeping so close behind him that when he stopped outside our home, I drove into the back of his car with a thud. He strode around and pulled open my door, dragged me out, threw me on the ground and beat me until I was barely conscious. Goodness knows why it took me a further six years to leave him. He kept persuading me that everything was my fault. And do you know what? I believed him. I only left after he perforated my ear drum. That was my wake-up call.

There were many tragic stories, and Claudia found she could relate well to these women, whose stories, whose tales of mental and physical pain she kept for her book. Her own salutary tale would, obviously, be featured as a warning on how a successful, independent woman could be completely bamboozled into handing control of her life to a scheming man.

On this beautiful spring evening, leaving the glass door open and moving towards her kitchen table, which was positioned to make the most of the view, Claudia opened her laptop.

She checked her emails. Some emails were from fans, other emails from her publisher regarding the design for her book cover. She examined the choices they had sent and grimaced. Would they ever take her seriously? This was the first factual book she had written, and the subject was a grim one. These proposed book covers were far too chick-lit for her taste. All that pink! She made a note to phone them the following morning. She knew she had very little say as regards the presentation of her new book; far less than one would imagine. But at least they had sent her four options. She disliked all of them. She wanted something more appropriately sinister. She envisioned a cover illustrating a woman with the shadow of a man looming over her.

A couple of articles from *The Irish Times*, *Washington Post* and *The Guardian* — all of which she subscribed to — caught her eye, and she read for a while. She hated to be uninformed about what was going on in the world.

Then, leisure time. She went to the fridge and pulled out an already opened bottle of rosato, as pink as the Adriatic Sea when the sun was setting, pouring herself a generous glass. It really was the colour of a Pugliese sunset, she thought. Pulling out a bag of *taralli*, those famous crumbly snacks so popular in Puglia, she threw a few into a small bowl and took the wine and snacks back to the table, opening Facebook for a look at what her friends were up to. The cool evening breeze gently ruffled her blonde hair, and she felt soothed and more relaxed than she had done in many years.

Apart from Anya and her father, of course, her priority was Olivia. She felt she owed her a great deal; her love and support had played a vital role as part of the hard work of restoring her self-esteem. She was anxious to know how her favourite cousin was faring and to see if there were any new photos of her on Facebook. She clicked onto Olivia's page and was gratified to see how beautiful and radiant she looked. She had posted a photo of Niccolò and herself at their wedding celebration as her profile picture, and they looked like the most glamorous couple imaginable, on their balcony with the Grand Canal in the background. Olivia was living the dream now, after a few extremely difficult years for her and for Niccolò. At last, they had entered calmer waters. It was reassuring to see her cousin so happy.

She scrolled down through Olivia's photos, updating herself on her latest comings and goings. Here was a photo of Niccolò pruning roses, another of him digging a trench. He was in his element, as garden design was his big love, and he had made a successful career from it, travelling everywhere to fulfil contracts to cater to his clients' dreams.

Now she looked at a photo in which Olivia was tagged so she would see it, from her old friend Daisy from London. Apparently, Daisy lived here in Puglia for part of the year, though they had never met. It was a selfie of a baby-faced girl/woman who was carefully posing for the photo. Claudia was about to pass on when she noticed someone in the background. She gasped and zoomed in on the photo. There, leaning back on a white metal chair outside what looked like a bar, glass of wine in hand, was a man who, she was positive, was Michel. Heart pounding, she picked up her phone.

***

Olivia answered on the third ring. 'Claudia! Darling! How are you?'

'Hi, Olivia. Oh goodness, I may have a problem. I need to talk to you.' Claudia's hands were shaking. 'I've just noticed a Facebook post by your friend Daisy, where you were tagged.'

'Ah, Daisy!' Olivia laughed. 'What has she done now? Have you met her yet? She's dying to meet you.'

'Michel is in one of her photos! I'm positive it's him. It's a selfie with him in the background.'

'What?' Olivia gasped and said, 'Let me have a look on Facebook, and I'll ring you back straight away. Five minutes, okay?'

They hung up, and Claudia drummed her fingers on the table, taking a fortifying mouthful of wine as she waited for Olivia to phone her back.

When it rang, Claudia listened carefully to Olivia, with her spirits plummeting as she heard what her cousin had to say.

'I don't know how to tell you this, but that appears to be Daisy's new boyfriend. Yes, it looks awfully like Michel, but he's a bit out of focus, so it's difficult to be sure. I don't know what to say. I'm horrified. I didn't put two and two together.'

'But how did she meet him? How has this happened? Does that mean he's here in Puglia?' Claudia's heart was pounding.

'I've been trying to figure out where the photo was taken.' She paused. 'I'm going to phone Daisy, but I'll have to approach this tactfully.'

A few agonising minutes later, Claudia's phone rang again. It was Olivia once more.

'Her phone is going straight to voicemail. I've left her a message to phone me the moment she gets it.'

'Michel is dangerous.' Claudia's voice was barely more than a whisper. 'I'm wondering if he followed me to Puglia. But your friend Daisy…'

'I see the photograph was taken just over a week ago, and she looks happy enough. But yes, if it is Michel, she needs to know what she's getting into.'

Claudia thought. 'Olivia, you know Puglia fairly well. I remember you spent some time here a few years ago, and I wondered if you could identify where the photo might have been taken. I think it looks like Piazza della Libertà, but I'm not sure. What do you think?' She waited.

'Hmm…' Olivia pondered a minute. 'I agree. I think you're right. I'm sure that's that famous ice cream parlour in the background. You know, the one that won the award for their amazing fig ice cream? I notice Daisy has a red rug draped around her, so it must be the bar next door.'

'Ah yes! I know the bar. They always have those huge olives for aperitivi. I was there recently. Do you think that's where they were?'

'It seems as though he's right there in Ostuni.' Olivia paused. 'Claudia, please be careful. You just don't know what he might be up to. I wonder how Daisy met him.'

'Well, I wonder what he's living on. He didn't have two cents to rub together when we split up. Do you know if Daisy is wealthy?'

'Oh, yes,' Olivia said. 'Very wealthy, I believe. Her mother, Lady Carmen Ariston Smythe, I'm sure you will have read about her in the gossip columns, a famous London socialite of Spanish descent, died last year and left her a fortune. She's been globe-trotting ever since and now plans to buy a house in Ostuni. I wonder…'

'I'm not sure how to handle this, Olivia.' Claudia felt herself on the verge of tears. She had devoted every moment of the past several months to finding and moving into her beautiful Palazzo dell'Aquila and to writing her new book. She just could not bear to have her life thrown up in the air once more. Her impulse was to jump into her car and drive as fast and as far away as she could manage. She tried to pull herself together. No. Michel would not win. She had to be strong. But the thought of his menacing presence staying, perhaps close by, was terrifying. She shivered, remembering his last words to her and all the threat and menace they implied. How on earth did he find her?

Her cousin was obviously deep in thought. 'I have an idea,' she announced. 'Niccolò's cousin, Gastone, has been staying with us in our country home in Galzignano, and he's at a loose end right now. I don't remember if I mentioned him to you, but you might have met him at our wedding party. He just sold his software company for millions and is now deciding what to do for the rest of his life. Not bad, when you consider he's still in his forties!' She paused, thinking it through. 'Perhaps he'd like to give you a hand. He's very capable and clever. He'll know what to do and being Italian will help. I'll talk to him. I'll be going down to Galzignano tomorrow for the next few days while Niccolò is in Ireland visiting his sister.' After a moment, sensing Claudia's silent anxiety, she added, 'Gastone has influential friends in Ostuni and knows the town well.'

Claudia's brow was furrowed as she tried to remember the name but came up blank. He was obviously some pompous businessman, she imagined, but she definitely needed some moral support.

'I wouldn't like to put Niccolò's cousin to any trouble,' she said finally. 'But thank you, Olivia. Let me know what he says. I could do with some assistance here, as I hardly know a soul yet. I've been so busy with my new home and writing my book that I haven't made any effort to meet people yet. I'm sorry for worrying you, and I trust your judgement.'

They hung up, and Olivia promised to phone her in a day or two to say whether or not she had located Daisy and if Gastone di Falco would be coming to her rescue in Puglia.

CHAPTER EIGHTEEN
JANET

Janet was home at last. Her sweet trullo awaited, and she could not wait to hug her dogs, put her suitcase down and, finally, kick back and relax in her perfect space. The last few months had been stressful, and everything had taken quite a bit longer than she had envisaged, but all she had needed to accomplish had been done, and now she could get on with her life.

It was dark when she arrived, but she could see the welcoming light over her front door as she exited the taxi and walked eagerly towards her gate.

As she pushed it open, making a mental note to oil the hinges, she was greeted, not by her own sweet little mutts, but by two aggressive-looking bull terriers. She stepped back in fright and confusion as the front door swung open and she saw a stranger standing there.

Janet looked in amazement at the tall man framed in her doorway. The two strange dogs were barking aggressively at her. One of them was eyeing her ankles hungrily, obviously aching to take a bite and only restrained by the sharp words of his master. At his command, they slunk back behind his legs, both growling softly, deeply and with menace in their every breath.

'Who are you?' she demanded, confused, too nervous to approach. The lights of the taxi shone straight towards the front of her trullo, its engine still running. She could see that he was very tall with light-coloured hair, cut very short, barely more than stubble. 'Why are you in my house? Where are my dogs, Gigi and Bella? And where on earth is Daisy, my house sitter?'

'Pardon?' His voice was deep, and he spoke with a French accent. 'This is my house. Who are you?' He sounded threatening. Menacing, to be honest. 'Get those car lights out of my face.' He was shouting now. Angry. His face shielded from the glare.

'My name is Janet, and this is *my* house!' She was becoming agitated now. A strange man in her house? Unbelievable. Asking the taxi driver to turn off the lights, she stood there under the stars, outside her house, the strange man backlit in her doorway.

'But no!' he exclaimed. 'You are confused. I rented this house just a couple of weeks ago, and I do not know anybody called Daisy, and these are my dogs. I know nothing about yours.' He sounded irritated. 'I think you should go; otherwise, I will call the police.'

Janet was stunned. She stammered. 'But who did you rent the house from?'

'From the Semerano family. I believe the lady who lived here died, and the house was divided between her three sons equally. I made them a rental offer, and they accepted. We signed some paperwork just two weeks ago, and I have been given first option to purchase it once probate has been finalised.' He paused. 'This is none of your business. Please go.' Janet could see that his patience was wearing thin.

'Oh no!' Janet exclaimed. 'Has Margherita died? I didn't know. Oh, how terrible!'

She felt as though she had been slapped. Hard. She could feel her face begin to burn, as though his hand had actually made contact with both cheeks at the same time. She decided to leave straight away and try to sort this out. There had to be some mistake. Otherwise, she was having a bad dream. Maybe she would wake up in a few minutes.

She turned to check that her taxi was still there. She need not have worried. The taxi driver was standing there, surrounded by her suitcases, obviously fascinated by this altercation. *Life as a taxi driver could be quite exciting,* he thought, as he watched the drama unfold.

It was now late in the evening, and she had nowhere to go. She would have to find someplace to stay.

'I'm going to have to clear this matter up straight away. Are my things in the wardrobe in the main bedroom?'

'There is nothing here except my own belongings.'

'May I come in and have a look?' She looked at him imploringly.

'Certainly not!' Curt now and the dogs, obviously sensing a change in their master's voice, growled more threateningly. The smaller one with the piggy eyes made as if to run at her, but the man's voice brought him back to heel.

'You'll be hearing from me.' She returned to her waiting taxi, and she and her bemused taxi driver got inside as the gate clanged shut. Her thoughts were a jumble of emotion. What on earth was going on?

As the taxi driver threw the car into reverse, they missed the hysterical scream that drifted out into the night air.

Driving into Ostuni, she directed the taxi to Mimmo's apartment. In the meantime, she phoned Donatella, who surprised her by telling her that she was expecting her and that her little house was ready, with all her belongings carefully stored. Janet let out her breath and felt herself relax slightly. At least she had somewhere to stay while she sorted out this mess, but she felt close to tears of frustration and bewilderment.

'And the dogs?' she asked.

'I imagine they must be with Daisy.' Donatella sounded anxious. 'But I'm afraid I really don't know.'

'I'm just going to see Mimmo to find out what's going on. I'll see you later. Thanks, Donatella.'

She had never visited Mimmo's apartment before but luckily knew his address. Checking the names on the row of doorbells, she pressed the one that said *Semerano*. After a moment, a woman's voice said, '*Pronto.*'

Turning to the taxi driver, she asked if he could wait and promised she would not be long. He was perfectly happy to see what the next episode of this adventure would bring and agreed to wait. No problem, he assured her.

In her halting Italian, she asked if Mimmo was there and said she needed to speak to him urgently. The woman's voice said that she could come up to the top floor and the door buzzed to let her in. She stepped into a very small glass-and-chrome lift and pressed the button for floor four. It creaked its way upwards, and she struggled not to feel claustrophobic. Her stress levels were causing her to shiver.

Exiting on the fourth floor, she came face to face with an anxious-looking Mimmo standing in an apartment doorway. She tried to sound calm but failed.

'What the hell is going on?' she demanded, her voice too loud in the narrow hallway.

Mimmo's eyes registered embarrassment, and he raised the palms of his hands in a defensive gesture, ushering her inside hurriedly, taking a nervous peep over his shoulder to check if any of the neighbours had heard her salty language. Satisfied that everyone was watching television or otherwise occupied, he followed her into the apartment.

His wife, Donata, was standing waiting and came forward to greet her. Janet shook her small, dry hand and then waved at two dark-haired children who were sitting on a fat grey leather sofa watching television. They had all obviously been sitting together when she rang the bell.

'Would you like to sit down?' Donata waved her hand at an armchair, and Janet sat, or semi-collapsed, into it. 'Can I offer you something to drink?'

'No, no, thank you. I have a taxi waiting outside.' Janet struggled not to sound impatient and wanted to skip the formalities, the good manners that all Italians showed when you entered their home. 'Who is that man in my house?' She rounded on Mimmo, who immediately held his hands up again as if to ward her off.

'I have been expecting your visit, Signora Janet,' he said. 'I just didn't know when.'

'You know I've been in Dublin to be with my grandmother, who has since passed away. I couldn't get back any sooner.' Her voice was loud and angry. The children looked at her, and she could see that they were anxious. She decided to try to speak in a calmer voice.

'Yes. I know about this. But I have bad news too. My mother has also died while you were away. Now the house has been rented to another party for a year. He came to me a few weeks ago and offered to rent the trullo for a price per month almost three times what you were paying me. He told me that Daisy said you would probably be away for a long time. There was no paperwork to show that we had an agreement, and he has signed on the dotted line, with an option to buy when probate comes through if he wants to. I was overruled by my brothers on the matter and had no choice but to sign my share over for sale. It is the law here. Everything is divided equally after death.'

'But...' Janet was speechless, but only for a moment. 'Your brothers? What about our agreement?'

Mimmo dropped his eyes and looked abjectly apologetic. 'My brothers know nothing about you,' he confessed. 'I thought I could sell it privately to you, but they found out. I didn't expect to hear from them ever again, but they were notified when Mamma died.'

'I thought you were Margherita's favourite son.' Janet was mystified. 'She only spoke about you. I thought she would have left her home to you in her will.'

'Things don't work like that in Italy.' Mimmo sounded regretful. 'My brothers live in Germany, where they found work when they were both still teenagers and have not been here for many years. They didn't even come home for Mamma's funeral. We have had no contact with them for so long that I was very surprised when I received a letter — a legal one — telling me that, as they owned two-thirds of the trullo, they wanted to sell it. At that time, we were approached by the new tenant, and I had to agree, or I would get into big trouble. I had no choice.' His eyes were evasive. 'I couldn't let them know I had been renting the trullo privately and had made my own arrangements behind their backs. You must understand.'

'Who is he?' Janet wanted to know.

'I'm sorry. I was instructed to keep his name confidential and must abide by that. It's part of the agreement. I'm not allowed to say.'

He was now sitting opposite her with his head in his hands. Janet looked at him disbelievingly. *Anything for an extra buck*, she thought and almost said it out loud.

'Where are my dogs?' Her heart ached to see Gigi and Bella, their trusting little faces, Bella's constant quiver, and she felt she needed to hug them both right at this moment. They would understand, in their doggy way, how upset she was.

'I'm sorry, but I do not know where the dogs are.' He looked pleadingly at her. 'The new renter's dogs are at the trullo and the last time I called, they tried to bite me.' Now he sounded indignant.

'They must be with Daisy.' Janet perked up. 'She was looking after them. Where is she staying at the moment? Or has she managed to move into her new casa in the old town?'

'I do not know where Daisy has gone.' Mimmo gave her his Italian shrug, palms out and shoulders up. 'She was gone when I got there. She has not left a forwarding address. But as regards your personal possessions,' he added, 'everything is safe at Donatella's.'

Janet put her head in her hands, leaning forward with her elbows on her knees. She sighed deeply. 'What's going to happen now? And, for crying out loud, why did you not let me know all this before?' She uttered a few ripe expletives at this point, and Donata looked anxiously at her children in case their brains might be infected by the colourful language of this Irishwoman.

Another shrug from Mimmo. 'What could I tell you that you wouldn't find out when you got back? You were attending to your grandmother and your divorce. I didn't want to upset you, and there was nothing I could do. You have been gone for almost three months.'

'What about the money I paid you for the trullo?'

'That was rent!' Mimmo sounded aggrieved. 'But your old rental in Casalini is ready for you with all your possessions installed once more. Donatella is waiting for your return. I will telephone her now to tell her you have arrived back.' He looked into her eyes with all the sincerity he could muster.

Lying eyes, Janet thought and said, 'That's okay, Mimmo. I've spoken to her already.' She stood up.

Mimmo ended the conversation with the pronouncement: 'You will either have to wait until the end of the new tenant's rental to see if he will purchase the trullo or begin to search for a new home once more.'

Janet felt beaten as she returned to her taxi and asked the curious driver to point it in the direction of Casalini.

She felt lost. What about her dreams? What now?

***

DAISY

The tall man closed the door behind him, thoughtfully. He listened to the taxi drive away, its tyres crunching on the dusty gravel road and turned towards the bedroom. He stepped inside.

On the bed was Daisy, dressed in baby doll pyjamas, attached to the wrought-iron bedpost with furry pink handcuffs. He eyed her hungrily and approached as she kicked out at him. He smiled. She squirmed, maybe seductively, maybe from fear. He could not tell and did not care. As long as she squirmed, he was happy.

'I heard you scream.' His voice was low. Seductive. Menacing. 'You might have been heard. I need to punish you.'

He removed his belt.

CHAPTER NINETEEN
JANET

Returning to the little house in Casalini was depressing but, as Janet sank into the familiar bed that night, she vowed to have a good night's sleep and deal with everything starting first thing tomorrow. She just could not accept that there was nothing she could do.

Donatella had greeted her with open arms and clasped her to her fragrant chiffon bosom. 'There, there, cara.' Her voice was comforting. 'All will be well.'

Janet was not so sure.

Bright and early the next morning, she retrieved her little car, which was parked on a hilly side street, and drove back out to the trullo. Ringing the bell at the gate she was greeted by the sound of barking dogs, but nobody answered. It appeared to be empty, and she could see no car in the driveway.

She decided to visit Angelo at the kennels in case the dogs had been handed in. She suddenly felt the need to see him anyway. It had been a few months since they had communicated, and she began to feel that she might actually be missing his reassuring presence in her life. Being back in Puglia was very different to being in Dublin, where all was familiar, and she had a circle of friends on whom she could depend. After ringing the bell outside the gate, the Englishman she had noticed on her previous visit came to greet her, surrounded by the usual swirl of enthusiastic canines. She asked him if he knew anything about her little dogs. He told her he knew nothing at all, but he would keep it in mind.

'Talk to Angelo,' he said. 'If there's anyone who might have an inkling about your dogs, he's your man. He'll be here after surgery, later this afternoon.'

'I'll call back,' she replied as she began to pull away in her car. The Englishman stepped forward.

'By the way, my name's John. John Rivers.' She stuck her hand out of the open window, and they shook hands. 'If you're not doing anything tomorrow evening, why don't you come over to meet my wife Penny and have an aperitivo.'

Janet was delighted, took directions, and promised to be at their home the following day at six p.m. She realised that this was the English couple who lived just down the lane from her trullo. It would be good to talk to them.

***

Returning to Casalini, Janet went onto Facebook to see if that provided any clues as to Daisy's whereabouts. She tried to phone her, but it went straight to voicemail every time she tried.

The last entry on Daisy's page was a selfie of her having a cocktail in Piazza della Libertà in the centre of Ostuni. Janet studied the photo, which was slightly out of focus. In the background was a man. He looked familiar. Could he be the man framed in the doorway the previous evening? She could not be absolutely sure. She had not got a proper look at his face, as the lights of the taxi had only briefly illuminated him, and then he had been in the dark with the light from the trullo behind him. It could be the same man, but she was wracked with uncertainty about what to do.

She could not sit still. Where were Gigi and Bella? She searched online for a full list of all the kennels in the area, and she emailed them patiently one by one. She looked at photos of abandoned puppies and dogs of all ages, shapes and sizes that had recently been found and drew a blank. Her heart ached for them.

She also wondered where Daisy could possibly be. She telephoned the estate agent who was helping her to organise her new apartment and drew a blank there too. He said he had not seen her for over a month and asked her to please tell Daisy that she needed to get her paperwork in order as soon as possible; otherwise, the seller would be forced to put the property back on the market. It was bound to be "snapped up" by another eager buyer, he insisted, wording his veiled threat in typical real estate parlance.

Janet remembered Daisy's excitement when she had found this little jewel of an apartment, as she described it, and became even more worried and perplexed. Surely, with all this going on, she would not have disappeared off to Bali or India.

She noticed that Daisy's old friend, Olivia Farrell, the famous interior designer who had married a count and lived a fairy tale life in a palazzo on the Grand Canal in Venice, was tagged. She sat back and thought hard. Then she clicked on Olivia's profile and sent her a message.

I am a friend of Daisy Smythe. Do you know where she might be? I am looking for her urgently.

Driving to the kennels late that afternoon to see Angelo, as much for comfort as the possibility that he might have a clue as to where her dogs might be, she suddenly felt how urgently she needed to feel his arms around her.

Angelo was waiting for her, knee-deep in whimpering, barking dogs of every shape and size. She had almost forgotten how handsome he was, with his dark eyes and muscular physique. She got out of her little car and rushed to him, expecting to be taken in his arms. He stood with his arms by his sides.

'You're back.' He removed his peaked cap, exposing his neat, curly hair. He seemed distracted. 'So, tell me, when did you return to grace Puglia with your presence once more?'

Janet stopped in her tracks. 'Angelo. I've missed you so much. I'm sorry I haven't been in touch. I've been in Ireland tidying up my old life. Now I'm back for good.'

She could see that his frosty demeanour was beginning to thaw, so she pressed on. 'Gigi and Bella are missing. I'm distraught. Please help me, Angelo. I can't handle this on my own.' Her eyes were brimming with tears. She just could not cope with a relationship problem at that moment. Now was not the time for posturing and pretending that everything was great when it was far from the case.

He breathed out as if he had been holding his breath, stepped forward and put an arm around her, giving her a reassuring hug. 'I'll do whatever I can to help. You know I will. But I have to tell you, I have no idea whatsoever where Gigi and Bella might be. Did you leave them with

Daisy?' He saw her faint nod, the tears now pouring down her cheeks. 'Where is she? Don't you know?'

'Oh, Angelo! I have no idea where Daisy is and what she has done with my precious dogs. I'm so worried about them. And her, of course,' she added hastily.

Then she made a decision. She would go back to her trullo to investigate. Maybe the dogs were in the area and were trying to find their way home. She needed to go and have a scout around. Telling Angelo of her plan, she turned and began to walk towards her car. He followed her.

'Wait!' He caught her by the arm and gently pulled her towards him. 'Give me half an hour to finish up here, and I'll go with you.'

At that moment, a red Vespa drew up beside them. Sitting astride it was one of the most beautiful young women Janet had ever seen. She looked like a supermodel, tall and slim with enormous blue eyes peering out from beneath her crash helmet. Angelo greeted her.

'Anya!' he said. 'Perfect timing. I need to go out and help Janet to find her dogs.' He turned to Janet. 'Janet, meet Anya.' he said, 'Anya's just begun to help with the kennels for a few months. She's hoping to become a vet.' He smiled warmly at the girl. Janet felt a tiny tug of unease.

Anya dismounted from her little motor scooter and removed her crash helmet. Janet watched the white-blonde hair tumble down her back as she shook it out and ran her fingers through it, seemingly unaware of the picture she made. She was even taller than Janet and so elegant in bearing that she managed to make Janet feel awkward and frumpy. Janet wondered if Anya knew the effect, she had on other people with her supermodel looks and watched Angelo's face as he looked at this young vision.

'How's your mother?' Angelo asked the girl as she tied her helmet to the handlebars of the scooter. 'When are you bringing her to meet your beloved puppy?'

'Within the next few days for sure.' Anya turned and was about to begin her feeding routine for the dogs, who were looking up at her with their ears perked and noses twitching at the smell of the food that she was unwrapping when Janet spoke.

She had heard the slight hint of an Irish accent and asked, 'Are you Irish?'

'I sure am!' Anya looked at her with curiosity. 'You too?'

'Yes. From Dublin.'

'We've been living in Galway for years, but Mum's from Dublin originally. Blackrock.'

'I'm from Phibsboro!' Janet was in her element. 'But I lived in Glasthule for eighteen years until I moved here.' Blackrock and Glasthule are just a few minutes apart to the south of Dublin along the coast. 'I didn't know there were any other Irish people living here. Or are you just on holiday?'

'We're here permanently. Well, Mum is. She's even got her Ostuni residency. I come and go; school, soon to be Trinity College, I hope. She's in the process of renovating a new home for herself in downtown Ostuni.'

Janet was immediately interested. 'Maybe we can meet up sometime soon. At the moment, I'm staying out in Casalini. I thought I had bought a trullo, but something seems to have gone wrong with the purchase. It's a long story.' She trailed off. Upset.

Angelo added, 'At the moment, we're trying to find Janet's two dogs which seem to have gone missing while she was away.'

Anya seemed sympathetic but soon moved away to feed the dogs who were, by now, becoming overexcited and impatient at the delay in proceedings.

'Oh, Angelo!' Janet said, turning to him. 'I'm so sorry I left them with Daisy now. I should have left them here with you or asked you to recommend good boarding kennels. But I wanted them to stay at home where everything was familiar, and Daisy was at a loose end at the time. It seemed ideal.'

At that moment, John Rivers arrived, also on a Vespa, a navy one this time. Janet thought to herself that this iconic Italian mode of transport was obviously very popular.

'A real get-together.' John laughed as he came towards them. 'Am I missing a party or what?'

'We're going to look for Janet's dogs, Gigi and Bella.' Angelo had opened his car door and was changing out of his work boots into a pair of running shoes. 'Do you want to come with us?'

John, who was always keen on a bit of adventure, agreed to come along. Waving goodbye to Anya and leaving her in charge of the kennels, Janet and John climbed into Angelo's battered Land Cruiser, and they headed out of town.

Just before they turned up the dust road towards what she still thought of as her home, John remarked, 'That's where I live.' Janet had not realised that he was probably her nearest neighbour until that morning when she figured it out.

As she looked at the familiar lane in front of her, Janet felt waves of desolation crashing over her. She could barely think about looking at her trullo again with all the hopes and dreams she had stored there.

Angelo parked his car out of sight in the entrance to an olive grove a couple of hundred metres away, and they walked in the direction of the trullo. It appeared to be deserted, but they could hear the two dogs scuffling around inside the gate and decided to have a look around the perimeter.

Splitting up, they went in different directions, calling Gigi and Bella softly as they walked. Janet crossed the grass and entered the copse at the back of the house, pushing branches aside as she approached the stone wall, *her* stone wall, she told herself, which was just slightly too high for her to see over. Perhaps she should take a closer look. She rolled a loose rock over to the wall, stepped on it, rose onto her tiptoes and peered over. There was her perfect garden. She sighed deeply. All appeared to be as she had left it.

Just then, out of the blue, one of the dogs, whom she had not seen approaching, flung himself snarling at her from inside the wall. She stepped back hurriedly and fell backwards off the rock. Sprawling on the ground, she realised that the earth she was lying on had been freshly turned. She rose onto her hands and knees and examined the red soil.

Giving a small, choked scream, almost a whisper, she realised what she was looking at. Partially exposed, mostly covered with red earth, perhaps dug up by a fox, she could clearly make out the bodies of her dogs, lying dead before her.

She sat on the ground, tears flowing down her cheeks, looking at her little friends, clogged with earth, still largely intact. They had surely been there for a couple of weeks, as far as she could tell. She was shocked to her core and began to shake violently, throwing up onto the grass beside her.

Blindly, she rose to her feet as Angelo rushed towards her and gathered her into his arms.

'You're in shock,' he said, taking off his jacket and wrapping it around her as she shivered, her teeth chattering.

Her hands and cheeks were streaked in earth from wiping her tears, and Angelo hugged her to him. As she stumbled back to his car, his arm around her, holding her up, she felt faint and weak with shock. Angelo helped her into the car and asked her to wait while he took a shovel and some tools from his medical kit, and he and John returned through the undergrowth to where the dogs had been buried. When they returned, grim-faced, Angelo climbed behind the wheel, and John slid into the back seat.

Janet felt her heart could break.

'I've taken some blood and tissue samples,' Angelo told her, putting the car into gear and beginning to turn it. 'I want to see how they died. It looks as though they were poisoned. We put some rocks on top of their grave and filled it in properly. I couldn't bear to leave them exposed like that.'

'Shouldn't we go to the police?' Janet finally found her voice. She realised that she hadn't uttered a word since she had made her grim discovery. Now she began to sob quietly as the tears streamed down her cheeks. Angelo patted her knee.

'What good would it do?' He manoeuvred the car down the narrow dust road, avoiding potholes. 'Nothing would happen. I promise. No,' he added, 'we'll deal with this ourselves.'

'Come on down to our house,' John piped up from the back seat. 'I've just phoned Penny and told her what's happened.' As they pulled into the gateway, a yellow light began to flash from the top of the gatepost, and the gates began to open. They crunched over the gravel driveway, and Janet noticed a large carport under which sat a camper van and a red sports car. Penny came down the steps to greet her, accompanied by two lively dogs, who immediately tried to jump on her and smother her with affection. 'Get down! Get down!' shouted John, but they paid no attention whatsoever.

Penny, tall and blonde, introduced herself, obviously distressed to see Janet's face covered in mud and snot, with her hands filthy, sobbing loudly. Penny put a motherly arm around her and guided her up the steps and into their welcoming home.

After cleaning up as best she could in their bathroom, Janet emerged and sat at a table, where white wine was already sitting in a cooler, and various bowls of nuts and savouries sat waiting for her. John filled her glass with a generous portion of the local verdeca. She accepted a glass gratefully and took an enormous swallow.

Janet, tongue loosened by distress and wine, told them everything that had happened to her over the past eighteen months, going right back to James's betrayal, then to Mimmo's crooked handling of the house sale and now to the disappearance of Daisy and the discovery of her two precious dogs buried outside the wall of her trullo.

John and Penny murmured words of sympathy, and Angelo patted her knee. She felt comforted.

As if sensing the story was about their furry brethren, John and Penny's two dogs, Basil and Sybil, came over to offer their sympathy. Basil, glossy and enthusiastic, almost managed to spill Janet's wine when he jabbed his nose under her elbow to demand she rub his head, while little Sybil cocked her head to one side, looking up at her as if to say, 'We feel your pain'. She petted both dogs in gratitude. Their loving natures and attention were just what she needed.

Arranging to meet later that week for "proper" aperitivi, Janet hugged Penny goodbye. She felt that she had found a caring new friend and was glad. Then, with Angelo at the wheel once more, they made the return journey to the kennels, where Janet's car and John's Vespa were waiting for them in the gathering dusk. Anya had already locked up and gone home.

**

'Angelo?' Janet rolled onto her side and placed her hand on his stomach. She had cried into her pillow for most of the night and was feeling dreary and sad. She had never considered herself a particularly sexual or earthy woman, but she was nevertheless moved to stroke his stomach a bit more and soon had his full attention as he turned to her, face sleep-filled, and pulled her towards him. Maybe she was changing, she thought to herself.

Still feeling wretched from their discovery, the night before, she was glad to be comforted and gave herself willingly to his embrace, able to forget her unhappy thoughts for a little while.

Later, while they drank coffee at the tiny table in the house in Casalini, they discussed her little dogs, Gigi and Bella.

'I'm expecting to receive the blood test results later today,' he said. 'John took them to the lab first thing this morning.'

Janet sat, silently grieving. She could not find the words to respond.

'You know my assessment. The dogs were poisoned, I'm sure of it. This result will be confirmation, and we can take the results to the polizia tomorrow if you really want to. But you know my opinion. It's a complete waste of time.'

'Who would poison two sweet little dogs like that?' Janet felt indignation rising with her voice. 'It must have been that blond man who's living in the trullo. Who else could it have been?'

'But why would he do that? Surely burying the dogs just outside the garden wall would lead the polizia straight to his door if we had called them. But honestly, that guy would have had some story or other, and the polizia have bigger fish to fry. It wouldn't have gone anywhere and just caused you more distress.'

'I wish I knew.' She felt despondent. Her little dogs were dead. She felt bereft in a way she could not remember feeling before, shocked too. It had been a gruesome discovery.

Angelo put his hand over her restlessly moving one. 'Perhaps you should get another dog soon.'

'Oh no!' she said. 'I couldn't ever have a dog again after this. It's too painful.'

He nodded, knowing it would just be a matter of time before she chose another dog. *Some people can't live without their faithful friends,* he thought. 'Come to the kennels with me. Let's keep each other company,' he suggested.

Janet nodded. She did not want to be alone today.

CHAPTER TWENTY
CLAUDIA

Meanwhile, Claudia was preparing to go to the kennels with Anya. She had volunteered to drop her off this morning, as she wanted to see the puppy that Anya was so crazy about. Claudia did not really want a dog in the palazzo at this point, while so much renovation was going on, but wanted to make Anya feel completely at home. She had had very few dogs over the years and feared the commitment it would bring.

She sadly remembered her very sweet Chihuahua, Paddy, who had been run over by a car and killed when he slithered through the bars of the gate of their Galway home as he tried to follow Anya to school. Anya had been so heartbroken that Claudia had resolved never to get another dog. But now, Anya had just turned eighteen and was mature enough to cope with the emotional attachment that a dog inevitably brings along to invade your heart.

Clattering down the wide staircase from their living quarters on the main floor to the inner courtyard, where they climbed into Claudia's Mercedes and used the remote control to raise the electric roller gate, they emerged into the sunshine and onto the street. Claudia was convinced that Corso Mazzini was the most elegant street in Ostuni, and she loved living there. It was close to the main piazza, with its many restaurants and bars, and a quick uphill walk brought her to the town park with its palm trees, skirted by a row of bank buildings with busy ATMs and then, a little further, to the main shopping street, Via Pola.

The morning was hot and sunny, readying itself for summer when temperatures could climb to forty degrees centigrade during the day. As they drove to the kennels, Claudia noticed how the grass was beginning to turn brown and how dusty green the olive trees were, with the occasional trullo poking its head over the sturdy stone walls. Turning off the main road, they drove along a sandy lane, creating a white dust cloud behind the car. Getting stuck behind a little Ape on their way, that three-wheel puttering vehicle so typical of rural Puglia, they decided, laughing, that though they might be charming for tourists to take photos of, they were not so sweet to get stuck behind on a narrow road.

They pulled into a turning circle at the gate of the kennels, and a cacophony of barking erupted as they climbed from the car. Anya went to the gate and, at the sound of her voice, the barking turned to a collective whimper of excitement, tails wagging with happiness to see that their friend had arrived; a special friend who signalled that food was in the offing. Claudia hung back. She was not sure how she could cope with this sea of about twenty dogs and was sure that some of them were already looking at her with suspicion. She eyed their doggy faces, alert for even the slightest baring of a tooth or a rising hackle.

Anya understood that her mother was a bit nervous. Many of the dogs were bigger than she was! She took her by the hand and spoke soothingly to her.

'It's okay, Mum. They won't touch you; I promise. Come on.'

She brought Claudia through the gate, through the milling dogs and over to meet Angelo, who was deep in conversation with a tall, dark-haired woman of about forty. Her curly hair looked unkempt and, Claudia thought, her skin-tight leggings and skimpy top left nothing to the imagination.

Angelo was a good-looking man in — what she considered — a typically Italian way. Tall, slim and tanned with navy shorts worn to just above his knees, oozing self-confidence. His snowy white T-shirt was emblazoned with the slogan "I ♥ New York". She noticed the woman bristle as they approached, and Claudia could see that she was possibly interrupting an important conversation.

Anya strode ahead. 'Angelo. This is my mum, Claudia.' He proffered his hand, and Claudia shook it. She could feel him looking at her appraisingly; his deep-brown eyes with their long lashes seemed to look into her very soul. *Hmm, a Romeo*, she thought.

'I'm Janet,' announced the tall woman, inserting herself into the introduction. 'You're Anya's mum? She looks just like you. Just a taller version.' She sounded friendly enough, thought Claudia, whose natural reserve always kicked into gear when she met people for the first time. She, being from Dublin, immediately picked up Janet's accent as being from north of the River Liffey, and her chin rose slightly. Years of bias just could not be undone, or so it seemed, and she felt slightly ashamed of herself. Surely, she had not turned into a snob! She, Claudia Farrell, came from what she liked to think of as the right side of the tracks, being a "Southsider" from the leafy suburbs. Old prejudices were hard to bury, she admonished herself, promising to do better in future. She was living in Italy now, for heaven's sake, not Dublin.

'Yes. I am. I'm here to see a puppy, I think.' She looked around for Anya, who was approaching with a small, furry dog in her arms.

Face to face with this little bundle of black and tan fur, Claudia put out her hand to let it sniff, whereby the puppy frantically licked her. That was it. Claudia felt an immediate connection to the little dog. 'Mum. Can we take her home?' Anya looked at her beseechingly, and so did the little dog.

'Absolutely!' Claudia laughed with relief. 'What's her name?'

'Trixie!'

'Perfect!'

And so, Trixie, a little dog who faintly resembled a Dachshund, if you did not look too closely, was the newest member of the Ostuni branch of the Farrell family and was about to make herself at home amongst the opulent furnishings at Palazzo dell'Aquila, barking at passers-by from the terrace, which, as Corso Mazzini was pretty busy, was to keep her occupied daily for hours on end.

***

JANET

Janet was thoughtful. It had been interesting to meet Anya's mother at last. She had heard that she was considered a great beauty and could see it now for herself. Claudia appeared to be quite shy and reserved, unlike her daughter, who was extroverted and lively. This woman was restrained and serious. Janet knew that Claudia was a famous writer of romantic novels and had been expecting someone more along the lines of Barbara Cartland, draped in pink chiffon and calling everyone "Dahling", but no, definitely not. She remembered reading one of her books and being disappointed that, what she had hoped would be a steamy romance, had been well written and polished, with sex scenes merely implied by a rustle of silk or a gasp of pleasure.

This was a serious woman, her blonde hair tied back into a smart chignon, and from the cut of her loose linen slacks and shirt, with the sleeves folded back and expensive-looking leather loafers, she was elegant and pared back in style. She was so dainty and small-boned that Janet felt the way she had done when she saw Anya for the first time: large and frumpy beside her. What was it about this mother—daughter combo? However, she was not too sure whether she liked Claudia or not. Possibly not. She thought she might be a bit of a snob, to be honest. Janet did not like to feel intimidated, but she noticed how Angelo paid close attention to the blonde, his eyes drinking her in, or so it seemed to her. Hanging on her every word, she thought. She felt uneasy, pierced by a stab of jealousy.

When Claudia had left with Trixie safely in a basket on the floor of the car, wedged in front of the passenger seat, promising to pick Anya up later on, Janet resumed her conversation with Angelo.

'Nice woman,' Angelo remarked, watching Claudia's car disappearing into the distance. 'Very good-looking.'

Janet gave him a withering look.

'But,' he added, gathering himself together, 'not as sexy as you are, darling.' He took her hand and turned his gaze to her. 'Let's go to the lab and pick up the results. They'll be ready by now.'

He called to Anya and greeted John Rivers, who had just arrived, this time on a smart racing cycle. John had removed his helmet, which had left a red mark around his chin. His black cycling shoes gave him a strange mincing gait as he walked over to park his wheels beside the office, pulling a pair of battered trainers from his bag, which had been slung over his shoulder. He quickly swapped his footwear and pulled on a blue boiler suit over his Lycra shorts and T-shirt, ready to clean out the kennels.

'Hi, Angelo. Anya,' he said in their general direction as he headed towards the hosepipe, picking up a large can of disinfectant and a yard brush as he went. 'Janet,' he added, 'I'm hoping you'll come over to us for a proper aperitivo this evening so we can chat. Penny walked past your trullo today for a snoop.'

Janet agreed that she was looking forward to the "proper aperitivo", whatever that meant. She could do with some uncomplicated company at this point, and the thought of John and Penny's home, with its large veranda, two friendly unjudgmental dogs and some wine and savouries gave her an inner comfort.

'I'll see you at six. We've invited a few of the neighbours to meet you too. They're coming at about seven, so it gives us a chance to chat first.'

'Absolutely. Can I bring anything?'

'Just yourself,' John said as he turned on the hose and began the task of cleaning several kennels and filling water bowls. He did all this for nothing, merely for the pleasure of spending his time among his doggie friends and talking Italian with Angelo.

Janet smiled. Then she turned to Angelo, who was pulling his car keys from his pocket and gesturing towards his Land Cruiser. 'Let's go,' he said.

Turning down a side street in Ostuni near the park, with the banks with their cash machines ranged alongside, Angelo parked the car in one of the spaces opposite the laboratory and, after putting a euro in the meter, took her by the hand, and they crossed the street together. The tarmac was warm underfoot, and Janet noted to herself that she needed sandals with thicker soles for the summer months. She was still learning.

Entering the cool dimness of the laboratory reception area, Angelo and Janet were greeted by an elderly man with a gentle manner. His white hair was swept back like an orchestra conductor, and he came out from behind his high counter to gather Angelo into a two-kiss embrace and a firm pat on the back.

'Angelo! How wonderful to see you! It's been ages since you've called around. What's happening? How are all the dogs?'

His deep-brown eyes alighted on Janet, and he looked at her appraisingly. She noted his attention and wished she had put a sweater over her skimpy blouse. Even a bra would have been a good idea, she thought, as she squirmed under his scrutiny.

Noticing his interest, Angelo introduced them to one another.

'Giuseppe, this is Janet. She's recently moved here from Ireland.'

'An Irish lady indeed!' He eyed Angelo with an open question, which remained unanswered.

'Janet is the friend I told you about, whose dogs were found dead a couple of days ago. We were hoping you might have the results.'

'Ah!' He seemed disappointed not to have garnered more information about Angelo's tall, sexy-looking companion but bustled off into a back room and began to go through a stack of paperwork on his desk. Finally, he pulled out a piece of paper and returned.

'They were your dogs?' he asked Janet, putting on his reading glasses and squinting at the paper in his hand. He moved closer to her, a questioning look of interest in his eyes.

'Yes. I'm afraid so.' Janet was feeling tense and was anxious to hear the result, not to play at being sociable at this point. 'Were they poisoned?'

Giuseppe looked at the piece of paper in his hand again. 'Yes. I'm afraid so.' He looked at her with genuine sympathy. 'They were poisoned with a rodenticide, in layman terms, rat poison. I'm so sorry. They wouldn't have had an easy death,' he added tactlessly.

Janet breathed in deeply and tried to compose herself.

The doctor continued. 'How could this have happened? Were they not showing symptoms for a day or so beforehand?'

'I don't know how this happened. I was away and had left them with a house sitter. We just found them the other evening. I've been looking everywhere for them.' She drew in a shaky breath, fighting for composure. *Gigi and Bella*, she thought. *My babies.* She was heartbroken and to think that they had most probably died in agony. It was unbearable.

CHAPTER TWENTY-ONE
CLAUDIA

Claudia's phone rang late that night, waking her from sleep. It was her uncle Daniel, Olivia's father. She raised herself onto one elbow and listened.

'It's your dad,' he said without preamble. 'He's taken a bit of a turn and is in hospital. Perhaps you'd want to come and see him.'

'Oh no!' Claudia was shocked. 'What's wrong? How bad is he?'

'Ah! He's fine. Just a touch of heatstroke. He was out all day with no hat on, and it's quite warm at the moment for Ireland. They're saying he's "comfortable", whatever that means.' He sounded as gruff as ever.

'I'll be on the next flight. Where is he?'

'He's managed to inveigle himself a private room in the Blackrock Clinic.' Daniel sounded mildly disapproving at all this extravagance, but Claudia was pleased about that. At least he was not lying on a trolley in a corridor someplace.

They hung up, and Claudia padded down the passageway to Anya's room. She was dreading imparting this information to her daughter, who adored her grandfather.

After they had hugged and cried a bit, overcome by emotion, Claudia went online to find a flight to Dublin from Bari. The only direct one was late the following afternoon, but she found she could get back to Ireland more quickly if she were on the first flight to Rome in the early morning from Brindisi on Alitalia and then onto Aer Lingus directly to Dublin, arriving around lunchtime. She promptly booked and went to pack her bag. She would need to leave within the hour.

'Go back to bed, sweetheart,' she said to Anya, who was looking lost and confused. 'I'll phone as soon as I've seen Dad. Don't forget, Uncle Dan said that he's fine. He'll be well looked after in the clinic, but I just want to see for myself. You know how Dan and Dad play things down.'

147

Anya picked up Trixie's basket and called the little dog, who was thrilled to be allowed to sleep in Anya's bedroom, bounding happily ahead of her, stopping every couple of feet, looking over her shoulder to check that Anya was following her.

Claudia looked at Anya and Trixie fondly. 'Well, you have each other for company while I'm away. Hopefully, I'll be back in a couple of days.'

***

When Claudia landed in Dublin, she rang the clinic to find out how her father was doing and was told that he was being discharged the next day. The heatstroke had been mild, and they were doing tests on him today and would see what, if any, follow-up was needed.

She got a taxi from the airport to the clinic, which was positioned close to Dublin Bay, south of the city, just outside the upmarket suburb of Blackrock.

Sean was sitting up in bed, concentrating on the cryptic crossword at the back of *The Irish Times*, his newspaper of choice. He prided himself on being able to finish Crosaire, as it was called, in jig time.

They hugged each other, and Claudia sat on the edge of the bed, holding his hand. A bag of clear liquid dripped steadily into a pipe leading to the back of his hand, where a needle had been inserted. She had virtually no medical knowledge and assumed this was some sort of restorative elixir that was dribbling into her father's system.

'They're about to do a few tests.' He patted her hand, trying to impart some reassurance, but Claudia could see he was upset and nervous.

'What happened, Dad?'

'I passed out on the golf course,' he told her. 'The lads, we were on the fifteenth hole, just a four-ball, phoned for an ambulance, and they took me here. Luckily, we were playing at Milltown, so we were only about fifteen minutes away.' He went on. 'The lads went straight to the nineteenth for a pint after the ambulance left. They lost the humour for golf when they saw what happened to me.'

'Perhaps I should go over to the apartment and settle in,' Claudia said, gathering her roller bag and trench coat together, standing up, feeling relieved to see her father apparently unscathed by his experience. 'I'll pop back over this evening.'

'Daniel shouldn't have worried you.' Sean looked upset. 'I hate dragging you over here like this, on a wild goose chase. I'm fine.'

'That's okay, Dad. I wanted to see you anyway, and this just got me here sooner. It's about time I told you some things that happened to me during my marriage to Michel. I've been writing about it, and I feel it's time I gave you the lowdown on what really happened, now that we can talk, just the two of us.'

Claudia let herself into her father's home, a large ground floor apartment in a secure complex with its own private garden, into which he had recently moved and saw that it was in a state of chaos. It looked as though Sean had stopped bothering to keep things in order and, now that he was officially "unwell", she felt she had the opportunity to organise some home help for him.

After calling an agency of carers, she promptly went to interview their suggested helper, a motherly middle-aged ex-nurse called Lisa and was satisfied that she would look after her father and the house perfectly. She would come in five mornings per week at nine o'clock and go back home at two o'clock in the afternoon, leaving him his evening meal in the oven waiting to be heated when he was ready to eat. As Sean was semi-retired from the wine importers for whom he had worked for the past thirty-five years, he was spending more time at home and was, obviously, not coping well alone.

Sean was, understandably, unhappy about this invasion of his private space, but Claudia talked him round, telling him that he would be sparing her a lot of worry if he were to capitulate on this point. So, he gave in and accepted Lisa, though with some reservations.

Claudia spent the next couple of evenings with her father after he came home from the clinic, and they talked long into the night. He cried when he heard about the abuse his precious daughter had suffered at the hands of — what Sean considered — a monster. She found some of it very difficult to talk about and glossed over the more intimate details,

149

but she told him enough to gain his understanding of how gruesome the entire experience had been.

'I needed to tell you everything,' she said, drying her eyes. 'Anya knows nothing of what went on. Because she was here in Dublin, I was able to protect her from the worst of it. As I told you, she did witness one incident right at the end, but I think she believes I did something to deserve it.'

'Don't you think she's old enough now to have this discussion?' her father asked, back home now and settling himself into his favourite recliner, accepting a cup of tea from Lisa, who had been clucking her way around the apartment, muttering about the state of everything.

Claudia nodded. 'I suppose I should tell her before much longer, but I wanted to have this conversation with you too. Dad, you were right about him. He was evil, and I am so glad to be out of his life.' She paused and gave a wry smile. 'Very occasionally, I get a tiny pang of guilt when I think of him losing everything, including his home, but then I remember how he behaved, how dishonest and bullying he was, how he ruined his daughter's life, and I know I had no choice. It was either sink or swim. And I'm not your daughter for nothing. I'm much stronger now.'

He squeezed her hand and looked hard at her. She had been to hell and back with that awful man, he thought. She and Anya were his life.

She went on to tell him about what she had seen on Facebook. 'I don't know if it's Michel or not, but I'm terrified that he may be in Ostuni and, if so, I fear for my safety and Anya's too. You must know how dangerous he is. Look, I'm not sure, but it does look like him.' She looked at his horrified and worried expression and was unhappy about bringing it up, especially now he was just home from hospital, but she felt she owed it to him to be honest.

'Olivia knows the woman he was with and is trying to contact her. It was just the other day, and maybe it wasn't him at all. Don't they say everyone has a double?' She tried to put a light-hearted spin on her fears. Being at home in Dublin, she felt secure, as danger was far, far away.

Next morning, Claudia was on the early morning flight to Rome, heading back to Ostuni. She would see her father there soon, as he planned to visit once the doctors told him he was fit to travel.

150

Early afternoon the following day, Claudia arrived back at her palazzo. After pressing the zapper for the up-and-over metal gate, she drove through into her inner courtyard and parked in her usual space beside Anya's Vespa. She opened her handbag, rummaging for the bunch of keys containing the big door key with the eagle stamped on the front, the Yale key and the blue zapper for the alarm. She came up empty.

'Oh, heavens!' she moaned. 'Where are they?' She tried to think. She had left home in such a rush she had probably left them behind on their hook in the kitchen. Or had she left them in Dublin? She had not been concentrating; her attention had been focused on her father's health and their pending conversation about Michel.

Claudia always kept her car keys and zapper separately from the house keys, which were too large and heavy to have them dangling from the Merc's ignition.

She climbed out of the car and rang the doorbell. After a moment, the buzzer sounded, and Anya let her in.

'Did you forget your keys, Mum?' Anya called from the top of the stairs.

'I don't seem to have them with me,' Claudia replied. 'Maybe they're in the kitchen.'

She hauled her overnight bag from the boot and began to climb the stairs. Their new housekeeper, Maria Grazia, appeared, cloth in hand as always, and took it from her, bringing it through to her bedroom.

She and Anya hugged, and they discussed Sean and his health problems. They sat together in the kitchen, where Maria Grazia had prepared a light lunch.

'It was lovely to see Dad,' Claudia said, lifting a forkful of tomato and snow-white, creamy mozzarella to her mouth. 'He was his usual self — perky and full of chat. But I won't be able to stop worrying about him until he's been given the all clear.' She dabbed the corners of her mouth with her napkin. 'He sends his love and is dying to see you. He's hoping to be over in a couple of weeks, doctors permitting.'

All thoughts about her missing keys were forgotten as she and her daughter talked through lunch. Afterwards, Anya prepared to leave for the kennels. 'I'll be home around five,' she said, as she lightly kissed her mother's cheek, picked up her bag and banged the front door behind her.

'I'm going to have a lie-down,' she told Maria Grazia as she headed to her bedroom. 'Perhaps you could wake me up before you leave?'

Maria Grazia bustled off, her cloth still firmly attached to her right hand, as if it were an extension of herself. The palazzo had never shone so brightly. It was good to be home.

For the moment.

Maria Grazia was Claudia's latest "find". A small, buxom woman with impossibly dark hair, shot through with unlikely copper highlights, and a pale, jaundiced complexion, enlivened by thin, darkly pencilled eyebrows, which gave her a permanently surprised expression. She always dressed in black, though she told her new employer that her husband had been dead for more than twenty years. Five mornings a week, she arrived at the palazzo, armed to the teeth with strange household tools, and always began by ironing bed linen and clothing. Claudia found that even her underwear was being ironed. Then Maria Grazia would tackle the floors and bathrooms with vigour. Claudia loathed housework with a passion and, though she had always had home help in varying degrees, she had never before seen anyone on their hands and knees scrubbing a shower and was impressed by how spotless the palazzo had become.

She remembered the moment when Maria Grazia first arrived for work. She was holding a tall instrument, like a loo-brush, but about two metres long. She looked like a spear-carrying Roman centurion soldier, Claudia thought. 'What on earth is that?' she asked out loud.

'It's for the *ragnatele*.' Maria Grazia seemed to be surprised to be asked such a question. Surely everyone knew a *ragnatele* remover when they saw one! 'For spider webs,' she clarified, just in case her new boss was in the dark about such essential equipment. Anything was possible, after all if you were not Italian, she thought.

***

'Mum!' Anya called from her bedroom. 'Have you seen my pink lace blouse, you know, the one with the white collar?'

'Your pink blouse? I'm sure I saw it recently. Check again.' Claudia could hear Anya opening and closing drawers and closets, searching for the missing garment.

'No. It's not here.'

'No, darling. Isn't it on the rail with your fresh clothes? Maria Grazia ironed it for you a few days ago.'

'I haven't time to search now; I'll be late at the kennels. It will turn up. No worries.'

Bounding from her room in another pink creation, a tight T-shirt with small, white polka dots, over tight jeans, Claudia was struck by her daughter's adult look. No longer her baby, she thought.

'We must begin to look for a car for you.' Claudia was ready to admit that her precious daughter was an adult and needed her own set of wheels to get about.

'Oh, Mum! That would be great. Just a little run-around to get me to the kennels and back. Nothing fancy.'

'Let's go to some of the dealers over the weekend and have a look.'

All thoughts of the pink lace blouse with the white collar were gone.

***

DAISY

'Put this on.' The man was imperious as he proffered the pink blouse, waving it at Daisy. Daisy stared at the blouse.

'Where did you get this?' She examined the pink lace with its innocent white collar. Her voice was slurred, and she felt as though she were in a dream.

'I said, put it on.' His voice raised slightly.

Daisy struggled into a sitting position and wrestled with removing the baby doll pyjama top she was wearing. The cool air of the trullo made her shiver. He helped her to put the blouse on, first one sleeve, then the other, as though she were a child. He buttoned it for her, and she looked up with a dazed expression in her vague brown eyes.

The man looked at her. 'Get onto your knees,' he instructed her. 'You've been a very naughty girl.' He began to unbuckle his belt.

153

CHAPTER TWENTY-TWO
CLAUDIA

Olivia telephoned that evening.

'Olivia!' Claudia was delighted to hear her cousin's voice on the phone. 'How are you, darling?'

'Oh, Claudia! I have fantastic news! I'm pregnant! We're pregnant! I'm so happy. Niccolò is over the moon. I've never seen him so elated.'

'That's wonderful!' Claudia was genuinely excited to hear about this pending birth and was looking forward to meeting her new baby cousin as soon as he or she was born. It really was something to celebrate.

'Due at the end of November. What a Christmas we'll have!'

'Olivia, I'm so very happy for you both. This is absolutely the best news possible.' She felt warm inside at the thought of Olivia's happiness.

'But first of all, two things,' Olivia announced. 'Number one, Gastone is going down to Puglia in a few days. He'll be staying in a small hotel almost directly opposite your palazzo and will ring you as soon as he arrives. He's decided to drive down and spend a night with friends in Abruzzo on the way. As far as I know, he's planning to leave in the morning. I had a long chat with him when I went down to Galzignano, and I could tell he was becoming restless, looking for something to do with himself now that he's sold his company. He's been kicking around a few ideas and, with nothing decided, he's at a loose end right now.' She laughed. 'All that energy! Poor guy. He's only beginning to get over losing his wife Patrizia; it's not quite two years since she passed.'

'How did she die?'

'A massive stroke,' Olivia replied, adding, 'Poor Patrizia. It was all very sudden. One moment she and Gastone were sitting together after dinner, apparently discussing a book that she had just read, and the next moment she was in an ambulance being rushed to the emergency room. She died before she got there. They did everything they could to revive her, but the poor thing didn't stand a chance. Gastone was terribly shocked.'

'Did they have children? Or, I mean, does Gastone have a family?'

'Oh yes. Two beautiful sons, both at college in Padova and both studying medicine. They're twins, not identical. I think they must be about twenty. They're living in an apartment in downtown Padova, and Gastone has a home in the countryside just outside the city, towards Treviso. He didn't really want to stay there so soon after Patrizia died, and he sold his business, so Niccolò invited him to come to the villa near Galzignano to give him a change of scenery for a while.'

'That's kind of Niccolò. Are they close?'

'Oh yes. Almost like brothers. Gastone was wonderfully supportive after all that trouble with the gondolier a couple of years ago. He came and stayed with Niccolò for a few weeks to make sure he was okay. He's a kind person. I like him a lot. I know I can trust him to help you to find out what's going on and also to keep an eye on you. You shouldn't be there alone if Michel is on the loose. Goodness knows what he might do if he ran into you!'

'Olivia, I'm staying put, whatever happens. I've been talking to Dad, and he's pretty horrified about what happened between Michel and me, and he's planning to come over shortly. And, anyway, I'm not going to be pushed out of my lovely new home.' A note of defiance had crept into her voice.

'Keep an eye on Anya, won't you?' Olivia was concerned, knowing how much Anya had loved Michel.

'I will. Thank you, Olivia. You're wonderful. You really are. Now, what was the second thing you wanted to tell me?'

'How would you like to be our baby's godmother?'

'Oh goodness!' Claudia laughed. 'There is nothing I would like better. How fabulous! I promise I'll be the best godmother on the planet. Are you sure? I'm not exactly known for my religious fervour.'

'Of course, we're sure. We have decided to give our baby four godparents: you; Francesca, Niccolò's sister; Gastone; and Paul, Francesca's husband. He and Niccolò are very close, as you know.'

'Any thoughts on names yet? I know it's early on, but, knowing you, I'm sure you must have some thoughts on the subject.'

'Oh yes. Several.' Olivia laughed. 'I suppose we'll know when we see him or her, but top of the list, at the moment, is Francesco. Or Bianca if it's a girl. Though that may change many times over the next few months.'

Finally, hanging up the phone, Claudia wandered to the tall kitchen window and looked out. In the distance, the Adriatic Sea was blue, with the horizon blending with the sky, so one could hardly tell where one ended and the other began. She could not help but wonder how Niccolò would react if this baby were a girl. Surely, nobody could ever replace his daughter Sofia, who had died so tragically just a few years previously.

Her thoughts were interrupted by a movement below. She looked down at the street. Whatever it had been was no longer visible. She shook herself. *No paranoia, please*, she told herself. *Nothing to be seen.*

She should have looked more closely; eyes watched her from a darkened doorway.

***

JANET

Janet arrived at John and Penny's house just before the sun set behind the hills surrounding their house, Casa dei Fiumi, among the olive groves.

Once more, the dogs, Basil and Sybil, gave her a tumultuous greeting while John cried, 'Get down! Get down!' to the enthusiastic pair, who appeared to be suffering from temporary deafness. Janet was perfectly happy to let them jump all over her but raised her knee slightly to discourage them from clawing at her favourite jeggings, those skin-tight jeans that she loved so much. They rushed ahead into the house, then turned, panting, waiting for her at the front door, ears raised and tails wagging.

Penny had walked her dogs past Janet's erstwhile trullo that day to see what she could spy. There was a car parked in the driveway. It was a distinctive sapphire-blue Toyota SUV. Brand new, she could tell by the registration, she surmised it was a rental. She saw nobody, though she could hear dogs barking as she walked past. She heard or saw nothing else.

John poured her a large glass of white wine. This time, Penny had gone to a lot of trouble, and there were pieces of quiche and little pastries filled with shrimps in a delicious sauce. Sausage rolls, the last thing Janet expected to see in Italy, were steaming in a dish. So, this was what was meant by "proper aperitivi". She felt at home straight away and was relaxed with this warm couple.

As Janet unwound, wolfing down some sausage rolls and quiche — Penny encouraged her, telling her there were plenty still in the oven for the other guests who would arrive soon — they discussed their next move. Having discounted telling the police, they wondered what had happened to Daisy. John got out his computer, and they logged in to Janet's Facebook account. Clicking onto Daisy's page, they ran through her photographs and saw the recent one of her with a strange man with ash-blond hair, slightly out of focus, whom Janet thought might be the man living in her trullo, though she explained to them that she was unsure. They wondered if Daisy could possibly be there with him and realised that they needed to investigate further. Perhaps they could go there when he was out and try to look inside, but what about his two vicious-looking dogs? They were going to pose a problem.

Just as Janet was about to sign out of her Facebook account, she noticed that she had a message and clicked on it. It was from Olivia Farrell, Contessa di Falco, telling her she was sorry she didn't have a clue where Daisy was, other than she had noticed that she had been in Ostuni a few weeks ago. She mentioned that she had tried to contact Daisy herself recently but had had no luck.

Janet was disappointed, but she had not been expecting a miracle. She logged off and tuned back into the conversation. John was putting forward an idea and was full of enthusiasm for the adventure ahead.

'How about we throw a dead rabbit over the back wall and use your keys to dash in through the gate and front door?' John mused. Janet was unsure whether or not he was serious; he always looked as though he was joking. 'We could pick one up at the butcher shop. I think that once we're inside, the dogs will be a lot easier to handle. They enjoy snarling at the gate and making a racket. Just doing their job!' He chuckled.

At the sound of his laugh, Basil launched himself onto John's knees. John looked at Janet to make sure she was watching and suddenly threw back his head and howled. She was momentarily bemused until she heard Basil join in with enthusiasm, his nose pointing towards the ceiling. It was loud.

'The neighbours will wonder what's going on.' Penny made a shushing motion, and John laughed.

'We don't have any neighbours,' he said. 'Luckily.'

After this diversion, they continued to discuss the problem of the dogs at the trullo and how they were going to get in and out without being savaged.

Obviously, John was highly experienced with dog handling from his voluntary work at the kennels. He added, 'I'll bring along some restraints, and we'll manage them. Even an old blanket would help. I could throw it over them long enough for us to get out again.' He thought for a moment. 'I suppose Angelo could always tranquillise them, if necessary. But that would take time to wear off, and just suppose this guy arrives back before they come round properly. That could be dangerous. We don't want him to become suspicious.'

Janet pondered the plan, reaching for a Pringle and munching it thoughtfully. She was nervous at the thought of meeting the blond man again and said so. 'There's something really threatening about him,' she said, taking a large swallow of wine and picking up a couple of crunchy *taralli*. 'I'm not sure I want to risk running into him. But, I suppose, if you and Angelo are there with me, even if he does come back unexpectedly, I should be pretty safe. But it's not ideal, for sure.'

'Danger?' Penny asked. 'Do you think he's actually dangerous?'

'Yes, I do. Look at how my dogs ended up. Do you think they poisoned themselves?'

'I have no idea,' John said. 'Perhaps there was rat poison on the property, and they found it. It's always a possibility. I find it hard to imagine anyone being evil enough to deliberately poison two friendly little dogs like Gigi and Bella.'

'I'm not sure at all.' Janet felt deflated. 'But we must find Daisy. Perhaps she's in danger.' She noticed John and Penny looking at her doubtfully. 'Perhaps I should have another word with Mimmo first.'

At that moment, the doorbell rang, and the dogs rushed, barking, towards the front gate with John dashing after them shouting, 'Get down! Get down!' while the dogs ignored him.

A Belgian couple had arrived, musicians turned olive farmers, who lived close by. She had noticed their house, set back from the road, as she had often passed it on her walks and admired their extensive vegetable garden, while their chickens clucked and scratched around the base of several pine trees, which provided shade and privacy for their home.

Their dog dashed through the barely opened gate, up the steps, around the living room at high speed, pausing to take a quick drink from Basil's bowl and sniff to check there were no scraps on the floor by the bin, then back out again, before his owners had even managed to get as far as the steps. He waited for them there, his tongue hanging out, panting, a tail-wagging ball of tan fur.

'Stuffi!' Penny greeted him warmly. He was obviously a regular visitor. Basil and Sybil were delighted to have another dog to play with, and they were soon rushing around the garden together.

Lucas, the ex-musician, sported a thick grey ponytail and a warm smile, while his wife Emma, slim and fit from working in their olive groves, held out a firm hand to Janet and welcomed her to the neighbourhood. Janet noticed that Emma's straight brown hair fell to below her waist and was envious, running her fingers through her short curly bob; her own hair seemed to grow out and not down, as she would have preferred. They sat down together around the table on the veranda, where Penny did magical tricks by producing freshly cooked quiche and more sausage rolls.

'We were wondering when we were going to meet you,' Lucas said, picking up his newly filled glass. 'We have seen you many times walking by with your little dogs.' At that moment, as if at the word "dogs", Basil and Sybil dashed into the house, accompanied by Stuffi. 'You didn't bring your dogs along?' he queried, obviously unaware of the situation as he saw Janet's face suddenly stiffen.

Without going into detail, Penny told them that Janet's dogs had been mysteriously poisoned. They were full of sympathy and said they hoped it hadn't put her off the idea of living in the countryside here in the Valle d'Itria.

They were interrupted by another commotion at the gate, and a local Italian couple arrived with their little terrier, Peppa. Warm, friendly, and full of local information about everyone and everything that Janet could possibly need to know, this exuberant couple, Oronzo and Elena, lived in yet another trullo that Janet had walked past on an almost daily basis. Their orchid collection was famous, and their greenhouses and gardens were visited by groups of enthusiasts on a regular basis. Janet was fascinated by Elena's enormous blue eyes, set off by a thick mop of curly white hair and the warmest manner possible.

Who knew that so many wonderful people lived behind these limestone walls! She was intrigued to learn that she had so many, previously unknown, neighbours, and it made her even more determined to reclaim her trullo at all costs. She felt that she belonged among these relaxed, friendly people whose goals in life coincided so perfectly with her own.

Penny rushed around with more and more food, all piping hot from the oven. Janet popped yet another tiny vol au vent filled with egg and prawn into her mouth. *Goodness!* she thought. *I won't need to eat for a week!* John refilled her glass, his elbow high in the air, telling her he'd make her a coffee before she left.

Towards the end of the evening, she found herself chatting to Penny.

'Can I give you a word of advice?' she asked Janet. 'Oh, maybe I should just keep my mouth shut, but I worry about you.'

'What is it, Penny?' Janet felt anxious as she leaned towards her new friend.

'Well. How keen are you on Angelo? Is it serious?'

'I like him a lot. I think you could probably say we're a couple at this point.' Janet took another sip of wine, wondering where this conversation was going.

'I was afraid of that.' Penny topped up her glass of rosato and put her hand on Janet's. 'You know he's got quite a reputation with the ladies?'

Janet was surprised. 'I didn't know that. No. I know he was divorced many years ago and is devoted to his work. Other than that, no.'

'Don't count on him to be faithful. That would be a mistake. We've known him for years, and he's always got a woman on his arm. Mind you,' she added, 'he could have changed since he met you. I don't know.' She trailed off.

'When did you last see him with another woman? Can you remember?'

'Oh yes. Just about a month or so ago. Before you got back from Ireland, I mean, after all, you weren't here.' Penny was now becoming uneasy. Had she put her foot in it? Perhaps.

Janet was surprised, but after her experience with James, she realised that she needed to take stock of the situation. She didn't know her true feelings for Angelo at this point. It was early in their relationship, and there was time for them to sort out their feelings for one another when this drama had played itself out. She would not let this affect her.

'Thank you, Penny. For the warning.' She squeezed her new friend's hand. 'I'll bear that in mind. Luckily, you've given me this heads-up now, before my relationship has gone too far down the road.' She was genuinely touched by Penny's gesture, as it must have been difficult to articulate such information about the handsome Italian.

When she collapsed onto her bed in Casalini later, she felt better than she had done in ages. As her head swam and she began to drift off to sleep, she thought maybe it had been the best evening ever. She knew now that moving here to the stiletto heel of Italy had been the right move.

She would fight to get her trullo back, and all would be well.

But that was just a dream, for now.

CHAPTER TWENTY-THREE
DAISY

It was dark and damp. Daisy looked around but could only make out vague shapes. Her head ached, but she was awake.

Sitting up with effort, she put her hand on the wall beside her. It felt cold and clammy. The only furniture appeared to be the bed on which she was lying, a basic camp bed with a musty coverlet over the mattress and no pillow. Was she dreaming? The room swam about her, and she lay back down again, too dizzy to stand up.

As she turned her head, she could just make out the shape of a door set into a small portion of the stone wall. She sat up again and, this time, tried to stand. She felt her bare feet touch the floor, which was slimy underfoot, and realised that she was clad in some sort of towelling dressing gown.

At first, she staggered a little, but groped her way towards the door, lured by the light at its edges. It looked as though the sun was shining outside. What was she doing in here? Where was she? Every muscle and joint in her body seemed to shoot darts of pain as she tried to move towards the light. She struggled to stay upright.

The door was metal. She gave the handle a feeble tug, but nothing happened, and it remained rigid. All she could hear were the two terrifying dogs that the man had brought home a few days previously. They were sniffing around outside the door, which was firmly locked. She was confused and returned to the bed, lying down once more on the lumpy mattress. What if she screamed? Would anybody hear her? Tears streamed down her cheeks, which took her by surprise, as she had not realised, she was crying.

Daisy tried to think about the last thing she remembered. Her head felt as though it were full of fog. She closed her eyes and retreated into drowsiness and sleep. As she did so, she thought she heard a girl sobbing.

But she had probably imagined it.

CLAUDIA

Her mobile rang. 'Claudia Farrell?' a male voice enquired.

'Yes. Claudia here.'

'Hello. It's Gastone di Falco here. I think you might be expecting me?'

'Oh yes. You're in Ostuni?'

'Yes. I arrived earlier today. May I come and see you?'

It was evening. Claudia had been planning to have an aperitivo on her terrace. The sunsets were magnificent, and she enjoyed sipping a glass of rosato wine, its colour a perfect match for the coral-coloured dusky sea. She stifled a sigh. Did she really want this man coming into her life? He was probably a fat, boring, self-satisfied businessman, but then, Olivia loved him dearly, so he must be okay.

'Yes. Join me for an aperitivo. Do you know where I live?'

'I'm outside your front door right now.'

'Oh! I'll buzz you in.' She walked over to the front door and pressed the intercom button on the wall.

The footsteps on the stairs — surprisingly light for a fat businessman, she thought. Trixie dashed forward, barking, her long ears flapping.

As Claudia opened the door, she could hear the *clip-clopping* of his leather soles on the long flight of stone steps. Then he appeared. A tall man, his black hair straight, floppy and parted in the middle, with two white wings brushed back over his ears, came to an abrupt halt when he saw her. Trixie greeted him like an old friend, whimpering around his handmade brown loafers and pawing at his cream chinos.

'You!' His face froze in mid-greeting as he registered surprise. 'We met at Niccolò and Olivia's wedding reception.' He put out his hand to shake hers, adding formally, 'Gastone di Falco. I don't think we were introduced.'

Remembering the incident when she had covered him from head to toe in expensive Prosecco, then rudely disturbed him at the di Falco mausoleum on the island of San Michele the following day, she took the proffered hand with only a moment's hesitation, which he noticed. 'Claudia Farrell. Pleased to meet you.' She was embarrassed and tongue-tied for once but pulled herself together and ushered him through to the salon, where she had put the bottle of rosato, a dish of cashew nuts and another of *taralli*, while she fetched a fresh glass from the cabinet.

'Planning to drink alone?' He smiled, with what she felt was disdain and an implied criticism. 'Lucky I came by.'

Claudia bristled. If this was his attempt at humour, it had failed in her estimation. She sat down and waited for him to do the same. Trixie was still entranced by the stranger, who now bent to stroke her head, but remained standing, looking around the huge room with its frescoed ceiling and a fireplace, where you could hide a couple of large men, if that was your bent, and the floor-to-ceiling windows leading out onto the terrace, overlooking the old town and, beyond that, the Adriatic Sea, now turning a darker shade of orange in the setting sun.

'This is magnificent.' He picked up the proffered glass of wine and proceeded to open one of the terrace doors. 'May I?' His manners were formal and — Claudia thought, though loathe to admit it — old-fashioned in a way she appreciated.

She joined him on the terrace, and they raised a toast to Puglia. She found herself looking at him as he admired the view and sipped his wine, seemingly transported onto another planet. She noticed his tall, slim build and air of complete relaxation.

'I have missed the sea,' he said. 'I have been spending a great deal of time in the Euganean Hills recently, which has a very different beauty.' He finally looked at her. 'Olivia is such a wonderful hostess. So generous with her time. And, of course, Niccolò, who loves the villa in Galzignano like nowhere else. Have you been there?'

Claudia shook her head. 'No. Not yet anyway. Maybe next time I visit. I just heard the great news about Olivia's pregnancy, so perhaps I will get there when the baby is born.'

'Niccolò telephoned me earlier with the wonderful news. He's very happy. I'm glad for him.'

'Apparently, we are both to be godparents.'

He looked at her, his raised eyebrows seeming to display mild disapproval. 'You are to be a godmother to Niccolò's child?' He sounded incredulous, and Claudia could feel her hackles rise.

'Yes, indeed.' She felt an immediate need to justify herself. 'Olivia and I have always been close, and it's not just Niccolò's child, by the way. Her father and mine are brothers.'

'I see.' He returned his gaze to the sea, which was now a deep coral as the sun sank, and the sky darkened to navy blue.

After more small talk, Claudia had decided that she did not much care for Gastone di Falco. He appeared to be full of his own importance, stiff and, apparently, deeply conservative in his views. She was surprised that Olivia found him so wonderful. She vowed to make sure that his visit to Ostuni was as brief as possible. *How arrogant he is!* she thought to herself.

Finally, Gastone addressed the reason he was in town. 'So, tell me,' he began, 'who is this man of whom you are so frightened? Olivia told me that he is your ex-husband and that you broke up under difficult circumstances. Apparently, you suspect that he is in town.'

'Michel Reynard,' she began. 'My second husband, in fact. My first husband, Philip, died many years ago, and I married Michel just over two years ago. The marriage lasted barely one year...' For some reason, she felt that this must make her seem like a loose woman, something she had never felt before, until this moment.

'Why are you frightened of him? Olivia gave me very few details, as she said you would want to inform me about what happened in your own way.'

'It's hard to explain.' She patted Trixie, who was, apparently, trying to climb onto her lap and encouraged her to lie in her basket instead. The little dog looked indignant and, head held high, huffed along the terrace to bark at the passing strollers below. She continued, 'Have you ever heard of the expression "gaslighting"?'

Gastone looked at her intently. 'Yes, I have. Isn't that when someone wants to control another person, they work at making them feel stupid and worthless, even mad? I remember the old movie *Gaslight*; it's years since I saw it, but I think that's where the word comes from, if I'm not mistaken. The heroine thinks she's going mad because her husband keeps moving things around and makes her feel as though she's imagining things.' He stopped to think, to remember. 'Well, something like that, I think.'

'Exactly. What he did was make me feel as though I was going crazy. He would tell me outrageous things...' She remembered the incident in Menton and the photograph of the wine club, where he had pointed out all the women he had slept with. Her cheeks burned at the memories. 'Then, when I reacted by becoming upset, he would tell me I wasn't well and needed to take something. He had me on all sorts of tranquillisers and anti-depressants. I was like a zombie and felt completely inadequate.'

For the first time, she saw a glimmer of sympathy in Gastone's eyes. He could see that she was becoming upset just reliving those memories. 'Go on,' he said.

'Two things woke me up. First of all, I discovered that he had sexually molested his daughter, Freda. Then he tried to steal my investments, fraudulently. But when we finally split up, he said that he would get even, if it was the last thing he did.'

'Are you really afraid that he meant what he said?'

'Oh yes. If you had heard him, the way he spoke, spitting the words at me, you would understand. Now he appears to be in Ostuni. I spotted him in the background of a photograph where Olivia was tagged on Facebook. I'm almost positive it's him. The photo was taken, I'm certain, just up the street in the piazza. Honestly, I'm absolutely terrified.'

Gastone looked thoughtful. 'How do you know he molested his daughter?' He reached for the bottle of wine and, with an enquiring look, to which she nodded her response, he topped up their glasses. He sat back and looked at her intently while she gathered her thoughts.

'She wrote to me. I wish I still had the letter, sordid and all as it was, but Michel burned it when he saw it.' Claudia found it difficult to tell her story to this stranger and tried to sound as cool and collected as possible.

'And stealing from you?'

Claudia began to relate the story of Michel's failed business, how she tried to prop him up, believing that his divorce had decimated his finances. Then the story of the stolen documents. 'It's humiliating to admit it, but he married me for my money. Nothing else.' She gave a wry little laugh, self-deprecating and bitter.

By now, it was almost completely dark. The terrace lights had come on outside and, on the street below, smells of cooking were coming from various restaurants. The front doorbell rang. It was Anya.

'Sorry, Mum! I left my key behind. Can you buzz me in?' Then she came running up the stairs to be greeted by an overexcited Trixie, who acted as though she hadn't seen Anya for weeks.

Gastone stood up to shake hands with Claudia's beautiful daughter, who looked nonplussed to see her mother sitting in the salon, drinking wine with a strange man, her head swivelling from one to the other in confusion.

'Gastone is Niccolò's cousin. He's visiting Ostuni and staying in a hotel just across the street.' She tried to speak calmly, as she had not told Anya anything about seeing Michel's photograph. She supposed she should have told her, but she had not wanted to disturb the ease with which her day-to-day routine with her daughter had progressed and had no idea where this was going. She wanted to avoid creating anxiety for Anya at all costs.

She flashed a look of warning at Gastone, who realised that Anya knew nothing about Michel's possible re-emergence, nor, apparently, about his threat to Claudia when they parted. He held his tongue and chatted with Anya about her work at the kennels and her pending studies at Trinity College in Dublin.

'What's for supper, Mum?' Anya asked the inevitable question after they had been discussing Olivia, Niccolò and the pending arrival of the new member of the di Falco family for about half an hour.

'Oh!' Claudia had completely forgotten that she had two fillets of swordfish marinating in the fridge, potatoes to peel and vegetables to prepare. 'I'm sorry, Anya. Supper went completely out of my mind.' Anya looked at her mother closely. This was so out of character that she could hardly believe it.

'Okay! What would you think if I just popped out and got a few pizzas?'

Claudia looked questioningly at Gastone. Surely this wealthy aristocrat would turn up his nose at the very idea of a takeaway pizza, but no. 'Make mine an Amatriciana,' he said, smiling for the first time that evening. She noticed that his entire face changed, from formal and slightly arrogant, to warm and friendly, and she realised how very handsome he was. She decided it must be the mention of food, as all Italians automatically cheer up at the thought of anything culinary.

'A small Margherita for you, Mum?' Anya knew that Claudia rarely ate pizza, but she felt justified in ordering in on this occasion due to her mother's memory lapse. Who was this stranger who had the power to make her mother forget to cook, and why was he really here? She narrowed her eyes and looked at both of them.

'Er... yes. Perfect. Thank you, darling.' Claudia tried to relax, but it just did not feel right to her to be sharing her daughter and their home with this slightly formidable man. *Will he expect a plate, knife and fork?* she wondered. *Even a linen napkin?* Surely, eating a pizza straight out of the box, with paper napkins from the pizzeria, would be out of the question.

As Anya left, clattering down the marble stairs, Claudia bustled about in the kitchen. Gastone followed her, carrying the wine bottle and glasses. The evening was balmy, and she put knives, forks, plates, and napkins on the table on the rear terrace overlooking the garden and lit two large candles.

His eyes registered the comfortably decorated family sitting room through which he passed on his way to the large stone terrace as he placed the half-full bottle of wine on the table.

'This is a truly beautiful property,' he said, as he admired the vines, jasmine, and wisteria growing lushly over the balustrade and overhead pergola.

'Thank you.' Claudia was always pleased when anyone admired her new home.

'I seem to have taken over your evening.' He sounded apologetic. 'I should have made an arrangement to come to see you tomorrow morning, but I was keen to meet up so I could report back to Olivia as soon as possible. She's been fretting about you.' Now he sounded impatient. *Women!* he seemed to be saying, with a sneer.

Claudia tried to relax, though she was still wary and unsure about what she thought about him. One minute he appeared friendly, the next arrogant. She was uncomfortable as she realised, she had told this stranger so much about herself; she rarely confided in anyone, but she felt as though she had had no choice. Confused, she longed for the evening to be over so she could go to bed and think.

CHAPTER TWENTY-FOUR
JANET

Angelo looked up from his laptop as the slam of a car door reached his ears. He was in the tiny office at the side of the kennels, which looked out over the driveway. The dogs were whimpering excitedly at the gate, so whoever had arrived was well known to the milling canines. That could only be Anya or John.

Janet was sitting on the one and only armchair in the corner, trying to read a book and waiting for him to finish up so they could go over to the trullo again to see if there was anybody there. If it were empty, they would let John know, and he would join them. He had a butchered rabbit in his fridge, which, he said with a chuckle, made Penny squeal every time she opened the door to get out the butter or milk.

As Angelo sat at his desk, Janet noticed him look out the window. She heard a car drive away and raised herself onto her elbows to peer out too. She saw Anya approach the gate and watched Angelo crane his neck to see who had dropped her off. Trying to damp down jealous thoughts, she was sure he had been hoping it might be Claudia, as he had obviously been impressed with her the other day. She was convinced that he now looked at her, Janet, with a guilty expression on his face, which confirmed her opinion on the subject. She would have to be careful, as that woman could be dangerous, she thought, dismissing Penny's revelation of Angelo's womanising.

However, what Angelo had seen when he looked outside had made him start with alarm. It was a sapphire-blue Toyota SUV with a man behind the wheel. As the car drove off, he saw Anya turn towards the gate and enter, chatting to the dogs, who were obviously thrilled to see her. What had she been doing with this man, who appeared to be the owner of a car, identical in colour, make and model, to that driven by the new inhabitant of Janet's trullo? What on earth was going on?

Angelo got to his feet and exited the office. Janet got up immediately and joined him outside. Anya was approaching, her lovely face smiling at them happily.

'Welcome!' he said. 'Have you got a new friend? I haven't seen you arrive in that car before. Where's your Vespa?' He tried to sound casual, but Janet heard genuine anxiety in his tone and wondered.

'He's an old friend.' Anya sounded reserved. 'My Vespa is at home.' She said nothing more, and Angelo was not sure how hard to press her on the subject as he turned to Janet with a questioning look on his face.

Taking her arm, he moved back towards the office, telling Janet what he had seen. She had missed seeing the car itself but was stunned at what he told her.

'It's an identical car to the one at your trullo.' He looked over his shoulder to ensure that Anya was out of earshot. He need not have worried. Anya was surrounded by a crowd of ecstatic dogs as she went to the storeroom for their food, chatting to them in a language they obviously understood, as they waited impatiently for her to fill their bowls. 'And the man driving it seemed to have light-coloured hair, though I didn't get a good look at him.'

Janet was stunned. 'You mean it could be the man who's living in my trullo? The man who drove Anya here this morning? But how can that be true? I don't understand.' She thought about it for a moment or two. 'I'm going to ask her what her connection is to him. Maybe she knows where Daisy is, what happened to Gigi and Bella.' She turned to follow the girl.

Angelo caught her arm. 'No! Don't confront her. I'll find a way to ask her myself when I have the opportunity. I don't want her to become alarmed. You can't just walk up to her and begin an interrogation. Let me handle this.'

But Janet's anxiety had overcome all logical thought, and she strode after the girl, leaving Angelo standing by his office doorway with a bemused expression on his face.

Catching up with Anya and wading into the sea of eager, wagging tails, Janet called to her. 'Anya. Who did you come here with this morning? Who drove you here?'

Anya looked at her interrogator, her face impassive. 'Janet. Why do you ask? What is it to you who I came here with?' Janet could not read her face, though she thought the girl looked upset; maybe she had even been crying.

'Erm…' Janet was taken aback by the girl's apparent coldness. 'Sorry. I just thought I recognised the car…' The realisation dawned that she was handling this incorrectly and she should have gone along with Angelo's suggestion.

'I'm sure you couldn't possibly know the driver of that particular car, and it really is a bit odd to be questioned about who drove me here this morning. Very odd indeed,' she added, for good measure, turning back to filling the dogs' bowls with kibble and what looked like a type of minced meat. 'My personal life is absolutely none of your business,' she added and turned away.

Janet stared at Anya as though she might see the answer to her question written on the back of her T-shirt, then, abandoning further questioning, returned to where Angelo was still standing, looking annoyed.

'Did you really have to talk to my excellent helper like that?' Yes. He was definitely annoyed. 'You can't go around interrogating people, especially my staff. That's seriously out of order, Janet.'

'Sorry,' she muttered.

'Now, you know what you've done? You've made it impossible for me to ask her, as she will realise there's something up. I know you're anxious about Daisy and what happened to your dogs, but there's no need to stir up unnecessary trouble.' He turned on his heel and entered the office, flopping himself down behind his desk, running a distracted hand through his thick black hair.

***

DAISY

Daisy woke up. She was groggy and peered around with half-closed eyes. She was in her cosy bed in Janet's trullo. She began to relax, then remembered her previous waking moments in the cold, damp room when she had tried to open a metal door to escape. It was a vague memory, without substance.

Had she heard a girl crying? She couldn't be sure; her thoughts were disjointed.

It must have been a dream, she thought, trying to move, then discovering that one of her wrists was cuffed to the bedpost. *What's going on?* She struggled to free her hand, but it was tightly bound.

She looked at herself. She was wearing a childlike party dress, all frills, flounces and glitter. On her feet were tiny pink ballet pumps. She was deeply confused.

Footsteps outside the door. It opened. The man entered. He was carrying a toy wand, pink and covered in glitter. It sparkled in the dim light from the hallway. He approached her slowly as she tried to struggle into a sitting position. Terror overwhelmed her.

'Time for some magic tricks around here.' His voice was silky with menace. He raised the wand.

CHAPTER TWENTY-FIVE
CLAUDIA

'Anya!' Claudia had overslept, and it was time for her daughter to leave for the kennels. 'Anya! Time to get up!'

She pushed open the door to her daughter's bedroom and stopped in the doorway. The room was empty, and Anya's bed was neatly made.

She must have got up quietly and let herself out, Claudia thought, as she moved towards the kitchen to make a cup of strong tea, her favourite brand in its dark-green box, brought especially from Dublin. She put water in the kettle and turned it on. *Toast this morning, I think. With some of that organic apricot jam. Yes.*

After having drunk more than her usual quota of wine with Gastone the previous evening, Claudia was feeling less than fresh this morning. Sitting at the kitchen table in front of the long window onto the terrace, she allowed herself to think about the fact that she had actually eaten a takeaway pizza with this aristocratic Italian. She felt it had all been slightly surreal. Unsure whether she actually liked him or not, she decided to reserve judgement until she got to know him better.

He was good-looking, cultured and successful; those were a given. He was also arrogant and a bit stuffy, she told herself. She sipped her strong brown tea and reflected on the positives and negatives of Gastone di Falco, though she knew she should give him the benefit of the doubt at this point. After all, as she had told herself previously, Olivia thought he was wonderful. Was she matchmaking? Claudia considered the possibility and knew she could not rule it out. That would be typical of Olivia, in the nicest possible way, of course. She smiled to herself as she dearly loved her cousin.

Suddenly, she heard the main door on the lower level click shut. The sound echoed up the stairwell. 'Anya?' she called, rising to her feet. There was no sound. 'Anya?' She opened the hall door and called down, this time from the top of the double sweeping set of stairs. Silence.

Claudia ventured down a few steps until the big main door came into view. There was nobody there. *I must have imagined it,* she thought, puzzled. She was certain she had heard the front door close.

Returning to her table, she sat and mused for a couple of minutes, then tried to put it out of her head.

Time to sit in the sunny courtyard, she thought, as she headed to the steps leading to the garden, still in her dressing gown and a pair of furry mules. She had her pen and notepad to hand so she could jot down some thoughts regarding the outline of her next book. She had a few ideas she wanted to put to the test.

As she sat down, she suddenly had a flashback to half an hour previously that caused her to dash back up the steps to the stone terrace. Rushing through the palazzo, she remembered what it was that was out of place.

As she opened the front door and looked down at the lower level for confirmation, she saw that, just as she had just imagined it, inside the big up-and-over roller door, Anya's Vespa was still there, neatly parked beside her navy Mercedes.

Removing her phone from the pocket of her dressing gown, she dialled Anya's number. She answered on the fifth ring.

'Hi, Mum! What's up?'

'Where are you? Are you at the kennels?'

'Of course! Sorry I left without saying goodbye this morning, but when I checked in on you, you were out for the count. I decided not to disturb you.'

'How did you get there? I see your Vespa is still in the garage.'

There was a slight hesitation, and Anya replied, 'I got a lift.'

'Really? With whom? I didn't know that anyone else even knew where we lived.'

'Just a friend. Nobody special.' Claudia could tell that Anya was being evasive and wondered why. Surely, her daughter had no secrets from her. Mind you, she was growing up fast and was of an age to make her own decisions. Perhaps she had a boyfriend. Claudia knew that with Anya's stunning good looks, she had a fleet of admirers back in Ireland, but she was a good, trustworthy girl, and Claudia knew when to back off. No interrogation was necessary.

'Okay, sweetheart. How are you getting home?'

'Oh, I'll cadge a lift with John. He says he has to go into Ostuni later to pick up some meat from the *maccelleria* just down the street from us. Apparently, his wife wants to roast some lamb this weekend.'

'See you later then. Bye for now.' She ended the call and tried to put any lingering anxiety out of her mind. Anya would tell her what was going on soon enough. She pulled out a chair in her cobbled courtyard, sat down and looked around, savouring the sweet scents of blossom from the pots of orange trees that lined the high wall that surrounded her garden. She loved this private, enclosed space with its huge terracotta containers of red geraniums, the wisteria that was in bloom right now, its heavy, mauve flowers hanging from one wall of the terrace, and the jasmine that curled its way across the trellis over her head. It was heavenly, she thought, as she sat in a half dream, all problems put to the back of her mind at that moment.

She lay back and closed her eyes, pulling the edges of her robe apart. She was naked underneath and revelled as the sun caressed her body with its warmth. She relaxed deeply and dozed. Suddenly, she was awoken from her reverie by the sound of a deep groan. It came from behind the wisteria at the far end of the terrace. She hurriedly pulled her robe around herself and sat up.

'Who's there?' she said, trying to sound in control, hiding her nervousness beneath an authoritative voice.

There was no response. Perhaps she had imagined it. After all, nobody had access to her terrace, and Maria Grazia was not due for another hour. Anyway, it had sounded like a man. She got up and had a look behind the plants, but there was nobody there.

On impulse, she phoned her father in Dublin. He told her he was in his car on the way to the office for a meeting and that he was stuck in a traffic jam on the M50, that busy motorway that orbits the city of Dublin, from north to south.

'How are you?' Her father was always concerned about his darling daughter and granddaughter. 'How's Anya? Any more news about Michel?'

Claudia reassured him that all was well and wondered why he was going back to work so soon, a notion that he dismissed, saying he was perfectly fine and was looking forward to his visit soon. Claudia made a mental note to order another bed and some furniture for the third bedroom, which she had not yet got around to decorating. She pulled her notebook over and began to make a list as she listened to her father bringing her up to speed with the Irish political situation, a subject of which he never tired.

'A bunch of muppets!' he declared.

They hung up, and Claudia began to plan a trip to the large furniture store, which was just off the main highway on the way to Bari.

Then she thought about her upcoming meeting with Gastone. He was to call over that afternoon after having made enquiries locally. The previous evening, she had reluctantly dug out a wedding photo of Michel in his best suit. The camera had also captured a moment when she appeared to be looking at him lovingly. She had given the photograph to him, feeling embarrassed, tempted to cut herself out of the picture.

He was also going to check with the rental car companies but was not sure whether he would be able to find out any information due to Italy's strict privacy laws. He planned to call on his friends here in Ostuni too, to try to find out the best way of going about looking for someone. Not being a detective, just an aristocratic, well-connected Italian, he had a lot to learn and was open about the fact that this was going to be difficult. But, at the very least, he said, he would be there if she needed him if, for example, Michel were to come calling.

About an hour later, having written not one single word of her new plot outline, she climbed the steps to the first floor and headed for the bathroom. Dropping her robe, she stepped beneath the hot rain shower and lathered herself with scented soap. As she turned off the tap, there was silence. The shower doors were steamed over, but she thought she saw a shape moving in her bedroom. She froze.

'Who's there?' Her voice quavered slightly. There was silence. Perhaps she had imagined it. Maybe it was a reflection of herself from the mirror. She was becoming paranoid, she thought.

She stepped out of the shower and pulled her towel around her body, peering into the bedroom. It was empty. Out of the corner of her eye, she spotted something on the floor beside her chest of drawers. It was a black lace camisole. Had she dropped it earlier? But no. She picked it up and opened the drawer which was full of lace and silk underwear. Had someone been looking in there? Impossible. She returned the camisole to the drawer and looked for the set of lingerie she had decided to wear that day.

Claudia often thought she had a slight underwear fetish. Pretty lingerie and shoes were her favourite items to buy. And cosmetics, of course. She had a vast collection of expensive bras, panties and negligees, right there in the dressing room area of her bedroom.

She could see that something was out of place. Her favourite lacy rose-pink set with the matching negligee were not to be seen. She rummaged for several minutes and gave up as she realised, they were missing. She sat on her chaise longue, trying to remember when she had last worn them and was certain she had worn them about a week previously. Where could they be?

She shivered nervously, too terrified to put her fears into words.

***

Promptly at three o'clock that afternoon, Gastone rang her doorbell, and she let him in. She was still perplexed about the missing underwear and the fact that she had become even more certain that someone had been in her home. She was frightened and was keen to share her worries with him.

He had barely managed to sit down on the terrace when she told him her fears. He looked perplexed.

'But how would someone get in?' A logical question needed a logical answer, and Claudia was unable to provide one.

'I can't understand it. I've invested in a top-class security system here, so unless someone has their own set of keys, it's inexplicable.' Her large blue eyes began to fill with tears, and she felt that she must look pretty silly to the sophisticated Gastone who, she judged, was struggling to take her seriously. 'I have a deadbolt as back up for the original lock on the front door and the back door is inaccessible except through the courtyard or garage. Both are securely fastened, and there's no sign of a break-in.' She added, 'I checked carefully.'

Gastone still looked sceptical.

Changing the subject, she enquired, 'How did you get on today? Any sign of where Michel might be?'

'No luck yet,' he admitted. 'I've been asking around, and nobody recognises the photo you gave me. I printed the photo from Facebook too and even asked at the bar where it was taken and nothing. Though the owner and his wife both recognised Daisy.' He added, 'Apparently, she's a regular there.'

He looked despondent. Claudia began to feel guilty about the fact that Gastone was in Ostuni at all, running around trying to find her ex-husband. 'I'm sure he'll turn up sooner or later. If he is here, perhaps it's just a coincidence, and maybe it's got nothing to do with me at all.' She sounded hopeful, but she felt in her heart and soul that she was being threatened in some subtle way that she could not quite get a handle on. Somehow, she could feel Michel's evil presence in the very air she breathed.

'If it is him, I wonder what he wants.' Gastone mulled over the problem. 'He sounds like the worst sort of criminal. What on earth were you thinking of marrying the brute?'

Claudia heard the criticism in his voice and felt irritated. Her hackles rose immediately. Who was he to judge her?

'We got married too soon. I didn't really know what I was letting myself in for.'

'But your daughter? How has this affected her? Did you not think about her welfare and safety when you took such a huge, life-changing step?'

Claudia stiffened with indignation. 'Honestly, I thought I was doing the right thing for her. Philip died when she was only seven years old. Surely, she needed a father figure in her life. I trusted him, but I was fooled. As I told you before, he married me for my money. I realise that now, shaming and all as it is. I thought he was devoted to me.' She looked away. Her brimming eyes were about to overflow. She dabbed at them with a tissue, and Gastone looked mollified. But only a little bit. She thought he still looked dubious, as though he must think her the most stupid woman on the planet. She sniffed again. Perhaps he was right.

He stood up. 'I'll leave you now to get on with your day.' His voice seemed cool, as though she were not showing enough gratitude for his morning's endeavours. 'Please telephone me if you are worried in any way. I'm meeting one of my friends for an aperitivo and will discuss the matter with him. He's an attorney and knows everybody, including the mayor, and I'm hoping he will have a few suggestions.'

He gave a stiff little bow and left. Claudia sat there, half numb, half deep in thought, until, much later, she heard the doorbell ring; Anya had forgotten her keys again. She waited until she heard her feet running up the staircase.

Time to prepare dinner, she thought, as she went to greet her daughter.

CHAPTER TWENTY-SIX
JANET

Janet drove back to Casalini to have a shower and get changed for the evening ahead. Would they be going to the trullo or not? Whatever happened, she needed to be prepared.

She knocked on Donatella's door, which was just a couple of streets away from her rental. Enveloped in a floral, purple embrace, she was warmly whisked inside the house, full of lace, old-fashioned still life paintings and dark antique furniture. They sat together on the button-back velour sofa to chat.

Getting straight to the point, Janet asked Donatella to tell her about the last time she had seen Daisy.

'It was about three weeks ago,' Donatella recollected. 'I called to see if she needed anything, as I had been doing almost every week since you went away. She answered the door.'

Donatella paused to think. Janet sat beside her, not speaking, wanting her to keep up the flow.

'She seemed a bit odd. I thought maybe she was drunk. She was very impolite and asked me what I wanted, as though I was a complete stranger. She didn't even invite me in!'

Recollecting this major misdemeanour on Daisy's part caused Donatella to clutch anxiously at the locket she always wore around her neck. The one with the photo of her late husband inside. Janet waited.

'She told me to go away! "Don't come back!" she said to me, closing the door in my face. I couldn't believe it. I knocked again, but there was no reply.'

'My goodness! That doesn't sound like Daisy at all. She's normally so sweet.'

'Well, it was definitely Daisy, I'm afraid. I won't ever speak to her again after that. I've never been so insulted in my life.' Donatella's ample bosom quivered with indignation.

Janet thought about it. 'Did she do or say anything that made you feel she might be under pressure? Was she alone?' She thought about the man and wondered. 'Did you see Gigi and Bella?'

'No. Come to think about it, I didn't see the dogs, but I presumed they must be inside, but there was no barking now you mention it. And you know how Gigi loved the sound of his own voice.' She smiled at the memory, then caught Janet's eye and hurried on with her story. 'She seemed to be anxious, though very rude. I didn't see anyone else there, but I couldn't very well barge my way past her to check.' She cocked her head to one side, thinking about the incident. 'There was a blue car in the driveway. Come to think of it, Daisy doesn't drive, does she?'

'No. She doesn't normally drive. She's terrified at the idea of driving here. A blue car, you said?'

'Yes. A big blue car. An SUV, I think. I was too annoyed to pay much attention to the details. But yes. A big blue car was parked outside.'

Janet mulled this over in her mind. 'So, she was there until three weeks ago, which means she was there two weeks before I returned from Ireland. And there must have been someone there with her. It must have been that man I met when I returned. Apparently, his car is blue too.'

'I'm sure you have tried emailing her?'

'Several times. And a million phone calls. In fact, her mobile appears to be off. Actually, I'm beginning to feel very worried about her. I had thought that she had left when the dogs were poisoned, out of guilt, you know, or something like that. But I'm just not sure.'

***

DAISY

'Now send that email.' The man loomed over Daisy as her fingers hovered over the *send* button on her laptop. She obediently pressed the fateful button, and the email was sent. She had a moment of horror, but goodness knows what he would have done had she refused. He told her constantly that he knew what was best and who was she to argue? She was nobody. He controlled everything in her life now.

He had dictated the essence of it, but he wanted it to be in her own words. It had to seem authentic.

Dear Janet,

I am so very sorry not to have been in touch over the past few weeks. I have been unwell and have left Puglia for Milan to visit a specialist and plan to stay here for the time being. I will fill you in on the details when we meet again.

I gather from your emails that you are back in Ostuni and have been looking for your dogs. I am very sorry to tell you that they found some rat poison, and both died before I could get them to the vet. I didn't want to trouble you about them while you were in Ireland with so much on your plate. I'm so sorry about this and will try to make amends at a later date.

I hope you are well and that you are not too angry with me.

Your friend,

Daisy xx

After Daisy had sent the email, she burst into tears. What had she done? Apart from the bald lie stating she was in Milan; she hadn't known about the fact that the dogs were dead until this moment. Putting her hands to cover her face, she screamed her grief and terror.

The man laughed.

***

JANET

She was incredulous. Reading the email for the umpteenth time, Janet could not believe her eyes. The brief note from Daisy informing her that she had gone to see a specialist in Milan was just about unbelievable. Perhaps she really was ill. She wondered what could possibly be wrong with her. She picked up her phone and dialled Daisy's number for the umpteenth time. Nothing. The line was dead. Perhaps she had changed her number when she left. Janet's thoughts whirled. She began to type.

Daisy,

Sorry, but enough of the BS. I've had it with all this nonsense. As you obviously know, I have been trying to get hold of you since I got back to Ostuni more than a week ago.

I must speak to you urgently. You need to let me have your mobile number — your old one doesn't work — and where the hell you are. Honestly, Daisy, this is not like you at all. And who is the man who is living in my trullo? None of this makes sense. I need an explanation asap.

I hope you are okay and that your illness is nothing too serious. Phone me.

Janet

Angelo! she thought. Janet needed to feel his warm arms around her and to show him the email she had just received.

Grabbing her car keys, she rushed out to where her car was parked at the side of the street and pulled out its wing mirror, which she had learnt to always fold in when she parked. Many of the drivers around here were less than careful when it came to manoeuvring their way up and down these narrow streets in their ancient, battered Fiat Pandas; little cars that appeared to wear their dings and dents like badges of honour.

She arrived at the kennels fifteen minutes later and pulled up outside in a cloud of white dust. The dogs all rushed to the gate, barking and whining for attention. Behind them, bringing up the rear, came Angelo, running his hand through his dark hair and looking surprised to see her. They had arranged to meet later at John and Penny's house when they hoped to visit the trullo to see if the stranger was there. If he was out, they planned to fetch the rabbit carcass from Penny's fridge, as John joked, saying that her squeals were beginning to get on his nerves.

'Angelo!' Janet rushed from the car and waited for him to open the gate so she could throw herself into his arms. As she ran to him, she realised that he looked uncomfortable and saw, over his shoulder, that Anya's mother, the ultra-sophisticated Claudia, was standing at the door of his office.

She stopped in her tracks. 'Hi, Janet,' Angelo said. 'What brings you here?' His voice was flat. Almost disinterested.

'I heard from Daisy.' She wished she had stopped to brush her hair and apply some eye makeup before she had left in such a rush. Claudia was looking dazzling. She bit back a feeling of jealousy. *Why did this woman make her feel like a big lump?* She growled to herself. Coming up with no immediate answer to the question, she put it aside and strode her long-legged stroll up to the office, leaving Angelo to lock the gate behind her. *Well, at least I'm a lot taller than she is,* she thought.

'Hello. Janet, isn't it?' As Claudia greeted her in a friendly way, her gold Rolex watch glinting on one slim, tanned wrist, Janet agreed that, yes, indeed, she had the name right. Claudia continued, 'I just dropped Anya off, and Angelo is kindly giving me some tips on how to train Trixie.' She turned to smile at him, including him in the conversation, and Janet froze when she saw the expression on his face. Raw admiration filled his expressive dark eyes. And not for her, but for the glamorous blonde.

Janet knew that she had not imagined Angelo's interest in Claudia. It was obvious to her that she needed to be on her guard. He was a well-educated man, dedicated to his life as a veterinary surgeon and kennel owner. And a hunk, in her opinion: tall, dark and handsome with his Latin looks and sexy Italian charm.

He had told her about his short-lived marriage several years previously and that it had broken down because, it seemed, his ex-wife did not enjoy playing second fiddle to his dogs. Or so he had told her, but now that she had spoken to Penny, she realised that there could be a lot more to the story than she had been told. His first wife had left within the second year of their marriage and was now married to one of the local bank managers, a man who worked regular hours and brought home a reliable salary every month. She had two children, on whom she doted, especially her teenage son, who was the apple of her eye and for whom no woman could ever be good enough.

She studied the body language between Angelo and Claudia. Was she leading him on? She was unsure, but her fragile femininity had Angelo hooked. That much was obvious.

He took Janet to one side, murmuring an apology to Claudia. 'I'll just be a moment. Janet has some news for me. I'll be right back.' He turned to Janet. 'You said you received an email from Daisy? What did it say?'

'Here. Read it yourself' She handed him her phone, with the email on the screen.

After a moment, he looked up. 'Milan? Ill? Do you think it's true? Would she do this to you? I thought you said she was your friend.' He was incredulous, his brow furrowing with a mixture of confusion and annoyance. 'And I'm horrified at her dismissive attitude towards your dogs. That's just unbelievable. What? She buried them and left them for you to find? It doesn't ring true. Not if she's your friend. Who does that sort of thing?'

'I don't know what to think or do. Obviously, I replied immediately and asked her to phone me. All I can do is wait to hear from her again.' Janet paced up and down the concrete walkway outside the office. 'I mean, what are we now hoping to find in the trullo if we go there? If Daisy's in Milan, we're wasting our time.'

'Let me think about it. I'll see you later. Now, allow me to see you out.' He moved ahead of her and, nodding over to Claudia, indicating he would be back shortly, escorted Janet to the gate and let her out. She moved to her car, throwing a backward glance at Angelo's retreating back and Claudia's smiling welcome.

Tips on training bloody Trixie, indeed, she snarled to herself as she turned her car and sped away in a cloud of dust.

Claudia looked after her with an unreadable expression on her face and then gave her full attention to Angelo. *This man is gorgeous,* she thought, her cheeks flushing at her thoughts, which were plainly visible to him. He was accustomed to female adulation, after all.

***

DAISY

Daisy knew she was in deep trouble. She had begun to have moments of clarity, just every now and again, but, after pressing *send* on the email to Janet, she realised that she had, somehow, allowed this man to take control of her life. She had begun to hate him and realised that he was keeping her prisoner. But why?

First of all, she now knew that he was giving her some sort of drug to keep her in a state of listlessness. She slept a great deal and viewed everything with a sort of detached apathy these days. When he had demanded she hand over her credit cards and debit card, complete with PINs, she had shown little resistance.

'Darling. You're not well. Let me look after you. I'll need to do the shopping and pay the bills while you're ill. Don't worry your little self, darling baby girl.' He stroked her hair, and his seductive words had soothed her at the time. But not any longer as she began to develop some tolerance for the drugs she was receiving. She was beginning to wake up to what was going on around her. And, if he was as wealthy as he said he was, why did he need her credit cards? This had not occurred to her before, though he had mentioned that they should share responsibility for household expenses, which were minimal.

She was now sure she had heard a girl sobbing here in the house. She realised that she herself must have been in the small trullo in the back garden at the time. Who was the girl? She sounded young. And why had she, Daisy, been in the little trullo in the first place? It was no more than a tool shed, with a scruffy camp bed its only furniture.

Daisy had begun to hide the pills he insisted she take "for her nerves" whenever possible. Unfortunately, she had figured out that he must also be using a liquid sedative in some of her food and drink, so she never quite knew where it might be hidden. However, every evening there was a pill before bedtime, which Daisy always tried to hide the moment he looked away. Sometimes she managed to do this, mostly not, as he watched her every move like a hawk. When she could, she tossed these pills behind the bookcase, stuffed them under the mattress, pushed them into her pockets, or wherever she could manage at the time, and her head began to clear to some degree, though she still rarely managed to figure out where the liquid sedative had been secreted, perhaps in her soup or her tea? She could not tell. But she always knew when she had ingested some, as her mind would fog over soon afterwards. As a result, she began to eat and drink less.

'Come on, baby girl.' He would entreat her to eat. 'You've got to keep up your strength. You need to get better.'

He would push plates of food in her direction, even lifting a forkful of mashed potato to her mouth, speaking to her like a baby.

'I'm not hungry!' she would say, wondering if the potatoes had been spiked.

'Here comes a little aeroplane!' he would say, the fork heading in the direction of her mouth while he made little engine noises. She was sure she had seen friends with babies entreating them to eat just like this. It was mortifying, terrifying, but he persisted.

She tried to vomit after eating. Sometimes she actually succeeded, but mostly she just could not manage to stick her fingers down her throat in time to make herself gag.

Every evening he took her to the shower, got her to stand inside and twisted the taps so that the hot water would stream from the rain shower overhead. He would massage shampoo into her hair and sponge fragrant gel all over her thin body, rinsing her off with the hand attachment. Then he would instruct her to shave her body, telling her how much he hated hairy women. Showering was the best part of Daisy's day, and she found herself looking forward to it, though she found it embarrassing to be scrutinised so closely as she washed which, as far as she was concerned, not unreasonably, should be personal and private.

What she did not like was afterwards, when the man would produce a piece of lingerie for her to wear. Today's was pink and beautiful. She wondered where he managed to procure these expensive items of underwear. Then she would see him lick his lips and narrow his eyes to a menacing glint.

Then she would let her mind go blank; it was the only way she could cope with the indignities that invariably followed.

What did he want with her? It couldn't only be sex; she was hardly a spring chicken, after all, and he was a tall, good-looking man who could possibly have his pick of the ladies. Fat, helpless tears coursed down her cheeks.

CHAPTER TWENTY-SEVEN
CLAUDIA

'Anya?' Claudia called. 'Coffee's ready!'

There was no response. Not even the usual groan of 'Mum! It's too early!' or 'Okay! On my way!' Silence.

Followed closely by Trixie, Claudia pushed open the door to her daughter's bedroom. Once again, the bed was made up neatly, and there was no sign of the occupant. She felt a creep of uneasiness as she looked around. Walking briskly to the front door, she opened it and peered down over the balustrade to see if Anya's Vespa was there. Yes. It was still parked neatly beside her car, just as it had been the night before when she was locking up.

She pulled the phone from her pocket and dialled her daughter's number. There was no response; it went straight to voicemail.

'Anya. It's me. Are you at the kennel? Please phone me back.'

This was the second morning in the past few days that her daughter had not been there for breakfast. She decided to give it an hour and then try again. She did not want to appear to be a hysterical mother, overanxious, possessive; her long list, mentally outlining the type of parent she did not want to be, scrolled through her brain, and she returned to the kitchen to have another cup of coffee.

The hour ticked by, and there was no return call from her daughter. She tried to quell the feelings of anxiety as Anya's phone went to voicemail once more.

She would phone Angelo at the kennel. Not wanting to seem paranoid or possessive, she thought she should ask him when Trixie needed her booster shots. She couldn't think of any other plausible reason for reaching out to him. She dialled his number,

'*Pronto.*' His deep voice sounded reassuring, and Claudia found herself veering away from her fraudulent reason for phoning and diving straight to the heart of the matter.

'Good morning, Angelo. It's Claudia here, Anya's mother.' She could hear the dogs barking in the background.

'Claudia!' He sounded pleased to hear from her. 'What can I do for you?'

'I was wondering if Anya was there. I can't seem to get hold of her on her mobile.'

'No. She's not here.' He sounded surprised. 'She told me she wouldn't be working today. Something about meeting up with an old friend, I think.'

'Oh!' Claudia was even more surprised by this revelation. 'I had no idea. That's odd. She didn't mention anything to me, but she's not here, and her Vespa is parked in the forecourt, so…' What else was there to say?

'She didn't tell you she was meeting an old friend?' Angelo asked. 'Perhaps it's an old boyfriend, someone she didn't want you to know about?'

'But I have no clue who that would be.' Claudia felt defensive. 'I know all her friends. Or, at least, I think I do.'

'Would you like me to ask John? He's here. Maybe she said something to him.'

'Please, Angelo.' She paused. 'Anya's a sensible girl. I'm sure there's nothing to worry about. I just can't help feeling that this is a bit out of character and decidedly odd. She told me she got a lift there the other day. Did you see who it was, by any chance?'

Now it was Angelo's turn to pause as he remembered Anya's arrival a few days previously.

'She arrived in a blue car a couple of days ago, but I didn't see who was driving. I think it was a man, but I couldn't be absolutely sure.'

'Perhaps she has a new boyfriend.' Claudia thought about it and continued, 'That's so unlike Anya. We don't usually hide things from one another.' She thought guiltily about the reason for Gastone's visit to Ostuni and the fact that Anya knew nothing about it.

'Janet asked her about who had dropped her off, and Anya became a bit defensive. But Janet really shouldn't have been prying. Sorry about that,' he added.

Claudia felt her maternal hackles rising. 'Why on earth would Janet question my daughter?'

'It's a long story, but we thought that the car might have something to do with the man who is staying at Janet's trullo. But we're not at all sure about that.'

'I have no idea what you're talking about.' Claudia could feel herself becoming upset. 'I'm sorry to have bothered you. I'm sure there's a perfectly satisfactory explanation for all this. I won't keep you any longer.'

She hung up and proceeded to pace up and down the kitchen, trying to figure out what to do. Perhaps she should do nothing other than wait to see if her daughter would return for supper at the usual time.

Claudia climbed the stairs to her study. She had just begun to write a new novel, having spent the past month setting out the plot and characters. She realised, when she checked the timeline, that she had given her romantic heroine a fourteen-month pregnancy and needed to alter this before she forgot. If that managed to get into the final draft, she would be a laughingstock.

However, sitting at the desk in her neatly furnished study, she could not concentrate. Where was Anya? What was happening to her daughter? Heading off twice this week with a stranger with no explanation was so unlike her. She struggled to think.

She was interrupted by the sound of the buzzer at her entrance door downstairs.

'Yes?' It was probably Gastone, she thought. But no.

'It's Angelo. May I come in?'

Claudia was startled but pressed the intercom to let him in and went down from her study to the hall, opening the door in time to see him approach, up the marble staircase, from the courtyard.

'Hi, Claudia,' he said as he entered the palazzo, his eyes taking in the grandeur of his surroundings. 'I wanted to apologise for our earlier conversation. I didn't want to worry you, and I was really just thinking out loud. Janet had absolutely no right to question Anya the way she did, but she has been very stressed about the loss of her trullo and the death of her dogs.'

Claudia was mystified. 'I don't know anything about Janet, her trullo or her dogs.' She ushered him into the sitting room and indicated an armchair for him to sit down. 'Can you please tell me what's going on?'

Angelo told Claudia about Janet's much-loved trullo, her three-month absence and the fact that when she came back, there was a strange man living in her home, and her dogs were dead, and there was no sign of the house sitter. He told her that he and Janet had seen a blue SUV outside the trullo when they went back to search for the dogs and that it looked like the same car that had dropped Anya off at the kennels the other day, though they could not be sure. Janet had been overly anxious and had interrogated Anya in a tactless way, he thought.

Claudia sat back amongst the cushions on her large cream sofa, looking confused. Angelo looked at her and felt something stir deep inside him. She looked so utterly feminine and forlorn that he found it difficult not to leap up from his armchair, sit down beside her and take her in his arms to comfort her. Claudia looked at him as though she could read his thoughts. She seemed a little startled, her huge blue eyes showing surprise. He wondered what would happen if he took that step, as he stifled guilty thoughts about Janet.

He had no time to decide as the doorbell rang once more. This time it was Gastone, who came trotting up the stairs and into the sitting room, stopping dead in his tracks as he came face to face with Angelo. The two handsome men eyed each other up with suspicion as Trixie examined Gastone's loafers and, liking what she saw, promptly rolled on her back to be petted. He bent down to greet the little dog, who then rushed off to circle the room at a high-speed gallop, ears flying.

'Angelo, this is Gastone, a visitor from the Veneto who is staying nearby.' Gastone rose to his full height, which was similar to Angelo's, and the men shook hands and exchanged glances, each trying to weigh the other up.

They appeared to be wary of one another, or so it seemed to Claudia. 'Pleased to meet you, Gastone,' said Angelo. 'I hope you're enjoying your trip south.' He said this as though his new acquaintance had just arrived from Mars and not from a mere 1000 kilometres north in the same country. The rivalry between Northern and Southern Italy was something that Claudia was only vaguely aware of, but it apparently existed, from what she could gather from the body language of the two men standing in front of her, as they sized each other up.

She remembered hearing about the nicknames the North and South of Italy applied to one another. The southerners called the people who lived in the North of Italy *polentone,* meaning "polenta eaters", whereas the derogatory term *terrone,* meaning "of the land", was applied to those from down south.

'Gastone,' Claudia began, 'we're a bit concerned about Anya. She has not been to the kennels today and has been seen in the company of a man that nobody knows. She's due home shortly; at least this is usually the time she returns. We're waiting to see if everything is okay. Angelo kindly called by to fill me in on a few details.'

She turned to Angelo as if wanting him to verify that what she had said was accurate. He nodded in agreement. 'Hopefully, she'll appear at any moment. I just wanted to check that everything was okay.'

Gastone looked uncomfortable. He had obviously hoped to find Claudia alone and, sensing his uneasy demeanour, she asked him if he had had a good day. 'Yes, Claudia. It was an interesting day, but nothing that can't wait until later to discuss. Let's wait for Anya to return. Then we can chat.'

Claudia was feeling tense. 'Would you like an aperitivo while we wait?' She jumped up and headed to the kitchen to get a bottle of chilled wine from the refrigerator. Gastone followed her and got the glasses from the cupboard while she rummaged in the larder for a bag of *taralli,* which she poured into a bowl. With a grateful smile, she handed Gastone the corkscrew, and they returned to the sitting room, where Angelo was standing at the tall windows looking out onto the walled garden below. 'This is a fabulous property. Very impressive,' he said, barely turning around.

Claudia settled herself on the sofa once more while Gastone opened the wine and filled three glasses. It was a sparkling Verdeca di Gravina, and they raised their glasses, the light catching the bubbles. 'Here's to your new home, and welcome to Puglia,' Angelo said as he raised his glass towards Claudia, smiling warmly. She felt herself soften at his words and by the way he looked at her. Gastone watched the interplay between the two, his eyes displaying a strange unease.

'*Salute*, Claudia,' he said, sipping the wine appreciatively. 'This is a lovely wine.' He examined the bottle. 'I'm very fond of Pugliese wines.'

Angelo muttered something about the posh wines of the Veneto. All that expensive prosecco and cartizze grown in the hills up around Valdobbiadene. He obviously thought that Gastone was being patronising.

Oh dear! thought Claudia. *These men are not getting along.* She looked at both of them critically, as if from a distance. Gastone, relaxed and at home in the luxurious surroundings of her palazzo, was aristocratic and had a disdainful air, whereas Angelo appeared to be down-to-earth, honest and uncomplicated. But she was aware that she knew neither of them well, and it was too early to judge. However, she could not help her vague antipathy towards Gastone, who always made her feel on guard, as if he somehow disapproved of her, whereas she was drawn to Angelo in a way that felt natural. Whatever happened, she thought, she and Angelo would be friends. If not more. She brushed away the thought but noticed that he was looking at her with soft brown eyes, full of admiration.

She realised, by Gastone's expression, that he had noticed it too.

Claudia's mind drifted to thoughts of the tall woman in the tight leggings and see-through blouse that she had met with Angelo and wondered if they were together. Certainly, Janet appeared to be quite keen; she could tell from her body language. To Claudia's eyes, she appeared to be all over him like a rash. But Angelo? She was unsure.

The object of her thoughts broke the brief lull.

'So, Claudia, what brings you to Ostuni?' Angelo asked.

'I needed a quiet and beautiful place to live, basically,' she responded. 'I spent a few months here with my late husband many years ago and fell in love with the area.' She paused to reflect. 'My cousin Olivia, who now lives in the Veneto, also loves Ostuni. She loves the friendliness of the place.' She smiled at Angelo. 'She also recommended that I look at this palazzo, which belonged to a friend of hers. I did, and now, here I am!' She raised her glass. 'To Ostuni!' She was beginning to relax a little, but the question of Anya was at the forefront of her mind, and she still felt deeply uneasy.

194

Time passed, and Anya did not return. Claudia tried to phone her again and again, to no avail. She began to feel some serious worry about her. Where was she? Who was she with?

'This is so unlike her.' Claudia was now pacing the room, phone in hand, trying to reach her daughter.

The buzzer sounded louder than usual, as everyone was on heightened alert, and Claudia rushed to the intercom.

After the main door downstairs banged shut, footsteps could be heard mounting the steps to the main floor of the palazzo. The front door opened, and Anya appeared. Her eyes looked red and swollen, as though she had been crying.

'Anya! Where on earth have you been? I've been worried sick.' Claudia approached her daughter, who backed away with a strange expression on her face. It looked suspiciously like contempt, but no, she thought, it couldn't be. Something was obviously very wrong.

'What do you mean?' The girl sounded indignant. 'I'm not on a time-clock, am I? I'm eighteen years old, for heaven's sake. And I'm not particularly late anyway.'

'Where were you today?' Claudia did not succeed in keeping her anxiety out of her voice, which appeared to anger Anya.

'I was with a friend.' Anya turned on her heel and entered the sitting room, starting with alarm when she saw both Angelo and Gastone there, staring at her as she flounced into the room. 'Oh! Hi, Angelo. Gastone.'

Claudia had followed her daughter into the sitting room, where the atmosphere was now tense. Nothing was being said, but it was obvious that there were many questions flying around in the air.

Angelo broke the ice. 'Hi, Anya,' he said. 'Did you have a nice day? You must know your mum has been trying to call you, and your phone was off. She's been pretty worried.'

'My battery died, and I forgot to bring my charger.' She stopped as she realised that nobody believed that old story, the over-used fiction that people routinely used when they wanted to have some private time.

'That's not like you,' Claudia said. 'It seems extraordinary that your phone died shortly after you left this morning. I saw it on the charger last night when I popped in to say goodnight.'

'It hardly matters. I had things to do and didn't want you interrupting me. I wish you'd just leave me alone.' She suddenly burst into tears, much to everyone's surprise. 'I'm going to my room.' She blubbered, wiping her eyes with her hands and turning to go.

'Darling girl. What's the matter?' Claudia approached her daughter. She was overwhelmed by this turn of events. Her daughter was not given to emotional outbursts, much less subterfuge.

'Nothing. Well, nothing I want to discuss at the moment. I'm going to my room.'

'What about having something to eat?'

'I'm not hungry. I'll see you tomorrow.' She left the room. Trixie followed her as far as the door, which was closed by the time she got there. She sniffed underneath the door, making puffing sounds, but to no avail. Anya had retired to her room in tears. Trixie trailed to her bed in the corner, flopping into it with a sigh.

Claudia sank into the cushions once more and tried to meet the enquiring gaze of her two male companions. 'What was all that?' She shrugged helpless shoulders. 'I wonder what's the matter. Hopefully, she'll be in a more receptive mood tomorrow, and I can talk to her in a rational way. This isn't like her at all,' she added, almost defensively.

Angelo suddenly stood up. 'I must go,' he announced. 'I need to get back to check on the dogs and lock up the kennels. John will want to go home.' He looked questioningly at Claudia.

'I'll see you out.' She rose to her feet.

Gastone also stood up. 'Could I have a few words with you before I go?' He addressed Claudia, who nodded in the affirmative, as she joined Angelo at the front door, as Gastone stood looking after the two of them, an inscrutable expression on his aristocratic features.

Looking up at Angelo, so tall and broad-shouldered, she felt a longing for him to hug her, inappropriate and all as this would be. He was a comforting presence and, she felt strongly that she could trust him.

'Thank you,' she said in not much more than a whisper. 'You were very kind to come over today. I know how busy you are with the veterinary practice and the kennels. I really appreciate your kindness.'

He bent over and kissed her on both cheeks, in that courteous Italian way, but more intimately, she was sure, as she felt his warm lips on her cheek. 'I'll see you soon,' he said. 'And I'll keep an eye on Anya while she's at work. If I'm unhappy about anything, I'll let you know.' With those reassuring words, he turned on his heel and left.

Trixie joined Claudia at the front door, and they both looked fondly at his retreating back as he descended the staircase and left the building.

As the door closed behind him and he stepped onto the footpath outside, he was unaware that he was being closely watched from under a portico on the far side of the cobbled street.

CHAPTER TWENTY-EIGHT
DAISY

'I've got to get out of here.' Daisy knew that, somehow, she had to escape from the clutches of the man. She was bone thin, her hair was a mess, with pepper and salt roots showing more than an inch along the line of her scalp, she felt soiled and dirty after more than a month of being used and abused. It was time to plan her exit. She needed to find Janet, horrified at the email she had been forced to send. She was aware that her friend now probably thought she was in Milan and had known the dogs had been poisoned, yet not said anything at the time. And her trullo had been snatched from under her nose. She must be devastated by all these events. Daisy blamed herself. She should never have allowed herself to be manipulated by the man. Now she was his prisoner.

But how could she escape? She was handcuffed to the bedpost for large parts of the day, being escorted into the kitchen to cook and clean while he sat at the table observing her every move. They would eat together, and then he would sit looking at his iPad while she washed the dishes afterwards, then escort her back to the bedroom, or as far as the bathroom door if she needed to pay a visit there, where he would wait outside, knowing that escape would be impossible through the tiny window high up inside the dome of the trullo. The rest of the day was spent lying on the bed in a drugged haze, staring vacantly at the ceiling, wondering when the man would next appear and what degradations were in store when he did.

He was sexually insatiable. At first, Daisy had quite enjoyed this side of things, having been more or less celibate for a couple of years prior to meeting him. This was a state of affairs she had tried to rectify many times on her world travels and, apart from the occasional one-night stand which never went anywhere, most men she met appeared indifferent to her charms, no matter how hard she tried to be seductive. Now, however, she felt that she would be more than happy to regain her celibate status, even become a nun, she thought, anything but this constant violation of her person, her body.

She began to formulate a plan. Perhaps she had a way to turn the tables. She thought about her collection of sleeping pills and the tranquillisers that she had managed to pluck from the occasional sandwich, which she'd had a split second to examine before being forced to eat it under his watchful gaze. She would wait until he looked away, hurriedly part the slices of bread, find the pill and secrete it someplace handy. It was always a nerve-wracking manoeuvre, making her heart thump with fear, but she had got away with it enough times to have made a difference to her clarity of mind, and she had added them to her hoard of pills. They were different shapes, colours, and sizes, and she was unsure exactly what they were, all she knew was that if she took them, or if he managed to administer a liquid that she could neither taste nor see, which she often had no choice but to ingest, she was aware that the following hours would be spent in a twilight world that she could not avoid.

Sometimes she would wake and find herself locked in the little trullo, where Janet used to keep her garden tools, knowing that he must be out or that someone was with him. She thought that her best chance of escape had to be when he was away, except that she couldn't open that metal door. Unless — the thought terrified her — her only other option was when he was there, which would mean that she would somehow have to incapacitate him while she made a bolt for freedom. Or, if she could render him unconscious and could not leave, she might be able to send Janet an email telling her of her plight. She mused the situation at length and waited for the opportunity to do something to get away.

It came sooner than she had anticipated.

Next day, under the pretext of dusting the trullo, while the man sat typing at his iPad, she discretely gathered up a few pills from behind the bookcase and under the mattress, concealing them in her flowing summer skirt, where a small inner pocket made an ideal spot to store them. Today he had instructed her to make a ragu, slightly spicy as he liked it, and had bought a packet containing a mixture of minced beef and pork. She had carrots, onions and celery in the larder, a can of pureed tomatoes and plenty of fresh herbs and spices.

Pulling out Janet's mortar and pestle, standing with her back to the man, Daisy pulled out the assortment of pills from her pocket. She ground them to a fine powder with the cumin seeds and spices, creating a fine powder which she put in the pot, cooking them along with the spices and vegetables. She then added the minced meat and fried it up well, creating an interesting blend of meat, vegetables, herbs, spices, and pills. She was aware of a tiny pink fleck and hoped it would disappear when she added the tomato puree, which it did, much to her relief. Her heart pounded.

Three hours later, she removed the ragu from the hob and put it aside. It smelled fine, but, obviously, she couldn't taste it to check the flavour. As usual, after making a big pot of ragu, she put some aside for the deep freeze, but she hoped she would not be around for long enough for it to cool down.

Suddenly, she had an inspiration.

'Would you like me to prepare the dogs' food before we eat?'

He looked up from his iPad and grunted an assent. He knew that Daisy was afraid of the dogs. He had trained them to be aggressive towards her by encouraging them to growl at her, making her jump away when they were around. 'If you prepare their bowls, I'll bring them out.'

Very discretely, Daisy added two ladles-full of ragu to the dogs' food, one each. She had no idea if this would work, but she had been worrying about how she would get past them to reach the gate. She mixed it in carefully and put it aside.

Then she put the pasta water on to boil, adding a generous pinch of salt, and began to set the table. Forks, bowls, napkins, and glasses were neatly laid out, and she weighed the pasta: one hundred and twenty grams of penne rigate, which she added to the boiling water. She set the timer for twelve minutes, though she was afraid she would not hear it over the beating of her heart, which was now hammering in her ears. What was about to happen?

The man picked up the dogs' bowls and carried them outside, returning to his seat at the table, iPad put to one side.

He lifted the fork and tasted the ragu, to which Daisy had added to the penne. He reached for the dish of grated parmesan cheese and looked at Daisy.

'Are you not eating?' He looked at her penne, no ragu, just sprinkled with a little cheese.

'I'm not feeling great,' she replied, which was true as her stomach was churning with fright at what she was hoping to do. 'I might have some later.'

'Mmm,' he mumbled, his mouth full. 'Delicious. Maybe I'll keep you on as my cook.' He gave a rare smile, which reminded her of how very good-looking he was when his features were not distorted by an ugly sneer. Daisy hoped she was doing the right thing in trying to drug him as she watched, her face anxious.

After the man had eaten, wiped his mouth with his napkin, and drained his glass of red wine, he walked over to the back door and checked that it was locked, slipping the key into the pocket of his chinos. He sat down on the sofa, pulling his feet up onto the end cushion. 'I'm just going to nap for a minute,' he said, lying back against the cushions. 'I feel quite sleepy.'

Suddenly, he began to snore softly. Daisy was almost too terrified to do anything. She knew she had to remove the key from his trouser pocket and her heart thudded as she approached his inert form. She had no idea how deeply he was asleep or when he might wake up. Dropping to her knees beside the sofa, she carefully slid her hand into his pocket and felt her fingers close around the door key.

***

JANET

Janet's phone rang just as she was reaching for another slice of pizza. It was Penny.

'Hi, Penny!' she said, happy to hear her new friend's voice. 'What's up?'

'Oh! Hi Janet. I've just been walking the dogs up past your trullo, and the gate is open with no dogs in sight. It's odd. The car is still there. Maybe he's gone out with the dogs for a few minutes and didn't bother to lock up after himself, but I've never seen the place look so deserted.'

'Where are you now?'

'I've just arrived home. I want to lock up Basil and Sybil, and then I'll walk up there again for another look.'

'No!' Janet said. 'It might be dangerous. I'm on my way. I'll pick you up in fifteen minutes.' With that, she hung up.

Putting some cling film over the remains of her pizza, she grabbed her car keys and rushed out the door, grabbing her shoulder bag as she left. On her way, she tried to ring Angelo, but the call went to voicemail. 'Ring me when you get this. I'm on my way to the trullo. Penny says it appears to be empty at the moment.'

As she pushed her little car to the maximum, dashing up the laneway to John and Penny's house, she wondered why the trullo appeared to be empty. Where, for example, were the man's dogs? She could not wait to get there and find out. She swung into John and Penny's gateway, and the light on the pillar began to flash as the gate inched open. Janet, revving the engine, had not realised until this moment how slow it was. 'Hurry up, gate,' she muttered, drumming her fingers on the steering wheel.

Penny was standing there with a plastic bag held gingerly in her hands.

'I've brought the rabbit along in case we need it.' Her voice quivered slightly, and she looked as though she might throw up but was putting on a brave face. 'It's beginning to get a bit ripe, to be honest, so I want to get rid of it anyway.' She popped the boot and tossed it in. Janet registered the truth of what Penny had said as the sweet odour of rotting rabbit flesh began to permeate the car. She opened both windows and turned up the fan.

They drove up the dusty laneway, on the lookout for either the man or his dogs. It was almost fully dark now, but Janet was worried about turning on the headlights in case she attracted attention. She parked about a hundred metres from the front gate of the trullo and killed the engine. 'Let's go,' she said, and they exited the car as quietly as they could. Penny retrieved the plastic bag from the boot and began to carry it at arm's length towards the trullo. Janet had a torch, which she needed to turn on, as they could easily have fallen over the low wall to one side of the lane and landed upside down in the adjacent olive grove. The women linked arms, and Janet pointed the torch's beam at the ground, as she had seen night-prowling detectives do in the police procedurals she had once so enjoyed watching on television.

Arriving at the open gate of the trullo, all was darkness. No dogs, just silence. It appeared to be deserted. They crept to the front door. Penny had the rabbit at the ready in case they needed it.

'I'll leave this out here, shall I?' Penny deposited the offending plastic bag on the front step.

They contemplated ringing the doorbell and decided that they should, just in case. It rang hollowly inside the trullo, and Janet felt a burst of love for her little house — at least that's how she still thought of it. Nobody appeared. Janet touched the door with the palm of her hand, surprised to feel it give way and swing open. Inside it was dark, but there was a smell of cooking in the air. They could smell spices and cooked meat as they entered the kitchen.

CHAPTER TWENTY-NINE
DAISY

Daisy slid the key out of the man's pocket and got to her feet, heart pounding, stopping only to pick up a huge bunch of keys, including a dark-blue alarm fob, which were lying on a side table. She grabbed them, thinking of the gate key and eyed the car keys with the car hire logo attached. Should she take the car, she wondered, realising that she had no real plan. She answered herself in the negative; the last thing she needed was a car accident, especially as she had no time to search for her documents. She needed to go. Quickly. She made for the door, sliding the key into the lock.

As she slipped outside, she was on the alert for the dogs. Were they asleep too? Had the drugged ragu worked? She sincerely hoped it had, as she fumbled with the keys and managed to unlock the gate as silently as possible, cringing when she heard it squeal, while looking over her shoulder every minute. There was no sign of the dogs, and the door to the house remained closed. She slid away into the darkening countryside, leaving the gate open behind her, so anxious was she to escape.

Turning left, she walked as fast as she could along the lane that took her past Lucas and Emma's home. She believed they were Belgian, but she had never met them and felt that her panicked arrival on their doorstep might seem pretty odd, so she kept on going. Their dog, Stuffi, gave a small bark as she hurried past, but it was just a doggy "hello", and she willed him to be quiet as she struck out over a ploughed field, which she was sure would bring her to a lane which headed in the direction of the village of Casalini.

It was getting dark now, and Daisy wished she had brought a torch as she stumbled over the rutted field, passing an abandoned trullo, its darkened doorway creating sinister shadows. As she felt the firm surface of the lane underfoot, she breathed a sigh of relief and kept walking, terrified that the man had somehow managed to follow her. All was quiet on the darkening laneway; only her frightened gasping could be heard over the sound of the night crickets.

She kept going.

At the end of the lane, she turned left onto a narrow back road towards Casalini. She was not going to chance taking the main road in case the man had woken up and was out looking for her in the car. Also, it was unsafe in the gathering dark, without a hard shoulder to walk on.

As she had no idea where Janet might be staying, who could she turn to now other than Donatella? She remembered the last time they had met and how the man had forced her to get rid of her Italian friend at any cost, as he stood out of sight behind the door while she gave Donatella the brushoff. He was holding a poker and had threatened to use it if she did not do as he instructed her. She doubted he would resort to murder, but she just never knew what he might do. She could not take the chance. She had squirmed inwardly at the look on Donatella's face when she had told her not to bother her again. It had been painful, but she had had to get rid of her, and as quickly as possible.

It was completely dark when Daisy finally arrived at the outskirts of Casalini, and she was grateful to see the street lights ahead. It had been a difficult walk, but her eyes had become accustomed to the darkness, and she had managed not to fall over anything on the way. She climbed the narrow street that led up to the main piazza where Donatella lived, close to the post office, and arrived at the circular area where a few trees provided shade from the hot Pugliese sun, for the now-deserted benches, during the daytime. She stood for a moment, trying to remember which house belonged to Donatella. It was dinner time, and the air was heavy with the scent of cooking. Many of the front doors were open, with mosquito curtains hanging lazily in the evening stillness. Voices could be heard over the sound of the tree crickets, who were busy performing their night-time concert for those who cared to listen.

Donatella's door was open too, as Daisy approached. A curtain made of bamboo spheres rattled gently as she searched for a bell to push. Suddenly, the curtain was pulled back, and Donatella herself appeared, the bamboo balls giving her the appearance of a Rastafarian as they fell about her shoulders.

'*Si?*' Then she saw it was Daisy and, with much rattling, pulled back into the house. 'Go away!' she cried. The door slammed, and Daisy stood outside on the step, wondering what to do. She wondered, once more, where Janet could be. What would she do? She had no place to stay, alone, terrified and on foot. She rang Donatella's bell again.

'Please, Donatella! I need to speak to Janet. Please!' she called.

Finally, Donatella appeared. 'What's going on, Daisy?' she demanded. 'You can't speak to me the way you did a couple of weeks ago and expect me to forget about it, just like that.' She clicked her fingers in the air to demonstrate.

'I'm on foot. I escaped from Janet's trullo an hour ago. Please help me. Where's Janet?' Daisy was howling now, tears coursing down her cheeks.

Donatella realised that these were extraordinary circumstances and relented.

'Come in.' She guided Daisy into her home and made her sit down at the table. 'I'll phone Janet now.'

There was no reply from Janet's mobile, so Donatella left a message. 'Phone me urgently! It's Donatella. Come to my house as soon as you can.' She turned to Daisy. 'Would you like something to eat? To drink?'

Before waiting for an answer, she poured a large glass of deep ruby-red primitivo and put it in front of Daisy, ladling a large portion of deep-fried zucchini flowers onto a plate, saying, 'Eat, eat!'

Daisy obediently took a hefty swig of wine while her tears fell.

***

JANET

Janet looked around the empty room. It appeared as if the house had been occupied just minutes before, as there were two plates, unwashed and with food detritus, on the table and a large pot on the stove, containing traces of ragu. A portion had been set aside to cool in a plastic container, and it was still warm. There appeared to have been a sudden exodus of the inhabitants, and Janet realised that two people had eaten, very recently, at the kitchen table, as she examined the two place settings. She decided to have a quick look around and left Penny standing in the kitchen, keeping an eye on the door in case anyone returned.

Her feeling of loss was almost overwhelming as she moved quickly from room to room. The house appeared to be completely deserted. Opening the wardrobe in the main bedroom, she saw it was full of clothes, both men's and women's and… She stopped in her tracks. There were Daisy's Balinese shawls and fringed leather boots. She darted to the dressing table and pulled out a drawer, then another. The first drawer yielded an eye-popping amount of lacy underwear. She looked at this in amazement and moved on. Two beaten silver bracelets lay among the detritus of the second drawer. Daisy!

As she hurried back to the kitchen to tell Penny what she had found, she was unaware of eyes watching her from the dark recesses of the bathroom. The man began to lower his arm to his side and with it the poker he had been holding aloft.

The two women exited the house and closed the door behind them. Penny gave a frightened cry as a low growl startled them. Janet shone her torch in the direction of the sound.

One of the dogs had found the rabbit and had dragged it over to the corner of the garden. It had come in handy after all.

'I wonder where the other dog is.' Janet ran the beam of the torch around the courtyard, coming to rest on a twitching form on the cobbled paving stones. She looked closer and realised that it was the other dog, fast asleep, making tiny barking sounds, his lips puffing in and out, as his paws dreamily chased terrified rabbits and, probably, people too. 'That's so strange! He looks as though he's been drugged.' The women looked at one another. 'Let's get out of here. Something weird is going on.'

They hurried out, deciding to close the gate after them. They both agreed that it would be irresponsible to leave it open, as those two dogs would then be free to roam.

As they returned to the car, Janet felt her phone vibrate in her pocket and fished it out. It was a message from Donatella. She listened and was about to respond when she noticed a text from Angelo. *I just got your message. Let me know what's going on.*

She tapped out his number as she got into the car. 'Where were you? I thought you would have been at the kennels when I tried to get hold of you earlier.' She was stressed and could not keep the angry edge out of her voice. 'And you were out yesterday evening too. I went over to the kennels, and John said you'd gone out. I tried to call you, but nothing. What's going on?'

He cleared his throat. 'This evening, I was putting a pin in a little dog's leg. It was thrown down the stairs by a three-year-old boy, who didn't realise that the puppy wasn't a toy.' He said this patiently, in measured tones, and continued. 'And last evening, I went over to Claudia's home in Ostuni. Anya was missing, and she rang the kennels. She sounded frantic.'

'Really?' Janet could feel her cheeks redden with annoyance. 'A damsel in distress who needed you so badly you couldn't even answer your bloody phone?' She turned the ignition and put the car in gear as she gave vent to her frustrations. Penny looked out the passenger window, pretending she was deaf and, perhaps, invisible too.

Angelo sounded calm. Unruffled. He was accustomed to Janet's occasional cursing and knew she was in a stressful situation. 'Sorry, Janet, but I felt I needed to check that everything was all right. I'm not sure why you're so upset. Anya works for me, and I feel that I have some responsibility. After all, she's just a teenager. Also, Claudia is new to Ostuni and doesn't know many people here yet.'

'Did Anya turn up? Is she okay?' Janet began to turn the car with the phone jammed under her chin. Penny tuned into the conversation again, looking anxious.

'Luckily, Anya arrived home shortly before I left. A bit late, but unharmed, as far as I could see.' He added, 'The problem Claudia has is that Anya won't give an explanation as to where she had been or with whom, and it's all a bit of a mystery. So, what happened at the trullo? Did you go there?'

Janet filled him in on the details or as many as she could before she turned into Penny's driveway.

'Do you want to come in?' Penny seemed tired, and Janet said she'd take a rain check and see her in a couple of days. Both women exited the car and hugged each other silently before Janet drove away, her brain teeming with thoughts.

She just could not figure out what was going on. As she exited the lane and headed back to Casalini, she tried to analyse the situation. First of all, Daisy. If she were in Milan, how come she didn't appear to have taken her possessions with her? If she were still living here at the trullo, why would she have told Janet that she was in Milan? Why did she not tell her what was going on? It was a complete mystery. Who was the man? Who had drugged the dogs? Why had the house been left open and unattended? Why had her own dogs been poisoned? So many questions and no answers whatsoever to any of them.

She suddenly remembered Donatella's message and turned her car uphill to the piazza. Donatella was waiting for her at the front door, looking anxious. The sparkle of her dress was easy to spot as Janet rounded the final bend. As soon as she pulled up, Donatella dislodged herself from her position and rushed to the car, not waiting for Janet to climb out, so eager was she to speak to her friend.

'Daisy's here!'

'My god!' Janet rushed into the house.

CHAPTER THIRTY
CLAUDIA

After Angelo left, leaving Claudia feeling that she would have preferred it if Gastone had been the one to hurry off, they spent an hour or so discussing what to do next about Michel. Gastone told her he had an acquaintance currently visiting Ostuni, a retired police inspector from the Veneto, with whom he'd had various dealings over the years. He had heard that he was staying at a hotel in the historic centre and was considering meeting him for lunch the following day but was unsure how much to tell him. His name was Ispettore Vito Scallone, and he had been involved in the investigation into the death of Niccolò's daughter a few years previously.

Claudia was reluctant to involve the police. Somehow, in her mind, it made the situation more serious than it possibly was. She had, after all, no proof that Michel was in Ostuni, nor that he had entered her home. It was all to do with her instinct, a feeling so strong that she was convinced he was around, something menacing in the air. Now she had Anya to worry about too. What on earth was she up to? As if she didn't have enough on her plate!

'I could just talk to him off the record,' Gastone volunteered. 'He's very experienced, just coming up to retirement in a couple of years. He dealt with the potential scandal surrounding the death of Niccolò's daughter with kid gloves. That's when we became friends.' He paused. 'You'd like him.'

Claudia was still doubtful. She had begun to regret Olivia's enthusiasm for sending Gastone here at all. She was wary of him and his disdainful way of looking at her. He had obviously decided she was stupid, she thought, and that she was wildly exaggerating the situation. However, he seemed to be trying to help, as he was obviously very close to Olivia and Niccolò.

For all those reasons, Claudia found herself agreeing that he should discuss the matter with Ispettore Scallone, and if he wanted to meet with her to collect whatever details necessary, she would go along with the plan.

Gastone was pleased and said his formal goodbye, promising to call her the following morning. Just to check in, he said.

Claudia strode to Anya's room to try to glean some facts about where she had been that day and with whom.

'Mum! I'm an adult!'

Claudia was becoming tired of this refrain and said so. 'Well, start acting like an adult then,' she retorted. 'You're under my roof, and you'll have the courtesy to answer my questions. Now, where were you today and with whom? You need to answer my questions.'

But Anya remained stubbornly silent.

'What could possibly be wrong with telling me?' Claudia insisted. 'How bad can it be?'

'Maybe I shouldn't be here at all,' Anya suddenly shouted. 'I'm obviously in the way of your great new social life with men coming round every day. You're in great demand, by the look of things.'

Thrown onto the back foot by the attack, Claudia was stunned. 'You don't understand. Angelo was here because he knew I was worried about you, and Gastone is a cousin of Niccolò. As you well know,' she added.

'Well, he doesn't have to come sniffing around every day. Does he? And Angelo obviously fancies you too. I'm afraid you may be turning into a bit of a tart.' She flung the words at her mother, who cringed.

This is so unlike Anya, she thought. But her daughter was not quite finished.

'You discarded Michel when you saw his business was failing. You put him out of his own house. How could you? You're completely cold-hearted. Now leave me alone.' She flung herself face down on the bed.

Claudia was stunned. *Where did that come from?* she thought as a glimmer of unformed suspicion began to nudge at the edges of her brain.

She hovered over her daughter. This was the first time there had ever been a serious confrontation, and she had no idea how to handle it, especially as it concerned her relationship with Michel, which she had imagined, until recently, was a thing of the past. Should she sit beside her on the bed and try to talk things through, or should she leave the room and hope that things calmed down after a good night's sleep? She chose the latter, left the room quietly and returned to the kitchen to finish clearing up the glasses, promising herself an early night with a good book.

Her heart ached as she finally retired to her bedroom.

She thought about her conversation with Anya. Why did she bring up Michel's name? Was there a connection? She sat on the side of her bed and tried to think.

***

JANET

Daisy cried and cried. Janet had never imagined that anyone could shed so many tears. Her auburn hair, with its alarmingly give-away roots, was tangled and snagged with little twigs and leaves after her walk through the laneways in the dark.

Her ordeal had been terrible if all these stories about handcuffs and drugs could be believed, Janet thought.

'Do we need to call the police?' she asked, but Donatella urged caution. 'Then what can we do? We need to discuss this with someone.' She reached for her phone. 'Angelo. Daisy has turned up at Donatella's house. Can you come? She has quite a story to tell, and we don't know what to do about it.'

Fifteen minutes later, Daisy was on her third glass of primitivo and beginning to slur her words. 'He raped me,' she told them for the umpteenth time.

The rattling of the wooden beads at Donatella's front door heralded the arrival of Angelo, with a worried expression on his handsome face.

He stopped when he saw Daisy, wrapped in a blanket, sitting at Donatella's table, a huge glass of red wine in her hand, crying and telling them about her ordeal.

'Get her a coffee. Black and strong,' he told Donatella, who instantly busied herself carrying out his order as he gently tried to prise the glass from Daisy's trembling fingers. Not an easy task. 'Now, Daisy.' He turned to the small, pallid woman, whose eyes and nose were red from crying and who was now sporting a dark wine stain around her mouth, giving the illusion of a lopsided blackberry-coloured smile. 'We need to talk. Here, have this coffee, instead.'

Daisy nodded in reluctant agreement and took the coffee proffered by Donatella.

He sat opposite her and looked her straight in the face.

'Tell me exactly what happened. From the beginning. Leave nothing out.'

Daisy recounted her first meeting with the man in the piazza and how she had allowed him into her life.

'What about my dogs? Gigi and Bella.' Janet inserted herself into the conversation at this point. 'Did this man poison them? Do you know?'

Daisy looked grief-stricken and guilty. 'The dogs? I didn't know where they were. I thought they must have been brought to the kennels. I went to feed them… they were gone.' She gave Janet a helpless look.

'You mean you didn't know they had been poisoned?' Janet was incredulous. 'How can you be so irresponsible? You let a stranger into my trullo, and my dogs are dead…' Anger and indignation began to overwhelm her. Daisy looked as though she had been punched. Her brown eyes were wide with confusion, and her little hands clutched at the fabric of her skirt.

Angelo intervened. He held up the palm of his hand towards Janet in a gesture to get her to stay out of the conversation for the moment. 'What is this man's name?' His voice was gentle, encouraging.

'Misha,' said Daisy. 'I don't know his surname. He just told me to call him Misha.'

'Where was he from? Was he Italian?'

'No. I think he was French, but I'm not really sure. He spoke French most of the time or English with a French accent.'

'How come he was able to take over the trullo?' Angelo probed. There was so much he needed to know, but slowly, like extracting teeth one at a time.

'I don't know anything about that. Janet was paying the rent at the beginning and, when that stopped, I think Misha took over. I'm not sure. You'd have to ask Mimmo.' She thought. 'He took my credit cards, and I gave him the PINs because I was ill.'

Janet could not resist asking. 'You were ill? What was wrong with you?'

Daisy paused for a moment. 'You know, I'm not sure. I felt okay, but then I began to get drowsy during the day, and Misha told me I was ill. He spoke to a doctor who prescribed stuff. But then I realised that he was giving me quite a lot of drugs in my food too, and I began to get rid of them.' She remembered how she had drugged the man and worried that perhaps she had killed him. She was afraid to tell them about drugging the ragu.

'And what about your accusation of rape?' Angelo was trying to be patient. He had decided that she was the vaguest person he had ever met. Perhaps she really was ill, mentally ill. He tried to stifle the thought. 'I thought you said at first that it was consensual, but you've been crying "rape" since you arrived.'

'At the beginning, everything was fine. But then it wasn't fine anymore.' She burst into tears again. 'He whipped me with his belt and did all sorts of disgusting stuff; he even beat me with a magic wand.' At this, Angelo could not help but to roll his eyes in Janet's direction. The woman was obviously crazy, was the implication.

'A magic wand?' he repeated.

Daisy nodded. 'And he locked me in the garden shed — you know that little trullo where you keep the lawnmower?' She looked at Janet. 'Every time he went out in the car, he locked me inside it. It's cold and dark in there,' she added, almost a complaint.

Janet's face was a mask of fury.

CHAPTER THIRTY-ONE
CLAUDIA

'What time will you be home this evening?' Claudia asked Anya at breakfast the next morning.

Her daughter was unusually subdued as she pushed a poached egg around her plate.

'The usual time, I expect.'

Claudia bit back a comment about how she didn't really know what time that was any more. She didn't say it aloud but felt sad at this new distance between them.

'I thought I might ask a few people over for supper. That's all. I'd like you to give me a hand.'

Claudia was a good cook who liked to entertain. She thought she would like an excuse to invite Angelo over again, and Gastone was there, so he was an obvious person to ask. Perhaps she should invite Janet too, make it all look a bit better. Anya could then relax her attitude about all the men she was, apparently, swanning around with and, at the same time, she could have a look at the dynamics between Janet and Angelo.

'I'll be here.' Anya pushed back her chair, gave her mother a quick peck on the cheek and left, blonde hair swinging behind her.

As soon as Claudia heard Anya's Vespa start up, followed by the clang of the up-and-over metal door, she relaxed and reached for her phone.

Angelo first.

'Hi, Angelo.' He had answered on the second ring. 'I wanted to thank you for coming over the other evening when Anya was so late home.'

'Oh, that was no problem.' He sounded amiable. 'Are you okay? Is Anya coming in today?'

'Anya's on her way. But that's not why I'm phoning. I wanted to invite you and your friend Janet to come over this evening for a bit of supper. It's just a spur of the moment thought, and I'd love it if you could both come.' There, she thought. That all sounds above board.

'That sounds good to me.' He sounded delighted. 'I'll give Janet a buzz and check she's free. I'll phone you back shortly.'

Ten minutes later, Claudia's phone rang, and it was Angelo. 'That's great, just one thing. It's a long story, but Janet has a friend staying with her at the moment. Could she bring her along? She hasn't been well, and Janet doesn't want to leave her on her own.'

Claudia could hear a hint of doubt in Angelo's voice and decided that he was ambivalent about this friend of Janet's. 'That's fine,' she said. 'Of course, bring her along. We're just going to be on the terrace, very relaxed, no fuss.'

'See you later then. Seven thirty?'

'Perfect.' Then she phoned Gastone.

'That would be nice,' he said. 'I'll be having lunch with my friend Vito today. That's Ispettore Scallone. See you later.'

She felt anguished as she thought about the dreadful things her daughter said to her the previous evening. A tart! Bringing Michel into her attack! Hopefully, this evening, when Anya met everybody together, she would be able to see that these men were nothing other than supportive friends, something she lacked since she had left Ireland. She longed for her father's visit.

Claudia stood in front of the mirror. Which dress should she wear? She tried to put her problems with Anya to the back of her mind for the moment and concentrated on her appearance.

First of all, there was the cream linen shift. It came to just above her knees, was elegant and plain. She tried it on with cream espadrilles, and it gave her an elegant and understated look. *Not very exciting,* she thought, as she swapped it for something with a bit more pizzazz, a pale-pink wrap, which she discarded straight away. *Too matronly.* Next, she donned a silky top and skirt and thought, *Hmm, a tad clingy, but yes. I need to look a little bit sexy. Janet will probably have everything hanging out, as usual.* She thought again, doubtful this time. *Anya will think I'm trying to seduce the men in this number.* Her thoughts whirled. *But I'm wearing it anyway.*

She laid the silky clothing on the bed, selected some special underwear: a push-up bra and panties with "no visible panty line" — very important, she thought, especially under silk — and a pair of high-heeled silver sandals. She would wear diamond studs in her ears and leave her hair loose around her shoulders.

Claudia stepped into the shower and reached for her scented gel. She planned to look fabulous this evening.

Stepping out onto her bathmat, she smoothed scented lotion all over her body. The delicate almond scent soothed her nerves. Her first dinner party in her fabulous palazzo. And Angelo would be attending. She felt a frisson of excitement as she donned her towelling bathrobe and furry mules, hurrying to the kitchen to finalise dinner, switching on the oven. Maria Grazia had done the preparations earlier and would come back in the morning to help with the tidying up.

Everything was well under control, and she gave a last critical look at the settings around the table on the terrace, which overlooked the walled garden. Candles flickered in the evening light, and the delicate perfume of orange blossom drifted on the warm evening air. Everything was perfect.

She returned to her bedroom and began to get ready to face the evening.

Claudia had just finished applying a sheen of pale-pink lipstick when the doorbell rang. Her first guest had arrived. She ran her fingers through her hair, gave herself a final appraisal in the mirror and went to the door.

Gastone appeared at the top of the stairs and was greeted ecstatically by Trixie, who appeared to be overwhelmed with love for his handmade leather loafers once more. He bent to pat her head, causing her to rush off around the room for her usual high-speed race.

Standing up once more, he looked at Claudia appraisingly, his dark eyes warm. She felt his warmth and wondered at it.

'You look wonderful,' he said, adding to her confusion, as he bent and kissed her gently on both cheeks. 'Shall I open this?' He indicated the bottle of cartizze, which was covered in condensation, obviously freshly chilled.

'Thank you.' Claudia tried not to blush, without success. 'Yes, please, Gastone. That's a lovely gesture.'

By now, Gastone was accustomed to opening bottles when he visited Claudia's palazzo and was soon pouring a glass each, as he eyed her, his face serious.

'I had lunch with Vito Scallone today. He'll do what he can to help. He's going to take a look at CCTV footage from two cameras which take in the front of your home. He wants to confirm what dates he needs to look at, in particular.' He took a sip and nodded his approval. 'I gave him a few pointers. For example, the other evening when you told me you thought you saw someone in your bedroom and heard someone on your terrace.'

Before Claudia could respond, the doorbell rang again. It was her other guests, who trooped up the marble staircase and entered the vestibule, where Claudia came forward to greet them. Gastone hung back, taking in the scene.

Angelo entered, ushering in the two women. Janet was resplendent in a red, clinging, low-cut top and skin-tight, black, patent leather leggings. Towering black patent heels completed the ensemble. Her lipstick matched her blouse perfectly.

Behind her, long red hair half obscuring her face, brown eyes looking around in bewilderment, was Daisy. She was draped in a Balinese shawl and wearing an ankle-length skirt with leather thong sandals. She was tiny and childlike. Claudia was not exactly a giant herself, but this woman reminded her of a little mouse.

Angelo stepped forward. 'Claudia. This is Daisy Smythe.'

'Pleased to meet you, Daisy.' Claudia proffered her hand, and Daisy slid her tiny hand into hers, looking at her with an anxious expression on her face. She felt the insubstantial, seemingly boneless hand and wondered why this woman looked so utterly lost and defeated. Her name rang a bell, but she could not quite pinpoint why. It would come to her.

She was aware of Angelo looking at her, and she looked up and met his eyes. She could see admiration and something more on his features. Longing, perhaps. She tried not to react and looked away.

'Claudia,' he said, in a gruff voice, quite unlike his normal relaxed voice. 'You look absolutely beautiful.' He pecked her on both cheeks, his hand resting on her shoulder.

She noticed Janet look at him sharply and said, 'Thank you, Angelo. It's great to see all of you.' However, she thought he was looking pretty good himself, tanned and fit, in a sharply pressed, short-sleeved white shirt and cream chinos.

She escorted the group to the sitting room, saw to it that they were comfortable on various sofas and armchairs and watched Gastone pouring their drinks. He seemed completely at home as he filled glasses and handed them out, along with a dish of *taralli,* which he offered around, demonstrating his immaculate manners. She saw Angelo watching his every move, possibly thinking the same. Janet looked confused.

'You're here on holiday?' She addressed Gastone. 'Are you staying here with Claudia?' A tactless question, but her curiosity was getting the better of her, as usual. Janet never beat around the bush. Angelo eyed her nervously. He could never be sure what she would say next.

'I'm staying in a hotel nearby. A little holiday.' Gastone retrieved his glass and raised it in a toast. 'To Claudia and her wonderful new home in Ostuni.' Everyone raised their glasses.

At that moment, Anya entered. She looked like a supermodel, with her impressive height and figure, her white-blonde hair tumbling loosely down her back. She wore tight pink jeans and a loose striped T-shirt. She lit up the room. Everyone turned to look at her as Trixie danced around her silver sandals, apparently admiring her painted pink toenails. Anya greeted everybody politely, and Claudia saw her take a particular interest in Daisy as she sat beside the tiny woman and began to talk to her quietly. Claudia could see that Daisy warmed to her daughter immediately, and she felt good about that.

Claudia was over and back to the kitchen to check on the food, finally guiding everybody to the table. The crystal goblets seemed to shimmer in the candlelight, and the soft pink of the setting sun cast a warm glow. Gastone had opened a bottle of coral-coloured bombino nero rosato wine and filled everyone's glasses.

Anya and Claudia brought in the first course, a simple plate of melon with prosciutto crudo and a basket of warm rolls. Everyone tucked in, and the chat began to flow.

'So, what brings you to Ostuni?' Claudia addressed Janet. 'Have you been here long?'

Janet laughed. 'I was going to ask you exactly the same question.' She paused and broke off a piece of roll, popping it in her mouth. When she had finished chewing, she answered Claudia's question. 'I've been here for almost a year and a half, and my reason for being here is kind of tricky and difficult to explain. Basically, I wanted to get away. I think the saying is, "I needed to find myself". I thought here in the Valle d'Itria, I might find a peaceful existence. My needs are simple.' With that, she pointedly looked around the luxurious room where they were sitting. Claudia felt that Janet's comment held an ill-concealed barb and did not react.

Janet continued. 'I thought I had found my dream home. A trullo a few kilometres from town, but I ran into a few problems.' She looked quickly at Daisy, hoping she had not offended her friend, but Daisy seemed to be miles away and was looking at the orange trees in their large terracotta pots, with a dreamy expression on her face. 'Still, I hope that things will sort themselves out soon, with a bit of help.' She glanced at Angelo, noticing, to her discomfort, that he was staring at Claudia. 'Your turn,' she said to her hostess in a sharp voice, which made Angelo look at her in alarm.

'Let me take the plates first. Anya, can you help me, please?'

Anya rose and helped her mother to clear the dishes and take them to the kitchen. Daisy rose too.

'Can you tell me where the bathroom is?' she said to nobody in particular. Anya stepped forward.

'I'll show you,' she said kindly, guiding Daisy out of the room and down the hall.

Soon the main course, roast lamb, rosemary potatoes, and green beans, were on the table. 'Nothing fancy,' Claudia announced, but it looked and smelled delicious, and everyone waited for Daisy to return so that they could begin, though Claudia insisted that everyone help themselves before it went cold. Gastone topped up everyone's glass again, this time with a deep ruby-red primitivo.

Daisy entered the room once more and went to the sofa to get a tissue from her purse. Rummaging around inside, she removed a bunch of keys that were sitting on top of her packet of tissues. She put them on the arm of the sofa. Claudia glanced over, hoping she would come to the table before the lamb was cold. 'Please start, everyone,' Daisy said, but Claudia had stiffened.

'Those keys!' She had a look of mystification on her face. 'Daisy, where did you get that bunch of keys?' She rose and went over to Daisy, picking up the bunch of keys and examining them. 'These look like my keys.' She turned the biggest key over in her hand and looked at the crest. L'Aquila — the eagle — and the blue alarm fob. All hers. She stared at Daisy, who was frozen in place, looking bewildered, her mouth open. 'Now I remember where I've heard your name before.'

CHAPTER THIRTY-TWO
CLAUDIA

Claudia turned to Anya. 'Are these your keys, by any chance? The ones you told me you forgot a few times this week. Or are they mine, the set I left behind when I went to Ireland?' She examined them and saw the lucky charm, her birth sign: Sagittarius, a tiny silver archer nestling among the keys. 'Ah! They're mine! I've obviously been using your set since I got home. How did Daisy come by them?'

Anya coloured to the roots of her hair. 'Erm, Mum. I don't know.' Her eyes were downcast as she appeared to be carefully studying the birds on the placemat in front of her.

Claudia swung to face Daisy. 'Where did you get these keys?' she demanded. Daisy looked around helplessly, and Janet rose reluctantly to her feet, trying to swallow a delicious chunk of rosemary potato before she could speak. She hated to see food going to waste, especially roast lamb and new potatoes, but she could see that Daisy needed her.

Gastone intervened. 'Daisy.' His voice was gentle. He took her hand, which trembled like a trapped bird. 'Please tell us where you got this bunch of keys.'

'In the trullo,' she answered in a small voice, obviously terrified. 'Janet's trullo.'

Janet hurried over. 'Daisy. Where in the trullo did you find these keys? Whose are they? Do you know?' she asked gently.

'They belong to Misha,' she said.

'Who's Misha?' Claudia asked. 'And where did he get my keys?'

Daisy looked at Janet as if to get the all clear to speak. Janet nodded, and Daisy told them. 'I met Misha in Ostuni when Janet was in Ireland. We had a relationship, but then he stayed. I didn't really want him to, but he was very persuasive. He drugged me. He…' and burst into loud sobs.

Janet put her arm around Daisy's shoulders and said to the others, 'Daisy has had a horrible experience. She has been held virtually captive for the past month, or more, by a man called Misha, who she thinks is

French. A tall man with kind of ash-blond hair. It seems that he also poisoned my two dogs. It's my trullo, or at least I thought it was. I left Daisy house and dog sitting when I went to Ireland for a couple of months. I returned to find a strange man in my home and no sign of Daisy. Apparently, she was there the whole time, and I didn't know.'

Finally, the penny dropped. Claudia knew who had stolen her keys. She remembered Daisy from Facebook, the woman with the man who looked so like Michel. Everything made sense. But how did he get his hands on her house keys?

Claudia turned to Gastone. 'It seems as though it could well have been Michel after all, the person who has been entering my home, stealing clothing, underwear, spying on me and goodness knows what else. It seems as though I haven't imagined things at all.' She pulled out her phone, logged in to Facebook and brought up the selfie that Daisy had put online a few weeks previously. 'Look!' she demanded.

Daisy looked. 'Yes. That's him. Not a great photo, sorry.' She looked around at everyone, seeming to seek approval. 'You can see how good-looking he is and, to be honest, I wondered why he would have wanted to be with me. I'm not a young girl. I think he was on the prowl for somewhere isolated to stay, and I stupidly let him know that I was house sitting in the countryside, alone, for an indefinite period.'

Claudia turned to show the photo to Anya but noticed that she had vanished. She dashed from the room. 'Anya!' she called, walking briskly towards her daughter's bedroom. Pushing the door open, she saw that it was empty. Moving hurriedly to the wardrobe, she flung open the doors. Anya's backpack was gone, and she was sure that there were jeans and a jacket missing too. 'Anya's gone!' she cried out. She was frantic.

Gastone appeared in the bedroom doorway. She fell into his arms, gasping in panic, and felt his body tense up and then relax as he put his arms around her and held her close, stroking her hair. 'Try to stay strong, Claudia,' he said in a soothing voice. 'We'll handle this together.'

Angelo strode up to them. 'Anya's gone? She can't have gone far. I'll get the car and drive around. Janet, you and Daisy stay here with Claudia in case she comes back.' He looked enquiringly at Gastone, who had released Claudia and was tapping a number into his phone.

'Vito. We have a problem. Can you come over to Claudia's home, please?' He clicked off and turned to Claudia. 'That's my friend Vito Scallone, the police inspector. He's on his way. He'll know what to do.'

Angelo left hurriedly and ran down the stairs to the ground floor. Claudia heard the outside door clang shut and was suddenly struck by a thought. Rushing to the front door, she peered over the balustrade. Anya's Vespa was gone. She phoned Angelo, who answered immediately, and told him. He knew the scooter and said he would check the roads out of Ostuni.

Janet suddenly spoke. 'Perhaps she's gone out to the trullo. I think, perhaps, she knows this Misha guy.'

Claudia was startled. 'Oh! Of course!' She put her hands on her hot cheeks and said to Gastone, 'If it is Michel that she's been spending time with lately, she's in huge danger. He'll use her to get his revenge on me.'

'We saw Anya arrive at the kennels last week in a blue SUV,' Janet said. 'Oh, my goodness. It has to be the man from the trullo. The unwanted house sitter. Misha.' She paused. 'If that's his real name, that is.'

'Let's go out to your trullo and check.' Claudia grabbed Janet's arm. 'Let's go now!'

Gastone intervened. 'Perhaps you should talk to the inspector first. He'll advise you on the best course of action.'

But Claudia was having none of it. 'We're going. Ring me and tell me what he says. I believe that time is of the essence.'

Daisy began to sob again. 'I don't want to go. Can't I just stay here, please?' she implored.

Gastone put an arm around Daisy's shoulders and led her to the sofa, handing her a large glass of red wine that had been poured what seemed a lifetime ago. 'You stay there and relax. Would you like me to turn on the television? There's bound to be something good on Netflix.' He spoke as one would to a child, and Claudia looked at him with something akin to fondness. She realised how much she had begun to trust him, to count on his kindness and reliability. He was a reassuring presence in her life.

'Okay, Janet.' Claudia spoke briskly. 'Let's go.'

'Be careful,' Gastone instructed. 'Call me whenever you need me. I'll phone when I've spoken to Vito.'

The two women dashed down the stairs as Claudia pressed the zapper for the up-and-over metal gate, and they jumped into Claudia's Merc. She reversed out onto the cobbled street and sped to the bottom of the corso.

Janet looked at Claudia, her face tense as she negotiated the erratic traffic, heading uphill on Via Panoramica, the eye-popping view of Ostuni on their left, for once ignored.

'There's something going on here that you're not telling me.' Janet sounded sharp.

'Not now, Janet.' Claudia was able to sound sharp too. This was not the time or place to try to explain things, as she reached the roundabout at the top of the hill and turned right towards Cisternino on the SP17 at speed. As they turned up the lane towards the trullo, they saw a taillight ahead.

'I think it's a scooter!' Claudia exclaimed. 'It must be Anya.' She followed the Vespa and could see Anya's blonde hair billowing out below the crash helmet.

It was impossible to overtake due to the narrowness of the lane. Claudia flashed her lights and gave a small toot on the horn, but the Vespa kept on going. When it reached the open gate of the trullo, it sped inside. They ground to a halt outside and exited the car just as the gate was slammed shut and locked. They hammered on it with their fists. No response. Then they heard scuffling, growling and two dogs began to bark furiously.

'What shall we do?' Claudia was terrified. 'Anya is in danger.' At this point, Claudia was beginning to regret that she had not stopped to change her shoes, and so was Janet. They were both struggling in their high heels on the stony ground outside the trullo.

Janet suddenly thought. 'I'll phone John and Penny. John will think of something. He's pretty inventive. At the very least, he's male backup in case things get nasty.'

Claudia's phone rang. It was Gastone.

'I'm here with Vito, and he's just shown a few minutes of CCTV footage to Daisy, who recognised your intruder as the man who kept her at your trullo against her will. She has no doubt that it is he. Now I need to tell you something else Vito has discovered, and I hate to tell you this under the circumstances, but Michel Reynard has a conviction for paedophilia dating back to when he was twenty-one years old.'

'Oh no!' Claudia was deeply shocked.

Gastone continued. 'Apparently, he was jailed for six months, put on a year's probation and is on the sex crimes register. He molested his thirteen-year-old sister, and his father turned him in to the police. When he came out of prison and finished his probationary period, his father sent him to Canada to get him out of the way. He only returned to Belgium after his father died.'

Claudia was speechless. She said nothing, trying to breathe normally. And Anya was with him inside the trullo. She felt nauseous.

'Gastone…' What terrible scenario had she dragged all of them into with her foolish marriage to Michel? This was a nightmare. She pushed the hair back from her face and realised it was damp with perspiration. The stress was eating at her insides. *Anya!* she thought, looking at the trullo, squat in the dark, lit by the moon and a few stars. The silence around her was intense. Just the sound of the night crickets, humming away, unconcerned about the drama playing out beside them. She could hear her heartbeat in her ears, and she was aware of a crawling sensation at the sides of her forehead, like worms trying to burrow their way into her brain.

'Ring me when you need me,' he said. And they hung up.

In the meantime, Janet had moved a few metres away and was talking on her mobile phone. Claudia could see her patent leather leggings glowing in the moonlight,. She was talking to John Rivers. 'We don't know what to do,' she said, turning off her phone and turning to Claudia. 'He hasn't a clue how to handle this, but he's coming up to give us moral support.'

Claudia had met John briefly at the kennels, and the thought of any support, be it moral or practical, cheered her somewhat. They decided to sit in the car while they waited for something to happen, and she did not discuss her conversation with Gastone. She needed time to digest the awfulness of what she had just learnt. They both needed to rest their weary feet too and eased their shoes off in the comfort of the car. Claudia moved the car onto the verge opposite the gate, and they saw the headlights of another Vespa approach them, coming up the hill.

'It's John. On his scooter,' Janet said.

At that moment, the gate flew open, and the blue SUV backed swiftly past them, doing a quick turn, and speeding down the lane before they could gather their thoughts. Claudia tried to get a glimpse of the driver, but his face was in shadow. The squeal of tyres gaining purchase on the narrow laneway was followed by a sickening thud, and John flew, headfirst, into the low stone wall. The back wheel of his Vespa was completely crushed as the SUV picked up speed and disappeared from sight.

'Oh my god!' they both cried. Claudia wanted to tear off after the SUV; she had seen Anya's pale face in the passenger seat as it sped past, but they had to attend to John, so they rushed over to him, shocked. John was lying on his back against the wall. He was not moving. She dialled 1-1-8 and held for an operator.

The two women crouched beside John, afraid to touch him in case they made things worse. He was breathing; his face was covered in earth and grass. His eyes were closed. All they could do was wait and pray that he was all right. At least, he had been wearing his crash helmet, so they hoped that it would have helped.

It was the longest fifteen minutes either Claudia or Janet had ever spent. Janet rang Penny, and she arrived, panic-stricken, shrieking her husband's name, just before the ambulance arrived. The blue lights and siren were loud in the silent countryside, and John suddenly opened his eyes.

'John!' screamed Penny. 'Look, his eyes are open.'

By the time the medics had put him on the stretcher to transport him into the back of the ambulance, John was wide awake and insisting he had just bumped his head and had only been knocked out for a minute. The medical team insisted on taking him to the *pronto soccorso* at Ostuni Hospital to check him out. Penny said she'd keep in touch as she dashed to her car, ready to follow the ambulance.

At this stage, Claudia was frantic about Anya. 'What are we going to do?' she moaned. 'We'll never find them now. We've no idea where they've gone.'

Suddenly, Claudia's phone lit up with a brief text. Anya. It appeared that she had managed to dash off a message. It contained one word: Polignano.

'They've gone to Polignano a Mare!' She grabbed Janet's arm. 'Anya just texted me. Let's go!'

As they climbed back into the Merc, Janet phoned Angelo to fill him in on what had happened. 'I'll turn the car and head there too.'

Claudia's phone rang, her hands-free system kicked in, and she heard Gastone's voice. 'What's happening?'

'Anya has, it seems, gone in the direction of Polignano a Mare in, I assume, Michel's car. We're on our way there. The fact that she texted me must mean she's worried. Or frightened.' She tried to breathe, in, out, in, out. Her heart was still pounding in her ears.

'I'll leave right now and meet you there. I can park in the street that faces the entrance to the old town and meet you at the arch.'

'How about Daisy? Will she be okay on her own?' Claudia was concerned about this delicate little woman who appeared to have suffered a major ordeal.

'Vito is here now, and he can keep an eye on her. He's keen to question her too, and perhaps she'll talk to him about this Misha character. Or Michel, or whoever he is.'

'Okay, Gastone.' Now, on the SP17, she accelerated towards Ostuni. 'We should be in Polignano in about forty minutes.'

'How much of a head start did Anya get?'

Claudia thought. 'About fifteen minutes or so. See you there.' And they drove off into the dark night.

CHAPTER THIRTY-THREE
ANYA

'Oh no!' Anya screamed, twisting in her seat as the car sped down the laneway to the main road. 'You've knocked over poor John. Please turn around. We need to see if he's injured.'

He kept driving, disregarding her distraught state. In fact, the more Anya screamed at him to turn around, the faster he drove.

'Where are we going?' She was trying not to cry.

In answer, he grabbed her mobile phone and began to text as he drove. Just one word; she could see it was Polignano.

'Are we going to Polignano a Mare?'

His face was rigid. 'Your mother destroyed our lives.' He looked at her briefly, the lights of Ostuni as they sped downhill past the White City, illuminating his face. 'I know you agree with me. She should have stayed. One year of marriage, and she took my home, the only real home I have ever known. She didn't even try to work things out.'

Anya silently agreed, but only up to a point. She knew there were things that her mother refused to discuss but had no idea what they were.

Exiting the Strada Statale on the approach to Polignano a Mare, he parked close to the high-arched gate to the old town, a place that was special to Anya, and where she had always loved to spend time, perhaps to have lunch with her mother in one of the little restaurants tucked away in the side streets, or just to wander and browse around the pretty shops. She loved the town's paved streets and white houses, its bell tower and, most of all, its position on the top of the stratified cliffs where the international cliff diving championships were held each year.

Taking her arm, he hurried her past the gate and onto a high bridge which Anya knew gave a stunning view of the beach, surrounded by the famous cliffs. They stopped almost exactly in the middle, and she looked down onto the roofs of restaurants and at the path that led to the beach. There were several couples and small family groups wandering around, laughing, chatting, obviously enjoying themselves and having a late-night stroll after dinner. The street lights cast a friendly glow.

'Now we wait,' he said, holding her arm in a firm grasp as they leaned against the railings.

Anya's head for heights was not great, and she looked down at the drop with discomfort, made even more uncomfortable by the look on his familiar face.

'Let me go, please,' she asked. 'You know I can't stand heights. I'd prefer to get off this bridge if you don't mind, this railing is pretty low.'

He held her arm even tighter. She looked up at him and what she saw made her recoil with fear.

He said, almost cheerfully, 'Don't worry. You'll be leaving this bridge shortly. There's a moment of reckoning first.'

***

CLAUDIA

Polignano a Mare was a pretty Pugliese town, perched on top of spectacular, stratified cliffs on the Adriatic Sea. It was a town that most visitors to Puglia had at the top of their wish list and longed to see. Both Claudia and Janet had each visited a few times, for lunch or aperitivi with friends.

All three cars arrived at their destination within a few minutes of one another, all having managed to find parking spots along Via Martiri di Dogali and hurried across the street to the entrance to the old town. Gastone had been the first to arrive and was waiting for them patiently. Claudia and Janet arrived just as Angelo pulled up behind them.

As they stood there, trying to decide which way to go, Gastone broke into a run, dashing away along the street. 'They're on the bridge,' he shouted over his shoulder as he ran.

The high Ponte Borbonico, with its many tall arches, crossed the opening to the famous Lama di Monachile, from where the world-famous cliff diving could be watched. It was late at night now, but there were still some people having a postprandial stroll who turned to stare at the running man. In the middle of the Ponte Borbonico stood Anya, her back to the iron railings, high over the roofs of some restaurants, rocks and a cobbled footpath leading to the bay. Facing her, his back to them, was a tall man, his light-coloured hair lit up by the streetlamps.

Claudia, Janet, and Angelo hurried after Gastone, and Claudia called, 'Anya!' Her daughter turned in her direction.

Gastone now appeared to be strolling, trying to look like a regular tourist. He took a few photos with his phone and tried to give the impression that he was disinterested in the couple, who were pressed against the railings about halfway across. Gastone managed to get close, so close that when Anya saw him, recognition flooded her features, but she gave no other indication. The man was holding her by the arm. It looked as though he were about to throw her over the railing, and he barely registered Gastone, so focused was he on whatever it was he had in mind.

When he heard Claudia's voice, he turned to face her, still holding Anya firmly, his look challenging.

Claudia's voice was barely above a whisper as she realised who she was looking at. 'Jan! Oh, my goodness, it's Jan!'

Michel's troubled son, Jan Reynard, smiled at her as she walked slowly towards him. She saw that he had Anya's arm in a tight grip.

He looked intently at Claudia and focused his intense gaze on her face. He looked smug and self-satisfied, a look that Claudia remembered only too well. He gave Anya a brief shake, threat implicit as if to remind everyone that he was deadly serious.

'You got here quickly,' he sneered. 'Sending the text was part of the plan. So, we finally meet again.' Realising that people were getting too close to him he shouted, 'Stay back, everyone.' But Gastone edged closer, just out of Jan's range of vision, realising that he only had eyes for Claudia.

She was silent, and Jan spoke again.

'Ah! Claudia. I've been waiting for you. You're just in time to say goodbye to your precious daughter.' He gave Anya another nudge.

'What?' Anya, terrified, screamed, 'No! Jan! Let me go!' She struggled to prise herself out of his vice-like grip, but he just tightened his hold on her arm.

'It's Jan! Michel's son,' she exclaimed to everyone and no one in particular. 'But why? Why are you threatening Anya? What has she done?'

'Anya has done nothing; this is about making you finally pay for the way you treated my father.' He paused, and his eyes took on a gleam that looked like a film of tears. 'Papa's life ended the day you threw him out of his own home,' he announced. 'Everything that happened is your fault. Now it's an eye for an eye and all that that implies.' He tightened his grip on Anya, who looked terrified, her eyes bugging with fear, as he continued. 'After you forced him to leave Antwerp, he had to go back to Turnhout to live with his mother and brother. He was past his prime, too depressed to begin again. It was all too much for him. His life was over.' His voice rose. 'You know what you did to him.'

'Oh goodness!' Claudia was shocked. As much as she had loathed Michel, she would never have wished so much pain on him, but she had felt merciless at the time. Shock coursed through her body, and she began to shake. 'Please, Jan! Please let Anya go. How could you threaten her like this? To consider pushing her from a bridge. Your step-sister, as she is, after all.' She tried to keep her voice calm, even though she was quaking with terror. Anya would never survive such a fall. 'Take me instead,' she pleaded.

A crowd had begun to gather. A couple of phones flashed, and Claudia prayed that someone had called the polizia. But her terror over Anya pushed all other thoughts from her head.

Jan gave a weird smile. 'Papa always promised to make you pay dearly for what you did to him. So now I'm here to take the ultimate revenge.' The man was obviously mad.

Claudia, though terrified, decided to change tack slightly, perhaps to divert him, keep him talking. 'And what about poor Daisy?'

The man sneered. 'That stupid little woman. What a pathetic creature!'

'How did you know where we were?' Claudia wanted to get to the bottom of everything while he appeared to be forthcoming.

'Ha!' He giggled, sounding unhinged. 'That was simple! I contacted Anya through Facebook a few months ago. Too easy. She was happy to tell me everything: where you were, about your posh new palazzo. You had no clue, did you, how much she loved Papa.' He paused, grimacing.

Claudia kept silent. Waiting.

He continued. 'Then you went to Dublin when your dad was ill, and Anya gave me a guided tour of your grand palazzo. Poor Papa. He should have been there with you. I saw a set of keys hanging in the kitchen and pocketed them when Anya was out of the room. Simple!' Now his face darkened. 'It was good to enter your home when nobody was there, though even more interesting when you were actually there. You look very alluring when you're asleep on your terrace.' He gave a suggestive laugh. 'And all that expensive underwear!' He spat the words at her.

Claudia recoiled inwardly but kept cool as Jan was briefly lost in his sexual reverie. She watched, holding her breath, as Gastone lunged forward and grabbed Anya by her free arm, the element of surprise helping him to pull her abruptly out of Jan's grip. As she clutched onto Gastone, leaping away from the vertiginous drop, Jan lost his balance and toppled backwards over the railings, feet in the air, then out of sight. The crowd moaned, women screamed, people rushed to look over the railing. Gastone put his arms around Claudia and Anya, and they all bent to see Jan, on his back, arms and legs spread wide, fifteen metres below them on the cobbled path to Lama Monachile, the famous bay, for a moment about to be infamous.

Gastone held the two women tightly, feeling them shake. Claudia rested her head on his shoulder.

'Thank you,' she murmured and nestled closer. He tightened his hold on her, and they stood pressed together.

They were all deeply shocked. Angelo had his arms around Janet, and they stood beside their friends, finding it difficult to believe what they had just witnessed. They heard the sirens of the police and ambulance, and suddenly, the bridge and its surroundings were being cleared by uniformed men wearing white holsters attached to their belts, complete with guns. Only their little group was left standing isolated in the middle. Another ambulance carved its way through the growing crowd, lights flashing, siren piercing the still night air, and they soon found themselves wrapped in foil blankets and being treated for shock.

Claudia held her daughter's hand, both still trembling, aware of how much worse it could have been.

So, it had been Jan all along, Claudia thought to herself. *That strange young man became even stranger.*

Jan was pronounced dead at the scene, and a stretcher bore his broken body to the waiting ambulance, which had parked under the bridge. It was an eerie sight.

Much later that evening, well after midnight, they all trooped back to the palazzo. Vito had been waiting for them and took his leave, pleading an early morning ahead, before his departure for the Veneto.

Claudia thanked him profusely and hoped they would meet again under happier circumstances.

Anya went straight to bed, her face pale, her lips tight. Black circles shadowed her eyes, which looked haunted. The doctor had given her a mild sedative, and Claudia hoped it would help her to sleep.

She offered them a nightcap and they sipped Cognac from Waterford cut-glass tumblers as they sat around the sitting room in various attitudes of exhaustion.

Angelo, Janet, and Daisy stood up to go. The women seemed to be the worse for wear; a mixture of tiredness and, perhaps, an excess of alcohol had left them looking worn out. Daisy had cried and cried when they told her that Jan was dead. Angelo offered to drive them back to Casalini, and they gratefully accepted, leaving Claudia and Gastone alone together.

'I should go too,' he said, remaining standing after the others had left. 'I just wanted to be sure you were feeling okay.'

Claudia had had more to drink than she was accustomed to and wobbled a bit as she walked over to him and put her arms around his waist, her head on his chest.

'Thank you, Gastone. You're wonderful. Has anyone ever told you that before?'

He looked at her and held her close. 'I must go, Claudia,' he said softly. 'Just for the record, I think you're wonderful too.' He sounded so serious that she looked up at his handsome face, suddenly a bit more sober, a question lingering in the air.

He bent to kiss her and, as their lips met, she felt a surge of something that she could not quite identify. Desire, certainly, but also a warm sensation somewhere around her heart. Something she was unaccustomed to feeling. She wanted him to stay, to hold her all night long. But he pulled away. Gently.

'I'll see you tomorrow. Get some sleep. You'll have to have a long talk to Anya when she's feeling better.'

Next morning, she phoned her father to tell him what had happened, all the details. They spoke for about an hour, and he insisted on bringing his trip to Ostuni forward.

'I'll be on the next available flight,' he insisted. 'I'm fine now. The doctors have told me I can fly, just to take it easy when I get there.' He would brook no discussion or argument on the subject. He was adamant. 'I want to talk to Anya about all this. We can talk to her together.'

He was as good as his word, arriving the following day. She met him at Bari Airport and drove him to Ostuni, just over an hour's drive. 'I've taken some time off work; they need my input less and less now that I'm semi-retired. But I haven't had a proper holiday in ages, and I'm determined to make the most of my time here.' He mopped his brow. 'It's pretty hot here, don't you think?'

Claudia smiled. She was accustomed to the hot weather by now and regularly swam in the sea down at Bosco Verde, a long sandy beach with umbrellas and sun loungers for hire in summer. There was parking available under the pine trees and a nice restaurant where she loved to sit in the shade and have a light lunch with her Kindle for company. It made her feel calm, almost blissful. She decided to take her father there during his visit.

'We'll go to the beach, Dad. We can swim in the sea. That'll cool you down.'

He cheered up visibly, much to her relief. She wanted him to be as relaxed as possible.

Arriving back at her palazzo, Anya had just returned from the kennels, and she greeted her grandfather with loving enthusiasm. He hugged her to him. Goodness, she was taller than he was! How she had grown! Or had he shrunk? She didn't want to think about the possibility that her father was actually getting old.

That evening, Claudia cooked for the three of them; she had been tempted to invite Gastone but felt it was too soon for him to meet her father. All the same, just as she was about to pour an aperitivo for her family, the buzzer sounded, and it was Gastone himself. He had decided to call by, and she had to admit, she was glad to set a fourth place at the table.

Sean knew all about Gastone's involvement in the search for Michel, and they seemed to hit it off well, not alluding to the subject in front of Anya, who was silent for most of the evening, pushing her food around her plate, eating barely anything.

After dinner, as Sean sipped his soda water, he was not allowed alcohol for a while — doctor's orders — he informed them unhappily, he addressed Anya directly.

'We need to talk, my girl,' he said.

'So serious, Grandpa.'

'Very serious,' he agreed.

Claudia beckoned to Gastone, and they went outside onto the terrace to finish their digestivi. 'Dad wants to tell Anya the whole story. She needs to know, but she doesn't trust me on the subject of Michel, and we think she'll take her grandfather seriously. I can't even broach the subject any more,' she told him as they stood close together overlooking the pretty courtyard. The sun had already set, and there was still a mauve tint in the sky. 'Don't you think the sunsets here in Puglia are the most stunning ever, anywhere?'

Gastone took her hand in his and studied her face. He said nothing, but his eyes were tender. 'I must go soon. But I was thinking, before I return to the Veneto, let's do a bit of exploring with your father. How about we take him over to Alberobello and Locorotondo tomorrow or the following day? I'd enjoy that myself. I haven't visited these places for years.'

Claudia accepted gratefully, and they agreed on a trip for the following day. He kissed her goodbye gently and left.

Many tearful hours later, Anya climbed into her mother's bed and put her head on her shoulder. 'I'm sorry, Mum,' was all she said. No further words were necessary.

Next morning, they all got into Gastone's SUV and drove to Alberobello, the town of one thousand five hundred trulli, where they climbed the hills and explored the narrow streets, stopping to purchase a gold pendant fashioned from an actual leaf. This Claudia presented to Anya, a Pugliese leaf, to bring her good luck when she returned to Ireland. She gave her daughter an affectionate hug. 'All will be well,' she reassured her.

Lunch followed in the historic circular centre of Locorotondo. They strolled past tall, narrow white houses with steeply pitched roofs — *cummerse* — which were peculiar to this pretty town. On another day, they visited Cisternino, high in the hills and ate at a *braceria*, where they chose their meat and watched it being cooked, then ate it, washed down with a jug of the local wine, outdoors in the narrow street at a table with a red-and-white tablecloth. Braised lamb in Ceglie Messapica and puréed fava beans with chicory in Martina Franca meant that every town they visited yielded up further culinary delights.

Over the days that followed, apart from their visits to the hill towns of the Valle d'Itria, they spent time on the beach too. Gastone was always with them, as he and Sean had really hit it off and had become good friends. Claudia was pleased; her father's opinion meant a lot to her, and she was wary of falling in love again. She questioned herself constantly. Then she would look at the two men sitting together on a pair of sun loungers, talking about sport and politics, and she relaxed completely for the first time in many months.

CHAPTER THIRTY-FOUR
CLAUDIA

One week later, Claudia drove her father and Anya to the airport for their flight to Dublin, but not before Sean had voiced his high opinion of Gastone. 'A true gentleman,' he said. And that told Claudia a lot.

Anya was due to start college in a few weeks and had a lot to organise in advance. Claudia was happy to know that she and her father were together. They could support one another and heal in their different ways. She watched them disappear through customs clearance with a lump in her throat — her tall, slim daughter and her slightly stooped father, who still had a spring in his step after all.

Returning to the palazzo that afternoon, she showered and slid into her favourite silk kimono, then reclined full length on the sofa, windows open, and a slight breeze keeping the room cool. She picked up her notebook and began drafting some ideas for her new book. She felt ready to tackle it now, refreshed and full of optimism about the future.

The buzzer sounded, and Claudia reluctantly dragged herself to her feet. She was tired and wanted to rest. It was Gastone.

She led him through to the sitting room, and he sat opposite her on an armchair. She was conscious that she was wearing only a silky robe and gathered it close around her. 'I really liked your father,' he said. 'It was special to be included in all your family trips. Thank you.'

'Oh, Gastone! It was such a pleasure to see Dad coming out of himself like that. He must be bone-weary of always being surrounded by women.' She laughed, then stopped when she saw his eyes, the way he was looking at her.

Before she could react, he was beside her on the sofa, and his arms were around her. The kimono slid to the floor somewhere between the sofa and the bedroom, and the sun was high in the sky the next morning before they emerged for breakfast.

***

JANET

Janet rang the bell at Mimmo's apartment and met him, once more, on the landing as she stepped from the lift. It seemed like a lifetime since she had been here the last time but, of course, it had only been a month.

'Monsieur Reynard has died,' she announced baldly. 'I want my trullo back.'

Mimmo could not hide his shock. 'What happened?' he asked, his voice strained. 'I spoke to him just a few days ago when I collected the rent. He was fine.'

'It's a long story Mimmo,' Janet said. 'You'll read about it in the news. It only happened yesterday. An accident in Polignano a Mare; he fell off the bridge.'

Mimmo escorted her inside. The apartment was empty.

'Where is everybody?' she enquired politely.

Mimmo looked surprised. 'It's August,' he replied as if that answered her question. 'They're down at the beach. They've been there since June. I go down there every evening and at weekends. We have a small villa at Rosa Marina.'

It seemed to Janet that everybody from Ostuni, decamped to the beaches of either Rosa Marina or Villanova for the summer, and the entire town was taken over by hordes of visitors from Milan and Switzerland.

'I want to return to our previous arrangement,' Janet announced before she had even sat down. 'Except that this time I can pay for it in full.' She sat down on the red velvet sofa, which was as hard as iron, and tried to look as though she purchased houses every day and that she knew what she was doing.

Mimmo looked at her, his innocent eyes wide and his lips already forming the words. 'Of course, house prices have risen a lot in the past few months. People are calling Puglia the "New Tuscany". Everyone is looking for a house here at the moment. I can sell that for a lot more now.' He sat back on the armchair, where he had sat down facing her, his small hands resting on his tracksuit-clad knees.

Janet stood up. 'Okay then, I'll find someplace else.' She was terrified that she was making a mistake and that he was, in fact, telling her the truth. But she had to try. There was a limit to her funds, and she had to be careful. She turned as if to leave, whereby Mimmo jumped to his feet.

'But an agreement is an agreement,' he said. 'I am a man of my word and, of course, I will sell you the trullo at the originally agreed price. Sit down. Sit down.' He waved at the sofa, and she sat down once more.

Her relief was huge. The trullo she loved so much would actually be hers.

They agreed to meet at the Notary Office the following day, appointment permitting. Mimmo said he would get on with the paperwork straight away.

'Can I move back in anyway?' she asked. 'If it takes a few weeks to organise, at least I'll be there. And I can pay rent in the meantime.'

Janet and Mimmo shook hands to seal the deal and, with the key to the trullo safely in her handbag, she drove back to Casalini.

Daisy was waiting for her when she returned.

'Oh, Daisy!' she exclaimed. 'I can go back into my trullo straight away. Let's pack and go over there now.' She gave Daisy a hug.

Daisy froze, her face horrified. 'Oh, Janet.' Tears formed in her eyes. 'I don't think I could go back to the trullo yet. I don't think I could face it. It's too soon. I'm sorry.'

After chatting about it at length, they walked up the hill to Donatella's house and asked if Daisy could stay on in the little house in Casalini until the purchase of her apartment in Ostuni was finalised. It would only be for about a month, maximum.

Donatella swept Daisy into a soft, scented embrace and reassured her that she could stay as long as she wanted. Daisy cried again, this time with gratitude. With Daisy, tears were never far away, and she'd had plenty to cry about recently.

CHAPTER THIRTY-FIVE
CLAUDIA

Claudia had already invited Gastone, Angelo, Janet, and Daisy to her home for dinner the following evening. As they had not managed to get through the lamb on the previous occasion, due to the drama that had unfolded, she had decided to try again. She had also invited John and Penny. John was now fully recovered from his accident, though the Vespa had not fared quite as well, having been judged a write-off. He was considering purchasing another, though Penny's face fell every time he mentioned it, so he was biding his time. He knew he would have another one before too long. She always gave in in the end. Lucas and Emma had also been invited and were coming with John and Penny. They were all highly curious to see Claudia's palazzo, very different from their country abodes. And, as Janet was now back in her trullo, there was really something to celebrate.

***

JANET

The evening started well enough. Janet and Daisy arrived together and met John, Penny, Lucas, and Emma on the street outside. Janet pressed the bell, and the door clicked open. They all trooped in, their eyes taking in the big courtyard with the curved marble steps leading upwards to the tall front door, where Claudia was standing, backlit by a soft, flattering glow.

As Janet and Daisy had been there before, though that evening had been a blur, Janet noticed how impressed the others seemed to be by their opulent surroundings. Lucas had his hair pulled back into a white ponytail, and he tugged at the elastic nervously as he mounted the stairs. Emma was dressed in a long flowing white lace dress, her long dark hair

241

drifting behind her. Penny was in a filmy wrap-around dress and sandals, her blonde hair freshly styled, while John and Lucas were wearing cotton shirts, chinos, and sockless loafers.

Claudia greeted them warmly, and Trixie dashed around happily, checking out their shoes, especially thrilled by Janet's teetering red patents. Gastone and Angelo had already arrived. Janet had wanted Angelo to drive her there, but he said he had late surgery and would go to Claudia's palazzo as soon as he was finished. He was standing there talking to Gastone with a glass of bubbly in his hand, looking self-confident and, as they pecked each other on the cheek, she could smell his fresh cologne. He was looking well, she thought.

Gastone greeted everybody formally, introducing himself to everyone in turn. His manners were impeccable, and he had an air of sophistication that was hard to miss. Janet thought he could possibly be the best-looking man she had ever seen, taken in his entirety: looks, manner, way of speaking, how he dressed. She wondered how close he was to Claudia.

After everyone was seated on the terrace with a glass of bubbly in their hands, they raised a toast to each other, happy that Anya was safe and that the man who had threatened her was no more. Nobody seemed sorry that he was dead; only Claudia appeared to be reflective. Perhaps she felt guilty every time she thought of the unnecessary death of her former stepson, Jan. She took a gulp of prosecco and sat back, trying to relax. This was the first time she had felt in any way tense in the past couple of weeks. Perhaps this dinner party was too soon for all of them.

Janet began to notice that, all through dinner, Angelo's eyes were fixed on Claudia. She felt the beginnings of fury forming in her breast. This was not what she wanted in a man. Who needed to be with someone who couldn't take his eyes off another woman? He was obviously smitten by the elegant blonde. She appeared to be all he had ever dreamed of possessing — the rich lady in the palazzo who has everything. She tried to stifle bitter thoughts; it wasn't Claudia's fault that she was beautiful and desirable, after all.

Janet was troubled by the way things were shaping up. Angelo's visits were becoming scarcer and, when he actually did show up, he seemed to only have one thing on his mind: sex. He rarely stayed overnight any more, and their relationship appeared to be fizzling out. And how about Gastone anyway? He seemed to be a close friend of Claudia's, completely at home in her palazzo. She didn't know exactly why he was there, but he was a lovely man, and she felt a real frisson of envy for Claudia's effortless corralling of these two gorgeous men. Gastone was obviously smitten too, devotedly topping up everyone's wine and constantly asking Claudia if she was okay. *If she were a cat, she'd be purring,* she thought nastily, taking a large swig of wine to wash down a soft, brittle piece of fig crostata, which melted in her mouth.

After a particularly delicious dinner, they moved over to the sofas, and Gastone poured brandies or limoncello for everybody. A plate of biscotti was placed on the low coffee table, and everyone sat back and relaxed.

Except for Janet.

She'd had enough. Having just moved back into her beloved trullo, she couldn't wait to resume her interrupted experience of paradise. Giving Angelo a sour look, she thought, *who needs a man anyway? More trouble than they're worth.* Thereby, unconsciously, echoing the sentiments of women everywhere, especially those whose partners have a wandering eye.

'Daisy! Let's go.' She rose abruptly, startling Daisy, who was enjoying an especially large tumbler of postprandial brandy, her face dreamy and peaceful in these comfortable surroundings.

Daisy staggered to her feet and reached for Janet's proffered arm, clawing at her Balinese shawl, which was in danger of tripping her up. Angelo barely noticed that they were leaving, muttering a disinterested goodbye as they left the room, his eyes following Claudia's shapely rear as she got up to say goodbye to the two women.

The exit of Janet and Daisy worked like a dog-whistle on the others as John and Penny rose from the sofa, followed by Lucas and Emma.

They let themselves out onto the street, found their respective cars, and Janet hurried home to her precious trullo after dropping Daisy off in Casalini. She needed to be alone, to think.

***

CLAUDIA

Back at the palazzo, all was not well.

It seemed that both Gastone and Angelo were waiting for the other to leave. Claudia, who had been uncomfortably aware of Angelo's eyes wandering over her body all evening, wanted him to leave but did not want to be rude.

Angelo stretched lazily and looked at his watch. 'Time to go,' he finally announced and rose from the armchair where he had been draped for the past couple of hours. 'I'll let myself out. Don't worry. You stay there.' He disappeared through the sitting room door, giving a small wave.

Gastone sat and finished his glass of brandy. He looked utterly relaxed, and Claudia felt herself relax too. His presence had become a deep comfort to her.

She smothered a yawn, and Gastone immediately stood up, the soft lamps emphasising his elegant frame, and his longish black hair with the silver wings shone under the chandelier. Claudia suddenly felt a wave of something resembling love for this wonderful man who had saved her daughter's life just a few short weeks ago. She owed him a great deal.

They stood facing one another in the vestibule. He took her hand, looking down into her eyes with a warm smile. He lowered his face, and she felt his lips on hers. They kissed gently, and he slid his arms around her, holding her close. She felt herself melt with desire in his embrace. He then kissed the top of her head. 'I'll call you in the morning. Let's go someplace quiet and talk. There are some important things I want to say to you. To tell you.' He stroked her cheek gently. And with that, he was gone. Her arms felt empty.

Claudia turned off all the lights downstairs, just leaving a table lamp glowing dimly in the hall. She went through to her bedroom, closing the door behind her. She slipped into the bathroom and had a quick shower. Naked, she approached the bed, where she experienced an acute shock. There was someone there already. A head with neatly trimmed black hair lay on her pillow.

As she gasped, trying to cover her nakedness, the covers were thrown back, and Angelo beckoned her to join him. 'Come, my beautiful,' he cooed seductively, reaching for her. She jumped back, shocked and fled back towards the bathroom, grabbing the first garment she laid her hands on, a filmy negligee that left nothing to the imagination and threw it on. She then returned to the bedroom and stood far enough away from the bed that he could not grab her.

'Angelo,' she said. 'What are you doing here? Are you crazy?'

'Crazy for you,' he said. 'Come to me, beautiful.'

'Absolutely not!' Claudia exclaimed. 'Please go. You already have a girlfriend. This really is not appropriate.' She tried to sound controlled, but her heart raced with fear. What if he forced himself on her? She tried to pull the tiny silk negligee closer to try to cover her nakedness, knowing it was futile.

Angelo began to climb reluctantly from the bed, and Claudia had to avert her gaze when she saw how aroused he had become. She felt nothing but embarrassment for him, tinged with indignation at his presumption that she would have joined him in bed.

'I know I didn't misread the situation,' he insisted. 'You want me. I saw how you looked at me.' He added, his voice low and seductive, 'You don't know what you're missing.'

He advanced towards her; arms outstretched. He was, obviously, a man unused to being rejected by women. At that moment, the doorbell buzzed. Exiting her bedroom, moving as fast as she could in her bare feet, she approached the small screen beside the main door to see who it was. It was Gastone. She jumped back as though she had been electrocuted. Then she thought that at least he would provide protection from Angelo, as she felt threatened by him and was fearful that he might actually rape her. She buzzed the downstairs entrance and rushed to open the main door in the hall.

'I'm so terribly sorry to arrive like this.' He ran a hand through his long hair, looking distracted. 'But I left my phone behind. I know how tired you were, and I hope you hadn't gone to bed.' Claudia could see him take in her skimpy attire with interest. He reached for her, about to slide his arms around her.

Before she had time to tell him what was happening, she saw him look past her, over her shoulder, while his face changed to bemusement. She looked around. To her horror, Angelo was standing in her bedroom doorway, as naked as the day he was born. His hands cupped his genitals, and he smiled at Gastone, a knowing look on his face.

'What brings you back, Gastone?' he asked, his voice laden with irony.

'I'm sorry to have disturbed you,' Gastone replied pointedly. 'I left my phone behind.'

He strode into the sitting room and returned with it in his hand. Angelo had disappeared into the bedroom once more, and Claudia was entirely shocked and tongue-tied.

'Goodnight, Claudia,' Gastone said gently as he headed for the stairs.

'Don't go,' she said. But he had already left.

She dashed through to the kitchen and locked herself inside, waiting to hear what Angelo would do next. There was a knock on the door.

'I take it that's a no then?' Angelo chuckled in amusement. 'I'm not a rapist, by the way. I just thought that this was what you wanted.'

Five minutes later, she heard the hall door close, and he was gone. She sat in the kitchen for a very long time until the sun rose, and the kitchen filled with the dawn light. What had she done?

How had this man decided that she was the sort of woman who would happily get into bed with him, someone she barely knew? What sort of messages did she send out? Gastone must now think her a slut too. She remembered Anya's words when she called her a tart and put her head in her hands, her face hot. Was that how everyone saw her? She thought about Michel, now dead, she assumed and tried to recall Jan's exact words. Had it been her fault? She was unsure. Her father had tried to reassure her, but it was no use; she felt shocked and beaten by everything.

Next morning, she had a message from Gastone.

Decided to return to the Veneto straight away. Wishing you a happy life in Ostuni. Gastone.

She felt a lump in her throat and gulped it down. She had never felt so alone.

CHAPTER THIRTY-SIX
DAISY

Daisy had thought that she could never feel happy or excited again. But that changed when she visited the estate agent and asked if the little apartment in the old town of Ostuni was still available. It was. And, what's more, the paperwork was all ready for her to sign. It had been for the past month.

She clapped her little hands together in joy, just like she used to do before the man entered her life and took it over so completely. It had been difficult to feel anything since her ordeal, but now she had a new purpose in life — her little apartment.

The apartment, at the top of the old town, close to the cathedral, needed quite a lot of work to make it fully habitable. However, Daisy was so impatient to begin her new life and forget about the old one that she decided to move in straight away. Anything was better than sitting around revisiting the past.

Her estate agent recommended a builder who was accustomed to working in the old town. Giuseppe arrived to take a look around and organise a quotation. He was a tall man in his mid-forties, she guessed. His hair was very curly and neatly cut, and he had a kind manner. Unfortunately, he spoke not one word of English and Daisy's Italian was limited to ordering lunch or asking where the bathroom was. But Google Translate came to their rescue, and they managed to communicate quite well. She would set it to *English to Italian* and speak. He would read what she had said in Italian and would respond when she changed it to *Italian to English*, and so they communicated perfectly.

First of all, the bathroom needed new fixtures: a new shower, loo, basin, and bidet, plus tiles were first on the list, and she decided to tackle this project right away. She needed a new kitchenette too, and the shutters on the two windows with the stunning view of the Adriatic Sea were rusty and needed replacing. She also needed heating of some form or another, as she planned to spend most of the year there.

Giuseppe seemed so capable that Daisy began to rely on his advice, as he called every day to see how she was getting on. She saw him as a "real" man, someone she could count on to do manly things. He brought his men along to take the sanitaryware out of the bathroom. Her next-door neighbour told her she could use his bathroom for a day or two, and she gratefully accepted the offer.

Daisy stood there, staring at the bathroom, minus the old tiles and sanitaryware. She was terrified at how it looked, having never had to deal with a project like this before. Giuseppe was standing opposite her, also examining the floor and walls, but completely relaxed. Daisy looked at him for reassurance and their eyes locked. The look they exchanged was full of meaning, and her heart beat a little faster than usual.

Next day, Giuseppe's men arrived to install the tiles. He arrived later with a loaf of freshly baked bread. She was touched and gave him her "little girl lost" smile. He smiled back shyly, took out his mobile, and spoke into the translation app. 'Sei una donna molto bella,' he said. And she read, *you are a very beautiful woman.*

As Daisy soon discovered, it was incredible what you could say to the Google Translate lady who translated everything they said without so much as a blush.

***

CLAUDIA

Claudia's mobile rang. She pulled it out of her bag and saw it was Olivia.

'Olivia! How are you?'

'Am I speaking to Auntie Claudia?' A happy voice rang out. 'Your new nephew is looking forward to meeting you.' Olivia laughed.

Claudia was speechless. 'Olivia! You've given birth! A boy! That's fantastic.' Joy bubbled inside her. Her godson had been born.

Francesco Daniele di Falco had arrived within half an hour of Olivia arriving at the hospital in Venice. A large, healthy baby with a mop of black hair was put into her arms and, as she and Niccolò looked at their new baby son, Olivia felt completely happy. Her little family, she thought. *I'm going to be the best wife and mother ever.* The word

248

"mother" gave her a deep thrill. Suddenly, she knew that she now had a lifetime commitment to this tiny person wrapped in a blue blanket. She was sure nobody had ever felt this depth of love before, just like most new mothers do, in fact, though she wouldn't have believed anyone who mentioned that. Hers was surely a unique experience.

Claudia had told Olivia all about Jan's awful death. She had told Olivia about her deep feeling of guilt over the whole thing. She still cringed inwardly every time she thought about it.

'You mustn't feel guilty.' Olivia's voice was indignant. 'You had to get Michel out of your life, and it's not your fault that Jan felt he had to avenge his father's fall from grace. I think they must both have been mad perverts. Look at what Jan did to Daisy. Absolutely disgusting!'

Though Claudia agreed with everything Olivia said, she still couldn't help feeling guilty, but now was not the time to be negative. Olivia had a beautiful baby boy; she herself was going to be the godmother and would soon be going to stay at Villa di Falco in the beautiful Euganean Hills for the christening.

As if Olivia could read Claudia's mind, she asked, in a casual voice, 'How did things go with Gastone? He won't discuss his visit to Ostuni at all, no matter how much I try to draw him out. Did something happen?'

Claudia did not want to discuss what had happened with Gastone over the phone. Olivia was celebrating the birth of her baby son and now was not the time to burden her with such a sad tale. A love story with a sordid ending, she thought. She missed Gastone every day, thought about him all the time and wondered how she could put things right. But she could not erase from her mind the look of horror and disbelief that had transformed his gentle features when he saw Angelo standing naked, leering at him suggestively in her hallway.

'Let's talk when I get to the Veneto,' she said. 'I want to start at the beginning and tell you exactly what happened. It's not something I want to chat about over the phone.'

Now that Olivia had had her baby and Claudia was due to visit her, she decided to tell her cousin what had transpired that fateful night in the apartment when she had found Angelo naked in her bed.

CHAPTER THIRTY-SEVEN
CLAUDIA

It was early December, and the skies were clear as Claudia's flight from Brindisi arrived in Venice. Wheeling her suitcase into the arrivals hall, she was met by a well-dressed, dapper man who was holding a sign with her name. He identified himself as Antonio who, along with his wife Paola, worked at Villa di Falco in the Euganean Hills. He was warm and friendly, chatting happily about the new baby, as he drove her the one-hour journey to Galzignano.

Crunching up the gravel drive, which wound its way towards the villa, Claudia was excited to see the famous gardens, open to the public on certain days, the pride and joy of Olivia's husband Count Niccolò di Falco. Everything was immaculate. Against the backdrop of the Euganean Hills, the fountains sprayed shining plumes of water into the air and birds called to one another in the trees. Then the villa came into view. It was enormous; she could see the main house with two jutting wings, huge ornate chimneys, and it had a general air of grandeur and opulence.

As they approached the front door, it was flung open, and Olivia came rushing down the steps to greet her. Claudia jumped from the Range Rover and threw herself into her cousin's embrace. She looked up to see Niccolò approaching, arms outstretched, a welcoming smile on his handsome face.

'We've so much to talk about,' Olivia said, linking Claudia's arm and escorting her inside, up a wide sweeping staircase to the piano nobile, the main floor of the villa.

Paola, the long-time housekeeper at the villa, was sitting beside a crib on one side of the room. Claudia could hear happy gurgles coming from it and went to have a look. A tiny baby boy, his brown eyes shining, a thick thatch of black hair, hands and feet waving in the air, was the cause of the gurgling sounds. He froze, eyes widening when he saw

Claudia and looked up at her in seeming amazement. She took one of his tiny hands in hers and felt an immediate bond.

'Francesco Daniele,' she said. 'I'm your cousin Claudia, and I'm thrilled to meet you.'

He kicked his feet in acknowledgement of the introduction and went back to making cooing sounds and staring in fascination at his hands.

'Well?' Olivia was beside her, pride and happiness glowing from every pore.

'He's beautiful. Just beautiful.' Claudia put her arms around Olivia and hugged her. 'Well done, you clever girl.'

'And me?' enquired Niccolò with a smile. So, she hugged him too.

After dinner that evening, all three of them sat around the fire. Francesco was in his crib in the master bedroom, and a monitor had been installed so that they could see and hear him the entire time. Paola was hovering around, obviously thrilled about her new set of responsibilities. A new home help had been hired to assist her with the heavy work, and they would be staying there for the next few months. They would return to Venice around Easter, perhaps. Or not. Both Niccolò and Olivia felt that the countryside around the Euganean Hills was a healthy place to rear their son.

After a while, Niccolò got to his feet and stretched. 'I'll head upstairs and leave you two girls to chat. You've probably got lots of gossip to share, and I don't want to be a gooseberry.' He laughed in his good-natured way and bent to kiss Olivia on the cheek. 'See you later, *amore*.'

Olivia leaned forward in her armchair and topped up Claudia's glass with a splash of their homemade limoncello. 'Now, we need to talk about how things went with Gastone.' She smiled knowingly at Claudia. 'You promised you'd tell me.'

'Oh. Gastone.' She sighed and looked down at her glass as if studying it for imperfections. Finding none, she looked at Olivia. 'It didn't end well.' And she told Olivia about the feelings she had for him, how well everything seemed to be going between them in the early stage of their brand-new love affair, culminating in the disastrous evening when Angelo had appeared naked in the hall when Gastone had returned for his phone. 'Things were beginning to go well between us, to be honest, but I couldn't expect him to believe that what he saw with his own two eyes was not of my doing.'

'You didn't try to explain?'

'No. I felt it would have been pointless. The damage was done. We hadn't been together long enough at that point for me to have tried to justify a naked man in my home. I decided to let it go. It was just too humiliating. I'm positive he thinks I'm just a tart on the make.' She bowed her head, feeling ashamed.

'And Angelo? Have you seen him since?'

'Once or twice when Trixie needed her shots.' She smiled, thinking about her little dog of whom she had grown so fond. Trixie was having the time of her life at the moment, staying with John and Penny and doubtless driving Basil and Sybil to distraction with her antics. 'But not socially. No. It's strictly business. I can never forgive him for what he did, though he apologises every time I see him.'

Olivia was quiet. Then she said, 'Would you like me to talk to Gastone? It might sound better coming from me.'

'No, no. Please don't,' Claudia said. 'I couldn't bear to have to rake over the whole thing again.' She paused. 'I must say I was becoming very fond of him. He's so…' She searched for the word. 'Reassuring. He was marvellous during Anya's ordeal with Jan. I'm sure he saved her life.'

'Whatever you say, darling. I won't interfere. I found you a palazzo and almost found you the most perfect man.' She laughed. 'I got everything almost a hundred per cent right. Oh well.' She added, 'You know he'll be arriving tomorrow for the christening the following day?'

Claudia stopped breathing. 'Of course,' she said, her heart pounding. 'It's just for a couple of days. I'll be fine. Don't worry.'

Olivia was concerned. Two people she loved dearly and, as far as she was concerned, were made for each other, needed a bit of help to restart their friendship, wherever it might lead. She lay awake in bed that night, thinking about the right course of action.

Over breakfast the next morning, Olivia said, 'Claudia, won't you stay on for Christmas? It's only a week away. We'd love to have you with us. Please say yes.' She looked to Niccolò for support, and he agreed wholeheartedly.

'That sounds wonderful,' Claudia said, 'but I was going to go to Dublin to spend Christmas with Dad and Anya. Your parents will be there too and a friend of Anya's from college.'

'Well! There you are. You won't even be missed. Our parents will spend their time gossiping about us, so if you're there, they won't be able to do that. And Anya will be happy with her pal. You must stay. Please say yes. Please!'

Claudia was unable to resist the lure of staying here at the villa, the weather so perfect, walks among the vineyards and olive groves. 'Yes. Thank you, Olivia. I'd love that. Yes, I'd love to stay if you're sure I won't be in the way. Your first Christmas with baby Francesco, after all.'

'We'll have a wonderful time. I'm longing to show you around. Three days here was never going to be enough. Give your dad a ring. He'll understand perfectly.' Having already chatted to Sean earlier that morning, she knew he would not put up a fight.

Later that day, Claudia curled up in a comfortable linen-covered armchair in a corner of the piano nobile. She was reading a novel that she had found on one of the bookshelves and was deeply engrossed when she heard a car on the gravel below. She craned her neck and saw that it was a large black BMW which pulled up underneath her window. Her heart raced when she saw the elegant figure of Gastone climb out, open the boot, and take out a weekend case. He then disappeared out of her line of vision, and she could hear him greeting Paola in the vestibule downstairs.

The familiar sound of his leather loafers on the marble stairs gave her a jolt of recognition, and she sank deeper into the armchair as though she wished she could disappear inside it.

The footsteps came closer.

'Claudia?' His voice was neutral.

She looked up, and there he was — tall, dark, handsome, and much more than that. By now, her heart was hammering so loudly she was sure he could hear it. She felt her face grow hot and knew that she was blushing.

'Erm… hello, Gastone,' she said and rose to her feet, her book sliding to the floor. He bent and picked it up.

'You like Donna Leon, I see.' He was looking at the cover.

'Yes. I do.' She put out her hand for her paperback, and he handed it to her. 'How are you?' she enquired politely. 'I haven't heard from you since you left Ostuni. You must know how grateful I am for everything you did for Anya and me when you were there.'

Gastone nodded. 'That's okay, Claudia,' he said. 'Is Niccolò around, or is he outside chatting to his roses?'

'I imagine that's exactly what he's doing,' she said. 'He disappeared after lunch in his gardening gear.'

Gastone politely excused himself and hurried off to find his cousin. Paola came and retrieved his bag, wheeling it away to one of the guest bedrooms, of which there were several. Claudia took a deep breath, curled back into the armchair, unable to concentrate on one more word. She gave up, put her head back, trying to collect her thoughts, and looked out at the beauty of the tree-covered hills that surrounded the villa. She felt deflated. What had she been expecting anyway? The last time Gastone had seen her, she had been in a skimpy negligee, apparently entertaining a naked man. Her face burned with shame. How had she brought this on herself? Had she really been sending out the wrong signals to Angelo? Was she completely stupid? These questions were unanswerable, she knew.

Dinner that night was a strain for Claudia. The foursome sat around a small table in an alcove off the kitchen. The dining room was being set up for the christening the following day, and they had decided on a light meal before an early retirement. Beauty sleep was of great importance to the new mother. Paola had prepared *baccalà alla vicentina*, a great favourite of Olivia's, as it brought back memories of her first-ever lunch with Niccolò in Vicenza when they were getting to know one another. It was only a few years since they had met, but so much had happened since that it seemed like aeons ago.

Gastone was quiet over dinner and scarcely glanced in Claudia's direction. She was unaccountably upset by this and was relieved when Olivia rose, indicating that she was retiring. Claudia got up too, said her goodnights to Gastone and Niccolò, called her thanks to Paola, who was hovering in the background and retired.

The men planned to stay up to greet the family party, due to arrive at Venice Marco Polo Airport on the late flight from Dublin. This family group consisted of Olivia's parents, Daniel and Lucia, Sean, and Anya. Niccolò's sister, Francesca, and brother-in-law, Paul, would be there too. Gastone's twin sons, Matteo and Gianmichele, would be driving down from Padova sometime in the morning.

She was grateful for the silence of the great house, her four-poster bed with its crisp linen sheets and down-filled duvet for the cold Veneto nights in mid-winter.

As she drifted off, she vaguely heard voices in the hall outside her bedroom door, the rumble of suitcase wheels on the *pavimenti alla veneziana* — that wonderful terrazzo flooring, so popular in these grand Italian houses — and doors closing, murmured goodnights.

Next morning, Claudia dressed with care. Her cream linen suit with a silk blouse underneath, brown suede knee-high boots and a cashmere coat looked chic. She examined herself in the mirror. She had pulled her hair into a chignon at the back of her head, and her diamond earrings sparkled in the morning light. She had had tea in her room, preferring not to go downstairs for breakfast, as she knew Olivia was doing the same. She relished her last few minutes of solitude, as she was still feeling vulnerable in front of her family and had scarcely gone anyplace over the past couple of months.

A knock sounded at her door. It was Anya who rushed over to gather her mother into a hug. She was looking like her old self again. *Isn't youth a wonderful thing?* thought Claudia. *I wish I had that sort of resilience.* But she just hugged her daughter, then held her at arm's length while she inspected her gorgeous rose-pink coat and grey leather boots. Her hair was tied in a loose bun at the back of her head, with wispy tendrils of her long blonde hair artfully arranged on either side of her face, her blue eyes huge. She looked as elegant as her mother.

'Everyone's downstairs,' she announced. 'Let's go and join the family.'

Claudia paused to knot a long silk scarf around her neck and to pull on a pair of brown suede gloves in case the chapel was cold. She had been told that it was rarely used.

Anya linked her mother's arm firmly in her own, and they descended the stairs together. Several familiar faces turned to admire the two beautiful blondes as they approached, and they were soon enveloped in the warm hugs of their loved ones. Everyone was in a celebratory mood.

Claudia was especially happy to see Francesca. This warm, friendly woman had been a safe haven for Olivia a few years ago when times were difficult, and she'd always had a soft spot for Paul. They all then turned to admire Francesco Daniele, who was swathed in the precious christening robe that had been handed down through the last few generations of the aristocratic di Falco family. Olivia was holding him proudly for everyone to see as her proud father, Daniel, and her mother, Lucia, arrived to join them.

Two tall, handsome men were standing to one side with Gastone. They both looked just like him, though younger and taller versions and Claudia guessed they were his sons. Both wore their dark hair long, their faces clean-shaven, and they were wearing smart, well-cut suits, and silk ties. Gastone politely introduced his sons to Claudia and Anya. Matteo was, it seemed, very taken by Anya and looked at her with interest. Both young men were studying medicine at the University of Padova, and Matteo wanted to go on to specialise in paediatrics, whereas Gianmichele had not quite made up his mind which direction to take and was mulling over several options. Anya told them that she had just completed her first pre-med term of veterinary at Trinity College in Dublin.

They began the short walk to the chapel, strolling through part of the gardens, between clipped hedges on a smooth gravel path. The chapel was nestled amongst a grove of cypress trees, and Claudia thought it was the prettiest she had ever seen.

It was very small, but inside it was ornate, the walls and ceiling covered in colourful frescoes and lots of gilding. It was warm and comfortable too, the air perfumed by the cascading flowers everywhere.

The four godparents were called on by the priest who was officiating. Claudia, Francesca, Gastone, and Paul arrayed themselves on one side of the baptismal font, facing Olivia and Niccolò. Olivia handed the child to Francesca, who, as Niccolò's sister — a di Falco by birth — had a leading role in the ceremony. Francesco Daniele was quiet, looking around with interest until he felt the icy drops of Holy Water cascading on his head and decided to let fly with a few howls, whereupon everyone smiled at one another.

Claudia stood there, taking in the entire scene. The beautiful little church, the handsome, elegant people — her family — by whom she was surrounded and felt peaceful. She smiled to herself, then glanced up and saw Gastone looking down at her with an expression in his eyes that made her blush. She turned away, hurriedly, confused.

Later, everyone gathered in the huge salon at the villa. Paola and her assistant, plus Antonio, served drinks and canapés while the noise level rose dramatically. A group consisting of a combination of Italians and Irish was bound to be louder than most, Claudia thought to herself as she noticed Gastone approaching. She was talking to Francesca, who decided to leave the two of them to themselves and wandered off to chat to Gianmichele, who was, it seemed, feeling left out of the animated conversation between his brother Matteo and Anya.

'Claudia.' Gastone looked at her. 'I'm sorry. I should never have walked away from you that night at your palazzo. I should have trusted you, listened to you.' He took her hand as she closed her mouth, having realised that it had fallen open. 'Forgive me. Please.'

'Gastone,' she said. 'I should have tried to explain, but I just couldn't form the words, and then you were gone.' She paused; her face hot. 'It was just too embarrassing for words.' A sudden thought flashed into her head. 'Did Olivia tell you what happened?'

He smiled. 'Yes. She did — last night after you had gone to bed. She told me the whole story. She told me also that you felt very saddened about what had happened.'

It was Claudia's turn to smile, and she turned her radiant face to his. Out of the corner of her eye, she saw Olivia grinning mischievously as she leaned towards Niccolò and indicated the twosome smiling at one another. Niccolò smiled, obviously happy about this turn of events, realising that his wife had had a hand in this masterful piece of matchmaking between two very special people.

CHAPTER THIRTY-EIGHT
CLAUDIA

After dinner that night, Claudia and Gastone put their coats on and walked hand in hand in the gardens. Discreet lighting showed the fountains, their plumes dancing in the night air.

Pausing on a bridge, from where they could see a fountain spraying silvery droplets into the night sky, they held each other, and he told her that he had never expected to find another woman he could care about after his wife had died. He told her that his sons would find it difficult to see him with another woman who was not their beloved mother but that, surely, when they saw that he was loved once more and could put the last lonely few years behind him, looking to the future, they would come around in time.

He told her about the death of his wife and how lost and lonely he had been since she had died. 'I don't remember much about the first year after she passed, to be honest.' He looked down at the water below the bridge, inky in the dark. 'It's all a blur. That's why Niccolò and Olivia asked me to come here to their villa to heal, away from all the reminders of my past life. They saved me, really. Now that time has passed, I feel strong enough to return home. In fact, I have spent the past few months there since I returned from Ostuni.'

Claudia, in turn, told him she understood and about the fact that it had taken her years to get over the sudden death of Philip and how she had then made the greatest mistake of her life marrying Michel, imagining that he could give Anya the fatherly support she seemed to crave.

They clung to one another as though they were drowning. Claudia felt the sort of connection for Gastone that had been lacking in her life for all these years. She was going to do everything in her power to make this man happy and, in turn, she would reap the reward of being loved for herself in the way she had always wanted to be, but had never quite achieved since Philip had died, all those years ago.

For the next ten days, Claudia and Gastone spent every possible moment together. Under Olivia's benign gaze, they walked in the gardens, went Christmas shopping together in Padova, and played backgammon in the evenings. They climbed the steep mountain trails, went wine tasting at Olivia's favourite Villa Fiorita, and visited the famous olive oil producers of Valnogaredo. Everything was perfect, Claudia thought.

Anya had returned to Dublin the day after the baptism with Sean, Daniel, and Lucia. Francesca and Paul were remaining for Christmas Day, as were Gastone's two sons.

It was a merry group of family members who gathered around the tree on Christmas morning to open their presents.

The mound of wrapping paper was gaining in height as Claudia reached for a small box with her name on it. Sitting back down on her armchair, she ripped off the paper and began to open the box. Suddenly, Gastone was in front of her, down on one knee. *Oh no!* thought Claudia, as she said, 'Oh yes! Yes, I'll marry you.'

Everyone clapped and cheered. A bottle of cartizze appeared as if by magic, and a beaming Paola poured everybody a glass. Matteo and Gianmichele came forward and hugged Claudia. She looked at them nervously.

'Congratulations, Claudia,' said Matteo.

'I know you'll make Papa happy,' chimed in Gianmichele.

Claudia's heart felt full. Her life had taken a turn for the better.

But nothing is ever perfect, as Claudia would soon find out.

***

JANET

Roast turkey, honey-baked ham studded with cloves, roast potatoes, brussels sprouts, bread sauce, cranberry jelly — a traditional Irish, or English for that matter, Christmas dinner with all the trimmings. Janet stood over the stove in her kitchen, checking the sprouts with a skewer.

Her guests were sitting outside the trullo, enjoying the midday sun. She loved how mild the Pugliese climate was at this time of year. Her second Christmas in Puglia, and she was aware of how her quality of life was improving, day by day. Her previous Christmas had been spent with Donatella at her home in Casalini, surrounded by her family. It had been fun, but she had longed to have friends to cook for in her little trullo.

Daisy had just poured herself an enormous glass of wine and was watching the dogs playing together. Janet's two puppies, Mutt and Jeff, were dashing around with Stuffi, Basil, and Sybil, making a bit of a racket. A happy sound, she thought.

'You look incredibly content,' she said, topping up Janet's glass. Janet stood with her back to the stove and looked at Daisy — she was looking radiant. What a difference a few months could make. The fact that she appeared to have found a new love interest, a man she could trust, appeared to have been instrumental in helping her to relax and recover from her ordeal.

Janet herself had decided that the single life suited her well and had no intention of allowing herself to be drawn into a relationship again. She rarely saw Claudia these days. They appeared to have mutually agreed, but never said it aloud that, despite being possibly the only two Irishwomen living in Ostuni, they would never be close friends as they had little in common.

She looked past Daisy at her guests, all sitting or lounging on her garden chairs, drinking wine, waiting for the main course. Nobody was in a hurry. This was Puglia, after all.

Lucas and Emma were sitting together on her green wooden bench in the shadow of the largest olive tree, while John and Penny occupied two wrought-iron chairs. Penny had her face to the sun, and John was telling Lucas and Emma about his latest adventure with his cycling pals. Giuseppe sat quietly to one side, his eyes on Daisy through the open door. There was an atmosphere of utter tranquillity, and Janet savoured the moment.

Daisy was in the mood to chat.

'I'm so glad you've got your trullo back,' she said. 'And I'm in my sweet apartment and really in love for the first time ever.' She waved one little hand in the air; the other occupied holding her glass of wine. 'Though, I must admit,' she looked down at her glass, 'some aspects have been difficult after what happened, Giuseppe has been very understanding and patient.'

Janet raised her eyebrows in response. Time would tell. She hoped her friend would find happiness.

Daisy continued. 'That was a terrible experience back in August, very scary.'

'Well, mostly terrible for you,' Janet said, feeling affection for her friend. 'What a terrible thing to have happened. Who would have thought a young man, barely thirty years old, would have been such a perverted sadist?' She tried not to sound too venomous. It was Christmas, after all.

'Young?' Daisy sounded surprised. 'He was certainly over fifty.'

***

CLAUDIA

Boxing Day, or *Il giorno di Santo Stefano*, as it was known as in Italy, dawned crisp and clear in the Euganean Hills. Claudia climbed out of bed and donned a cream silk robe and pulled back the curtains on one of the tall windows that overlooked the magnificent gardens that Niccolò had created with such love and care.

She turned to look at Gastone's head on the pillow beside where she had been lying until a few minutes ago. His face looked relaxed in sleep, and a small smile played on his lips.

She had never been happier.

Her phone rang. She picked it up from the bedside locker and strolled back to the window.

She could see the call was from Janet.

THE END